My Reflections

Marcus Blake

A Collection of Marcus Blake's Work

My Reflections

A Mavericknes Media / Truesource Publishing Book

Published by arrangement with the author

The book cover and author photo of Marcus Blake is by Deborah Frances.

My Reflections was edited by
J M Almgreen and Carol Felder

Mavericknes Media : Dallas Texas
Truesource Publishing : Dallas Texas

www.truesourcepublishing.com

ISBN : 978-1-932996-60-9

Printed in the United States of America
Published in Dallas, Texas

For More information on Marcus Blake go to…

www.marcusblake.net
www.facebook.com/themarcusblake
www.twitter.com/marcusblake
www.thatnerdshow.com

This book is dedicated to...

Cecil Jordan

1952 - 2005

My teacher, My mentor, My friend.

What the teacher is, is more important than what he teaches.

~Karl Menninger~

A great teacher is much more than just a teacher; they are your friend and mentor when you least expect it. They teach not just from books, but from their hearts. They are hard because they demand excellence, and they can find the very best you have. They inspire you to be more than ordinary because they know you can be extraordinary.

~Marcus Blake

ABOUT THE AUTHOR

Marcus Blake was born in Chicago, Illinois in 1977. He grew up in Chicago and East Texas. His education is in History, Literature, Psychology, and Religion & Philosophy. Marcus Blake has studied at many universities throughout the United States, but his Alma Mater is Stephen F. Austin State University in Nacogdoches, Texas, which is also where he wrote his first book, The Music of Life. Marcus Blake is a Poet, Musician, Comedian, Writer, and Historian. His books are The Music of Life, My Reflections, Returning Home. Sex Game. The Lonely Girl, Stories From Wrigley, 30 Minutes: Trust and Lies, 30 Minutes: Guilty Until Proven Innocent, 30 Minutes: A Soldier's Song, and 30 Minutes: A Badge of Honor. He has taught in the public school system, served in the Army, and been a guest speaker at Education and Literary events throughout the world. Marcus Blake is also a Radio Host, his current show is Saturday Morning Nerd Show which can be heard on Saturday Mornings at www.thatnerdshow.com. He is a veteran of Rock and Roll shows as well as Political shows on the radio. Marcus Blake makes his home in the Dallas, Texas.

Other Books by Marcus Blake...

The Music of Life

Returning Home

Sex Game

The Lonely Girl

Stories From Wrigley

30 Minutes: Trust and Lies

30 Minutes: Guilty Until Proven Innocent

30 Minutes: A Soldier's Song

30 Minutes: A Badge of Honor

Ring of Warriors: Making a Fighter

TABLE OF CONTENTS

Why?

People ask me why I became a writer when I never set out in life to be one. I always stop and think about it because there are a great number of reasons why I became a writer. In short, I find inspiration knowing that words and ideas can still change the world. I like knowing that long after I am gone my words will still be alive and will live forever. I like knowing that my words can make a difference in someone's life; that they can influence change, and bring out the best in something. I like the fact that one can be lost within my words. The best place to be is lost, whether it's being lost in a place hidden from the rest of the world, or lost in a sea of change, or even within a love. Things like this can restore the energy of life, fill our souls with complete joy, and make us live each day anew.

For me, I am lost in the words, lost in the words of them. The words that fade away with passing breath and the words that will come again for this is why I write.

~ Marcus Blake

SHORT STORIES

My Life in a Thousand Words

The man stood outside the bar waiting, waiting for the man who ruined his life. He was beat down; tired, and suffering from the worst hangover in his life, but there he stood waiting. All he could think about was the man who destroyed everything he had and of course that's when revenge seemed possible. He had a true enemy in the man he waited for and his enemy had struck a deadly blow. The bar he was in front of was called Jake's downtown bar and it was the regular hangout for the man he waited for. Vincent was his name, the man who ruined his life, and he'd done it in a thousand words.

The man waited 20 minutes while patrons from the bar gave him dirty looks as they walked in and out; they gave him the same disdained looks as they would a junkie or homeless person. Finally the moment arrived, Vincent showed up for his afternoon drink, it was his daily break from the grind of deadlines and endless typing that never seemed to make sense. He said hi to the usual crowd that stood outside the bar and he knew like his own family. As he was shaking a friend's hand the man who had been waiting pulled a gun from his jacket and grabbed Vincent pushing him down to the ground. He waved the gun in his face. Vincent had a look of terror on his face, not knowing what to make of the situation. It wasn't the first time he'd had a gun waved at him, but other times he had been too drunk or stoned to care. They were his Hunter Thompson moments and now he was looking for one again, but this time he came up short as he was being forced to face his demons.

The man with gun waved the gun at the crowd outside the bar waving them back so he would not be crowded. He picked Vincent up and led him into the bar and then told everybody to get out or he would start killing people. A few moments later the bar was empty except the man with the gun, Vincent, and the bartender. The man with the gun after putting Vincent in one of the booths by force finally asked him.

"Why did you do it, man?"

"Do what sir?" Vincent asked him, trying to be polite at the same time as not to upset the man with the gun.

"You know what you did, you ruined my life."

"How did I ruin your life? I don't even know you and I think you have to know somebody to ruin their life."

"Don't be fucking smart with me."

"I'm not trying to be sir, but I honestly don't know what you're talking about."

"It's what you wrote man."

"I write lots of things, can you be more specific?"

The man with the gun walked over and hit Vincent in the head with his gun. Then he replied "I'm the cop you wrote about. The article said I hate niggers."

"I know who you are now and I never said that in my column."

"But you were thinking it and you implied it you fucking bastard. Do you know how much shit I have to put up with now, I can't even work thanks to you."

Vincent just stared at the man with a fun, he wasn't even afraid anymore, he was guilty and then in a moment's flash his guilt turned to anger. He replied to the man. "I don't write anything that isn't true."
When he said that, man with the gun got even angrier. He pulled the cocking hammer back on the gun as if he was about to finally shoot, but then he stopped. He said to Vincent "Fuck you, you still don't know what you're talking about. You can only right the truth if you really know what happened. You weren't there, how would you know?"

"There were witnesses to what happened, I have their accounts."

"I was alone when it happened, people will say what they have to just to protect themselves."

Vincent sighed for a moment. He adjusted himself in the booth to sit more comfortably. Then looked directly at the man with the gun and said. "Be honest with yourself, you could have done things differently, you could have done things better. You made a mistake and I called you on it."

"We all make mistakes, but in the heat of the moment when you're staring down the barrel of gun that's when we're our true selves and that's when we let the fear dictate our actions. What do you do when you're faced with that kind of fear?"

"I don't know."

"Exactly, you don't."

"But could you have done something differently?"

"Maybe, but I didn't. Should I be punished all my life for it? Does my life have to end with that one single moment?"

"You killed somebody; you can't just walk away from that. You should have to live with it."

The man with the gun started to drop the gun as he stared at Vincent at the utter shock at what he said.

He couldn't believe the arrogance and self-righteous attitude of Vincent. He lifted the gun again pointing it at Vincent to make him cower in fear then he stopped. He said to Vincent. "You know, you're right. So you'll have to live with the death of your friend." Then the man with the gun pointed it at the bartender and shot him three times. After he did Vincent screamed at him in anger to stop because it wasn't too late. The gun crazed man looked at Vincent and said his last words. "I hope somebody will write about this, it should only take a thousand words." He shot himself in the head after that. Vincent ran behind the bar to help his friend Jim – it was too late, he was already dead.

A SPANISH SERENADE

The plane touched down at the airport in San Antonio about 10:00 am on a very clear and humid day. The heat seemed to stifle the very essence of joy from the passengers on the flight, leaving only their discontent for having to come to such an uncomfortable place. For one particular passenger, it was the first time he'd been there in fourteen years.

The last time for this passenger was also the last time he had ever spoken to his father. He'd had a terrible relationship with his father, and like most troubled relationships with parents it was a haunting burden to have to hold onto. Greg, as he was known to his friends, was an infamous musician who had resorted to teaching music at a small college in the Boston area to pay the bills. Sometimes it seemed like a lonely life, but to Greg the reward of having his life filled with music compensated for that.

Even though he had music, which seemed to be his whole life, there was always something that was lacking. Greg had at one time tried to make it as a professional piano player, which also happened to be another thing that he and his father didn't agree on. It seemed that part of his life wasn't supposed to work out, but then again, when does life ever work out the way we want it to.

The passengers of the plane crowded each other and hurried out of it while Greg lingered at the back. He just couldn't rush himself to face what he had come back home to do. He slowly walked into the terminal and sighed, trying to figure out what the losing team feels like returning home from the loss of a championship. About two days before Greg had received the call that his father had passed away, and since he was the only living relative still alive, Greg had to settle his father's estate. He knew one day he would have to come back home and put things to rest, but in the back of his mind there was a small part of his past that he could just as well leave alone. He took a cab to the office of the attorney that was handling his father's will so he could finally get done what he had come home to do. It didn't take him long to reach the office and there wasn't even much to go over in his father's will.

Since Greg was the only living relative, he had received everything his father had left behind, although he could not understand why at the time since they hadn't spoken to each other in fourteen years. The attorney read the will to Greg and told him that his father's new house was his now, as well as about ten thousand dollars that was in his father's saving account. Greg was in shock about the money, and then the attorney told him about the car his father had left to him in the will, which became even more of a shock.

The attorney led Greg down the stairs to the back parking lot while asking all sorts of questions about Greg, his father, and the car that was left behind.

"So are you surprised about your father leaving his car behind?" the attorney asked with curiosity.

It was obvious the attorney knew a great deal about Greg's past relationship with his father, and Greg had to wonder if it was out of anger and spite that his father had dispensed his history with his son to the attorney. Whatever the reason, he also thought to himself that there was no need to be angry since there was nothing he could do about it anyway. Greg looked at the attorney as they approached the door and said to him, "If you must know, I'm really surprised he left the car to me, because all the time I was growing up it was his pride and joy, even more than me."

The attorney answered, "Well, after seeing the condition of the car it must have been a real joy to him while he was alive. He really took care of it."

They finally reached the parking lot and both men stared at a beautiful 1966 Cadillac Seville Convertible with the amazement and satisfaction of staring at a beautiful Greek sculpture. Greg peered over at the attorney and asked even though he already knew the answer, "Is that the car? If that's it then I have to hand it to my father for taking pride in something and preserving it till the end of time."

The attorney looked at him with a smile and said, "Your father had the engine rebuilt as well as the interior, and then added a new paint job about a year ago. To be honest, a bunch of us in the office were hoping he wouldn't put it in the will and might sell it. It certainly is a beautiful car and something worth holding onto."

Greg nodded at him and continued to stare at the prize with utter shock and said, "I could always remember my father saying to me again and again that if a man was going to be classy or live in style then he should always travel that way, too. A good car could always help your state of mind when it comes to being classy."

The attorney casually laughed and replied "I have to say that I agree with him, and that particular car is a good way to do it."

Greg stood there for a few minutes admiring the artistic expression that was in the form of a car and he thought to himself that he might still be in a dream, but then he touched the car, running his hand along the side to remind him that he was not in a dream. The caddie was more than just a car, it was part of his life. He had learned to drive in it and drove his prom date in it.

The only time he and his father were at peace with one another was when they were driving down the open road together in the car. Greg was always sure that his father loved the car more than him and maybe his own wife, too, but after something like this car being left to him he began to question his own notions about what kind of man his father really was. He thought that when his father finally died it would be out of spite that he would leave everything he owned to his neighbor or something of that nature, and at first Greg didn't even really want any of it.

After finding out all that had been left to him, he began to wonder a lot of things about his father, things he hadn't thought about in a very long time.

The attorney said to Greg, "Here are the keys. We're done with the reading of the will, so enjoy."

He handed Greg a set of papers and a map to his father's house, and then they shook hands. Greg looked over at the attorney with some kind of contentment and said to him, "Thanks for all that you've done, and if I have any questions I'll give you a call."

"That'll be okay," said the attorney. "I hope you have a pleasant journey under the circumstances."

Greg loaded up the Cadillac and slowly eased out of the parking lot, trying to preserve the vintage vehicle as much as possible. He tried to preserve time as much as he could before he and the car faded away from the building down the street.

It was about an hour later that Greg finally arrived at his father's house, and from the way it looked everything had been left alone for him to sort. He was slow to enter the house, afraid that all his childhood memories would come flooding back even though this wasn't the house he grew up in, but he was afraid nonetheless.

He did some exploring and was surprised to see that there was nothing in the house to remind him of his past. It was as if he was entering the house of a complete stranger, and for the most part he was. He decided that he would spend the night there and figure out everything in the morning. Greg didn't do much cleaning except to gather all of his father's clothes and get them ready to be delivered to the Salvation Army. He didn't want to start his summer vacation with having to sort all of his father's stuff; he wanted to start the summer with a little bit of happiness instead of sorrow, even though it seemed almost impossible to do so.

The night went by fast, especially after the six beers he drank. Soon he began to forget what he was doing back home. After a light breakfast Greg decided that the best place for him was on the open road in his new red chariot that he had inherited from his father, and just like a child again he decided to let the road take him to an unknown destination. He gathered his things and left the house pretty much the way he'd found it and headed toward a place that had always provided excitement for him in his youth.

Greg went to Mexico not knowing why, but he went while escaping to a paradise that had always brought him peace in his youth. It was some place near the open sea where dreams and visions disappeared and became reality. It was a place that one became lost in and it beckoned the soul while the question of why this happened could never be answered. Greg was seeking an escape from all that he known up to that point in his life, so he journeyed into a place where most had never returned, or at least if they did they were forever changed.

After a couple of hours of driving beneath the bright sun with the top down, he crossed into Mexico and immediately felt better since returning to this part of the world. He still didn't know where he was going, but he drove in the direction of the water like he was searching for something that was not meant to be found, but something that he was inspired to find anyway.

The day was winding down and time seemed to have no meaning for Greg as he continued southward with a warm glow upon his face. He returned to the childlike happiness of riding in the car with his father. It was a simple place where joy is often known and memory collides with true living, a place inside of us that we do not visit nearly enough. Greg usually experienced this same kind of feeling when he played music and perhaps this was why he chose music as his life.

Sometime in the afternoon Greg entered a little coastal town called La Pesca that was more or less a small fishing village, or at least that's what it looked like to him. It also looked as if the modern world hadn't found this place yet, but it carried a beauty within it that could only be found in simple serenities. He entered slowly into the town trying to take in all that he could from such a mysterious place that he knew nothing about, and it was this place by the sea that he seemed to be drawn to. Although he couldn't begin to say why this little fishing village beckoned to him, he approached within its celestial borders without fear and without any form of logic.

Greg hadn't eaten since early that morning so he decided to stop and see what he could find in the way of a restaurant. He turned onto a little side road that looked like it had a bunch of shops and cafés from a road that seemed to be Main Street. He drove slowly down the little road, not paying much of attention to the people that surrounded it. All of a sudden he stopped to avoid hitting some people that were crossing in the middle of the road. As soon as he stopped an old Buick crashed into the back of his car.

It was obvious to the passenger of the Buick that Greg was not very angry about being in a car accident, but this was an unusual place for Greg and not the kind of unusual that provoked fear. Both cars pulled in-front of a little grocery store that was surrounded by more produce stands than Greg had ever seen in his life. For Greg it was a place away from all common places and one that was rich in timeless treasures. He looked over at the passenger of the car that had hit him and saw for the first time that it was a young woman.

To his surprise, the very sight of her made him forget all that had happened so far in the day, for she was like a goddess that he had only read about and never believed could be real. He thought to himself that she probably was the most beautiful woman he had ever seen, something that was truly made by God's own hand. She looked as if she was a soft crystal-like snowflake that dances with the cold winter wind and never knows sorrow. He walked over to her car and spoke in a soft tone hoping to calm the anger that showed on her face,

"I'm sorry about having to stop all of a sudden; I was trying to avoid those people over there. Are you okay? You're not hurt or anything, are you?"

She looked at him and paused for a moment as the anger disappeared off her face then she casually smiled at him. She replied, "No, everything's okay and I'm not hurt, just mad that I crashed my brother's car. I figured you would be screaming at me right now for following too closely behind you and hitting your Cadillac."

Greg smiled and said, "I'm not mad since this whole thing is my fault anyway. I'm not used to driving in a place where people just walk in the middle of the road. Besides, it's just a car you hit, it's not like you hit a person like I almost did."

The woman gave him a sarcastic look and said, "In Mexico, a car like that is more than just a car, it's a reputation. You better get used to everybody walking in the middle of the road; that's just the way it is here. I take it you're from some place far away?"

"I'm actually from Boston and I decided that since I needed a vacation I'd come down here," said Greg.

"Well, you couldn't have picked a better place to vacation; it may not be known as much as Cancun or

Veracruz, but it is the best place to be lost in," she said, smiling.

Greg gave her a funny look and replied, "You think the best place to vacation isn't a place to relax and bask in the sun, but to be lost?"

She laughed and replied, "The best relaxation that can be found is the place where one can be lost and not always found. Most people who venture to La Pesca are generally looking for something, but usually it's not known what it is they are looking for. Some have even sailed out there into the sea and have never returned; at least that is part of the legend around here."

Greg, intrigued by what she was saying, addressed her with his eyes and asked her, "Do you think I'm one of those people?"

The woman looked at him with the most intent of gazes and said with a laugh, "Sir, all of us that live here are those kind of people and all of us that have come here have been lost in some way. Those that come here even for a visit usually end up staying here. Actually, I have only known of one man who left for a little while then came back here to stay."

"I knew that there was something to this place when I entered the town," said Greg, a soft smile spreading on his face.

"There's more to this place than you know."

"Wow, you're beginning to sound like a horror movie, but you've got me intrigued," said Greg.

"Don't worry, what I'm talking about is a good thing and one worth finding out."

They both looked over the damage to their cars, and since this was a different place and both of them were captivated by the situation neither of them exchanged any information.

The woman looked at Greg with concern and said, "I really am sorry about the damage to your car, and if you'd like, my brother owns a repair shop so I can get him to fix it. I would hate for you to drive around in such a beautiful car while it's ruined."

"Don't worry about it," said Greg. "This whole thing was my fault anyway and my car isn't that bad off. It still drives and it doesn't really mean that much to me anyway, since my father gave it to me in his will."

"That's quite a gift, and I know I would cherish a gift like that if it was mine."

"On most occasions," said Greg, "I would cherish something like this, but it all depends on the person that gives it to you."

"I can't imagine what kind of person could be hated so much that a gift like that car would not be cherished, except maybe a parent."

"Well, I must say you are very perceptive. Parents are something we all have in common, especially ones that we're not always very fond of."

Before she could go any further with her simple wisdom, Greg looked a little nervous or afraid and said, "If you're all right then I guess I'll be on my way and let you get on with your day. Thank you for the insight and I hope everything goes okay for you."

With that said he turned back toward his car and started to quickly leave, although he couldn't help looking back at her one last time. The woman just stared at him as he walked back to his car with a concerned look and smiled knowing that he was running from something; she had seen a lot of people like that come to La Pesca. She also knew that there was nothing she could do but let him go, even after such an interesting meeting.

The woman got back in her car and tried to start it up, but it wouldn't start, leaving her to swear in anger so that everybody around could hear, including Greg. He looked at her one last time before he was about to drive away and saw that her car wouldn't start, so he decided to be friendly and help her out.

She was still trying to get it started when he walked up to her and said, "Is there anything I can do to help? If you need a lift somewhere I'd be more than happy to give you one."

His kindness brought a soft smile to her face. "Well," she began, "I guess I could use your help since this is my brother's car and he promised me he got it working again. I guess sometimes you can't even trust your own family, or maybe this car is really just a piece of shit."

Greg laughed at her candor and said, "Nobody could ever claim you don't say what's on your mind. Let me just give you a ride and you can have your not so trusting brother get this piece of shit he calls a car running again."

She laughed at his comment and suddenly her anger was replaced by the satisfaction of being happy. She took him up on his offer and let Greg escort her to his car like some Prince Charming helping the helpless damsel.

He had to drive through the heart of the little coastal town while driving her home, and he got to see for the first time all the little treasures that made that place more beautiful than he had ever seen. La Pesca was a place of hidden treasures where advancement was not in her nature, but one that was filled with more wonder that sets heaven from reality. All the people that he passed seem to be caught in a fairytale, not responding to this new visitor riding in a shiny car. They all seemed to be only content to be in such a place as this. It struck Greg as very peculiar, but instead of being afraid as most people might be, he was very curious yet again, teasing the beckoning of his soul.

After a long comfortable silence and taking in all the beauty he could while driving this mysterious woman home he finally asked, "So, have you lived in this town very long?"

She smiled and replied, "No, I have only lived here a few years, but it seems that I've been here all my life, caught up in a dream of sorts."

"What's so special about a place that would make someone like you say that?" asked Greg.

"Oh it's just this place," she said, "and perhaps you will stay long enough to find out what I mean, for the reasons are different for each person. I've been to many other places here in Mexico and the U.S., and they don't compare to La Pesca. I couldn't see being any other place in the world."

"I just plan on passing through even though I don't know exactly where I am heading," said Greg.

"Sometimes," she said with wisdom in her voice, "a place has a way of finding us when we aren't looking; I guess it's a little like love."

Greg didn't know how to reply to something he knew was true, so he just gave a casual smile and continued to watch the road. After a few minutes of silence she looked over and pointed to a little house that sat on a hilltop overlooking the sea and instructed Greg to stop at that house. It was a small villa, very earthy and filled with simple beauty which matched its resident. What made the house such a great place to live was its small patio overlooking the water and when the time was right one could see the sun completely fade behind the curtain of the sea.

There were small blooms of flowers that surrounded the rustic place. It displayed the love and joy that goes into a home that is true; a home where someone could never be mistaken but for who they really are. Greg could not help but smile with joy and awe in such a wonderful place. He suddenly remembered one of his fellow musicians saying beauty is only found in what is real and is rich in its simplistic treasures. If one should compose a musical piece with beauty as the theme, then they have to see beauty in its truest form of expression and live the music with their soul. To Greg, seeing a place like this made that philosophy real, and so for just a moment he took pleasure in what he saw.

She got out of the car and started to walk towards the front door. Greg, ever the perfect gentleman, offered his arm and escorted her to the front door. She turned to him when they arrived at the door and with all the sincerity in the world she looked deep within him and thanked him for all that he had done. Greg just simply smiled and shook her hand then turned and walked away as if he was walking away from the most tragic of accidents. The woman watched as he headed for his car, waiting for something that didn't seem possible. As Greg was about to get into his car he turned to look at this beautiful woman he had just driven for one last time and then he froze for what seemed years even though it was only for a few seconds. He couldn't quite explain why he spoke up and he didn't even know what he was about to say, but in a moment of shear panic he asked her, "I don't know anything about this place so do you know where there's a good place to eat?"

She hadn't taken her eyes off of him since he'd left to walk to his car. "There's a place called Julio's Café not too far from where the accident was, but it's not the best."

Greg smiled and asked her, "Where's the best place to eat in this little town?"

"This is actually the best place to eat, not so much for the food as for the company of strangers. I only say that because I think you should let me make dinner for you. It's the least I can do for you after all the kindness you've shown."

Every impulse in his body told him to say yes, and he was smart enough not to ignore them, so he accepted her invitation. As he was walking her inside her home he said, "So don't you think it's time we introduce ourselves?"

She smiled and replied, "I think that would be a great idea. My name is Sierra Isabelle Leon."

"Now that's a beautiful name," said Greg. "I'm sure that there's a story behind that."

"There is, and if you stick around long enough I might tell you the story."

"Well my name is as simple as they come. I'm Greg Richardson."

Greg could sense that she was toying with him, but he sensed no harm in it. Contrary to the usual cautious feelings a man might feel when a beautiful woman like Sierra would toy with his emotions and his desires, he felt completely at peace with her. It was something he had not felt in a long time, and like someone searching for the oasis in the desert, he followed his emotions.

Sierra went into the kitchen to prepare a simple feast. She told Greg to make himself comfortable and he began to explore the small dwelling that was occupied by the angel in the kitchen. He was curious to find out everything he could about this mystery woman he had just been captured by; he took in all that he could from the surroundings, trying to breathe in the very essence of it.

The place was small and quaint, but it seemed to fit her. What made it beautiful was its simplicity, much like most everything he had encountered in La Pesca. Sierra had not decorated her home with lavish things and it had everything one might need to live. It had a couple of pieces of furniture and a small television, as well as a small desk in the corner of the living room.

Sierra was an artist and taught art classes at a small school in town so she was accustomed to the art of living a small intimate life. The only room that seemed to have many things in it was the kitchen. The sense of it was that it was the kitchen of a professional chef. She had every tool necessary and everything in its place to make the finest of meals. The one particular thing in the villa that fascinated him besides her was the patio and the view of the sea that it overlooked. The patio was not very big, and like the house, it was made from very old reddish colored stones that looked as if they had been there since time began.

The ancient feel of the place just added to the treasure of such a wonderful place and the view of the raging sea at sunset. As he was standing out on the patio and looking at beyond what seemed forever she walked up behind him and handed him a cerveza.

“This is one of the reasons I have this place,” she said, “because I can look out and lose myself in the view. Out there is hope and chance, which is the only thing that life truly offers."

"Chance and hope,” Greg began, “are the best things to ever have and without them life probably isn't worth living, but its looks like you already know that. I can see why such a place would be hard to escape from."

They continued to talk and watch the sun set behind the water while she prepared dinner. The two strangers talked about different things such the places they had traveled to, their passions, and even a little bit of their families, even though Greg did not get too detailed about his. They talked about many things a couple would talk about when they start to date, trying to find out as much as they possibly could before intimacy prevailed. It was that usual bullshit people talk about while trying to just get to the next moment with the other person. The night seemed to wind away as they talked.

Later on in the evening as they sat on the patio overlooking the sea, Sierra got very serious and asked Greg, "So tell me what really brought you here in this part of Mexico."

“I guess since we have talked about all the unimportant things that people talk about on first dates its only right that you get a chance to play fortune teller with me," he said.

“You like to make jokes a lot don't you? Seriously, what really brought you here?"

Greg smiled and said, "For you, I'll play along. I guess it was the women. I had heard that the most beautiful women in the world were in this part of Mexico."

“Come on, be serious,” she said.

"I am being serious," he said, still smiling. "If the most beautiful women in the world are here, then this is where I want to be."

Sierra was not amused at his sarcasm and let him know it. She gave him an angry look and got up from her seat to walk back to the kitchen. As she got up she replied angrily under her breath, "If you are just going to make fun of this then you might as well leave, because you're going to ruin this wonderful evening."

Greg walked over to her as she started to clean. Knowing that she was mad at him, he grabbed her hands to make her stop what she was doing. He made her face him looking deep into her eyes, looking deep inside her, and said, "I'm sorry, but the truth is that I don't know why I came here. Maybe it was because I had never been this way before and I just wanted the road to take me wherever it led. Ever since I left Boston and came back for my father's funeral I've been kind of lost, and don't know where I am going. I am just going along with each day seeing what happens."

Sierra smiled again. "Perhaps you're just searching for something that you desperately need, and whatever you're looking for has led you to this place. You know you're not the first to end up here looking for something and maybe you will be like many souls before you and find it."

"Hopefully you're right," he said, "but I do know that I'm glad I'm here with you instead of somewhere else alone."

Both of them just stared at each other for the longest time trying to make sense of all that they were and being there with each other. Then Greg slowly bent down and softly brushed his lips against hers, holding her close to him. He kissed her with all the passion he had and tasted heaven for the first time in his life. It was the first time he kissed a woman knowing that it was more than physical infatuation; it was a love he couldn't explain.

They stopped and Sierra asked, "Why did you do that?"

"Because I didn't want to miss any opportunities or anything that could be," Greg replied.

Both of them sensing the moment and the romantic atmosphere, they just stared at one another deeply. Sierra finally spoke up and said in a soft tone, "That was nice, and I'm glad that you're here."

At the same moment, a song came over the radio that happened to be one of her favorites and she led Greg back to the patio and told him to dance with her. He did the best he could to keep up with the graceful creature before his eyes and they danced like two autumn leaves beneath the moonlight and the harbor lights. He held on to her softly like it was his last breath, and it wasn't too long before they were caught up in time's playful journey.

They kissed each other like two young lovers exploring every inch of their faces and then she led him into her most sacred of temples. All he could do while standing in front of her inside her bedroom was gently run his hands down the silky skin of her arms. He slowly ran his hands over her body as if exploring a great work of art.

Finally, as she was caught in a dream-like trance from his soft touch, Greg reached around and unzipped her summer dress, letting it fall to ground. She helped him out of his clothes and then they stood looking at each other for the longest time as if they were standing in an art gallery studying every inch of a priceless work. After a long moment while ecstasy was at its height, they slowly fell into each other's embrace and each of them explored the godlike figure in front of them. Greg remained soft and patient with her, trying to take in all that she was, from the mountain of curls in her hair to the sweet scent that graced her.

They spent the remainder of the night exploring every part of their bodies and making harmonious love to each other. The sun began to creep within her bedroom when the morning descended upon them as they slept wrapped up inside each other. They just lay there beside each other in pure serenity while the moments were being etched into memory and there was nothing but complete peace.

Greg watched her sleep and hoped Joshua's time would prevail on this perfect morning. He also hoped that he could remember Sierra the way she was at that very moment, simple and graceful in sleep. He knew that the moment was over, so he arose from the bed and put himself together. Greg was not a total bastard about these kinds of situations, so he left a couple of roses on the empty pillow with a note that said "see you later".

He knew he was still on a journey of sorts, but for now it began with her so he decided to stay for at least one more day. He finally found a hotel and got cleaned up so he could start his day and decide what he should do for the time being. His bags were all packed and he was rested by the afternoon, but he knew that somehow he couldn't leave. There was something that kept pulling him back to this magical place. There was also something much more important that was making him stay, even if he was not ready to admit it.

At the end of the afternoon he went back to Sierra's place to wait for her. She arrived a little after five and saw him sitting him on her doorstep with flowers. He just smiled at her. Both of them didn't say anything to each other for a moment; they just stared in a mixture and disbelief. Finally she said, "What are you doing here? I thought you would have been halfway back home by now."

"I couldn't leave for some reason," said Greg. "Something just kept pulling me here, so I decided to stay and check out this mysterious place you speak of so often."

"I'm glad you came back. I was wondering if I would ever see you again."

"I know I didn't say goodbye after last night, but I didn't want to make that mistake again," said Greg.

"Then make it up to me by having dinner with me again, and then maybe you can stay for a while."

"I'd like that."

He helped her inside the house and then she began to make a dinner again. It was like the night before had never ended. The whole time she was making dinner, they kept stealing glances at one another. They looked at each other like a couple of school kids in love, just like when not even innocence could be completely destroyed. Finally Greg spoke up and said to her, "I can't honestly say why I'm still here, but I know that I want to be here."

"You don't have to know the reason why," she said. Not knowing why can still change you in the best way."

"I really don't know what I'm going to do this summer, but I guess I can compose music anywhere that I have the proper tools."

"You know, down at the art school I teach at there's a music room with a piano and some guitars. You could work there and maybe do some teaching."

"I guess I could," said Greg. "It would definitely be a good reason to stay, and being in a different place might give me some much needed inspiration."

"You never know about a place like this, and I know at least one person that would be glad to see you every day," she said.

"That goes for me too, but I have to admit that I'm a little scared because this all just seems too easy or too much like a dream."

"I'll put your mind at ease, this is not a dream and I'll kiss you just to show you."

"Kisses are always good, but who's making jokes now?" said Greg, playing with her.

"If you don't feel that I am being honest then let me just say this; I feel very comfortable with you and I would like for you to stay. This may sound a little crazy, but you might be surprised what good can happen to you if you stay here. You just seem like a person that needs a good thing to come a long."

"You're right about one thing, this is crazy. But like you said, crazy may not be that bad, it may just be the best thing for me. I guess I could stay for at least a little while."

They smiled at one another and then they kissed. They repeated their magical night together and left dinner alone so they could love each other. They stayed wrapped in each other's arms all night once again and let time cease to exist on their way to being lost.

This is how it began; a summer of romance just like when they had been kids just enjoying the summer with their significant other. Trusting his instincts, Greg stayed in there for a while and there wasn't a time that anybody saw Sierra without a smile. It only took a few days for him to move in with her and it was in La Pesca that their love affair began. It was in this place that his life began to truly change forever.

They spent their days at the school and their nights just being with each other. Where most people might have gotten tired of being with each other, they seemed to only long more for each other. They found something of themselves in each other, although it cannot be accurately said what it was. That particular treasure was theirs and theirs alone. It was a peaceful time for them, a great time where they both didn't know anything else but peace. And like most times like this, it would eventually come to an end. For both of them, there would be a time of reckoning.

The summer was winding down, and after a great summer affair Greg had to figure out what he would be doing for the next school year. The new semester at the college he taught at would be starting soon and the preparation he usually had for it seemed to escape him as did most things during his time in La Pesca. Greg and Sierra were sitting in the living room of her little house while the candlelight that filled the room danced off the walls. They were just sitting there in complete silence working on their own projects and enjoying the company of each other. Greg had been trying to figure what to do, because even though he liked where his career had taken him to teach, he also loved the place where he was at. At least it was a place not like any other that he had become quite fond of. He'd never had a summer like this and it was hard to imagine it being over. Finally, as he sat reading he just asked, "Sierra, how do you feel about Boston?"

Sierra didn't even look up from the book she was reading and replied, "I think it would be a nice place to visit, but if you are asking me could I ever live there with you, I guess anything is possible, though I probably wouldn't be completely happy there."

Greg smiled. It always made him laugh when she answered all his questions in one response before he even got to make his point. Greg still thought of himself as a complicated man, and to have her see through that could do nothing but make him laugh. Men always see themselves as highly complex and complicated creatures, whereas women, knowing that they could see the truth in everything through some maternal-meter, foiled those notions by proving that men were very simple.

"Well," Greg began, "I thought I should just ask, because in a few weeks I'm going back to begin the next semester. I wanted to know if you would come and visit or maybe stay for a while."

Sierra put the book down and looked at Greg seriously and asked, "Are trying to tell me that you want this to be more than just a summer romance?"

"You can't tell me that you haven't thought about us after the summer is over. And if I have to be honest, then I'll tell you I haven't known anybody like you in my life, and there's never been any time in my life when I've been so happy, and I don't want it to end."

"It doesn't have to end; you can always stay here," said Sierra. "I would hope that you have found what you were looking for."

They both paused for a moment and then Sierra said, "Honestly, Greg, I feel the same way you do."

They both just looked at each other hoping the other would say something that could stop the inevitable, but silence lingered. After a long uncomfortable silence Sierra finally changed the subject.

"Don't forget this Sunday we're going to my father's house for dinner, and most of my family should be there."

"Don't worry, I can't forget this Sunday. "After all, I'm still a little nervous about meeting your father and the rest of the family."

The sun was shining in brilliant majesty over the ocean as Greg and Sierra drove down the coast to the town that she was from. The place of her birth was a town to the south of La Pesca called Ciudad Madero, and even though it sat on the Mexican shore, there wasn't much to the town in the way of water ventures. About the only thing of major importance was that it was near an airport, one of the few in Mexico.

For a small town sitting on the coast, it was pretty industrial because of the more than one car repair shops and a small clothing factory. Her father and mother's family had lived in that town all their lives and its members had grown up together. They were all still happy and nobody saw any reason to leave. And since everybody from Sierra's two families were still close, many of its members met every Sunday for dinner. It was a special time for family, and like most families in Mexico that had strong ties, Sunday was set aside to embrace that. Sierra's mother had passed away many years before, but that did not stop the two sides of her family from getting together every Sunday for dinner and fellowship with one another.

Greg and Sierra were one of the first to arrive, and even though she had not been to one of these family gatherings in a long time she was embraced like she had been seen yesterday. Her childhood home was busy; a few of her aunts and grandmothers were starting to prepare a feast as usual. When she first got there she immediately introduced Greg to her father Jorge and her two brothers Raul and Alex.

As Greg was shaking their hands, Raul teased, "So this is the boyfriend we keep hearing about and you were afraid to bring around!"

Jorge gave a discerning look to his eldest son and said, "Be nice to your sister about this man. There will be plenty of time to tease her later."

They all laughed and exchanged pleasantries. The family gathering was more like a party for anybody else, but it was not unusual for Sierra's family gathering to be filled with music and dancing and laughter. There was enough food to feed a small town, and a few mariachi players in the family played music throughout the night, except for during the prayer and eating. The family gatherings for the Leon's were nothing short of feasts and joyous times. This was something that Sierra had always treasured about her family, even if there were times that she could not stand to be around her father.

By the time everybody else from the various families had arrived, it had taken the better part of a few hours for Greg to make the rounds and meet the members of her family, and most importantly to learn everybody's name. The family gathering was a little short unlike most Sundays, but still boasted enough people to rival any other party. Greg was not used to this sort of thing and especially everybody continuously asking him how he and Sierra met and other details about their relationship.

It was like the Spanish Inquisition, but Greg just laughed it off because he was doing good enough to learn everybody's name in Sierra's family. Although Greg was new to this kind of family interacting and the different people he met that night he quickly began to fall in love with many of the interesting characters he had met. Most of whom took every opportunity to tell some comical story of Sierra and how the town he was staying in was a great town to live in. It became like a sales pitch on why the best points to this part of the country and why he should stay. Greg with a humorous attitude couldn't figure whether there was some hidden motive behind it all, but none the less it was funny.

As the evening progressed and everybody was very relaxed from all the wine and cervezas that were being drinked, Jorge grabbed a couple of cervezas and sat down next to Greg offering him one. Through all that was going on he had not had a chance to talk with Greg. He was very interested in him and the relationship he was carrying on with his daughter like all fathers should be.

Jorge spoke up in a curious tone and asked Greg "so my daughter has mentioned you very little to me, but she has not told me how you two met or what you are doing in this part of Mexico."

Greg replied "I actually met your daughter my first day in La Pesca." I was driving slowly through the middle of town not paying much attention and she accidentally hit me from behind. After all of that, we ended up having dinner that night. As for my being down here, I had to go to San Antonio for some family business. Since I was on a summer vacation, I decided to drive through Mexico and ended up in La Pesca."

Jorge asked, "So you have family in San Antonio then?"

"No, not actually," said Greg. "My mother died when I was young and my father just passed away, so there's nobody else there."

"I'm sorry to hear about your father," said Jorge. "That must have been hard to just lose one of your parents."

"Actually it wasn't. I hadn't spoken to him in fourteen years. We weren't exactly close, and since he wasn't the best of fathers, I saw no point in having a relationship with him."

Jorge looked shocked. "Well, just because a parent isn't perfect is no reason to not try to have a relationship with that parent. I don't think any parent deserves to be cut off from the children that they love just because they may not be the ideal parent."

Greg replied morosely, "Well, no disrespect intended, but I don't think my father loved me very much and I don't think he deserved to have a relationship with anyone in his family. To me, that's something that has to be earned, especially when it comes to love. Anyway, that's enough about my father."

After a brief pause Greg changed the subject and asked, "So I understand that both sides of your family have been in this town for a few generations."

Jorge replied, "Yes, my family ties go back to my great-great-grandparents, and Sierra's mother's family goes back even further than that. This is a good example of how close everybody is and the strong ties Sierra has to her family. That is something I think makes a full person. Without a strong family there are some important things a person may lack that might make them a good person."

Greg knew after a few drinks that Jorge's protective nature for his daughter was making him antagonistic towards him, but he let it slide since this was the first time they had met each other.

Greg finally said, "I think you make a good point; family is very important in a person's life and the great family you have here has certainly made a profound impact on Sierra's life. Although I don't think that everybody who doesn't have strong family ties is a ruined person, some can be better off. I like to think that I'm a pretty good person and well adjusted."

"But you cannot say for sure," said Jorge. "Maybe you are really not that great of person, and only fall victim to your delusions."

Greg picked up on Jorge's sarcasm and responded in kind. "Well, I haven't murdered anybody or committed some immoral sex acts toward people or even resorted to stealing, so I think I'm a pretty decent person despite the misjudgments of others."

Jorge looked angry. "I don't that is funny at all. There is more than just murder or rape or theft that makes a person bad. And besides, what makes you think I have misjudged you?"

Greg replied, "I didn't know I was talking about you, sir."

The two gentlemen just sat there with angry looks on their faces and finally Greg told Jorge he was going to get a couple of more cervezas for the both of them. Greg handed Jorge another cerveza and with a more pleasant tone Jorge asked Greg, "So I hear you teach music in Boston, so do you like teaching there?"

"I love what I do and Boston is nice, but I have to admit that I will probably miss Mexico. I've had a lot of fun this summer and I'm very glad that I met your daughter."

Jorge looked serious. "So I guess your plans here were not long term with Sierra?"

Greg, trying to keep his temper in check replied, "I was only staying here for the summer; Sierra and I had not discussed anything yet."

Jorge was mad by this point, and even though he could have stayed out of his daughter's business, he continued with his questions regarding her well-being. "But I thought you and my daughter were living together, because if that is true that means that the relationship is pretty serious, close to marriage if you ask me. She has done this before with guys and they have not been so respectful of her; you know, just wanting some kind of fling with her, so I'm trying to find out whether you are just like them or different. If you're just going to stay with her for the summer, sleeping around and then going home probably never talking to her again, then I guess you would be no different, right?"

"No offense sir, but I didn't come here tonight to be given the third degree, and what is between Sierra and I is our business."

By this time everybody around could hear what was being said between the two men and Jorge had stood up to face Greg. Jorge responded to Greg, "Look gringo, there is no reason to get angry; I am only looking out for my daughter. If there is something between you and marriage is the possibility, then there is a proper way to deal with it."

Greg, noticing that everybody around was looking at them responded, "I understand that, and I mean you no disrespect, but whatever is between your daughter and I is our business, not yours."

Jorge replied angrily, "My children are my business, and I am not going to let some Chico Juego take advantage of my daughter while he is on some summer vacation."

"How dare you judge me and accuse me of trying to take advantage of someone I care about very much. You don't know anything about us and what has been going on....I tell you again, it is none of your business what happens in our relationship."

Sierra came out of the house to see what was happening and walked over to her father and Greg to calm the both of them down. She walked up to her father just as he was pointing and saying to Greg, "By living with my daughter there is no telling what else you are doing, but you are already living in sin. I think I have every right to judge you because just maybe I need to put a stop to any other immoral acts you are committing towards her."

Before Greg could say anything Sierra was already face to face with her father and saying to him, "What are you doing? Are you trying to start a fight with my boyfriend just because you don't understand what is going on with him and me?"

Jorge replied, "Do you even know what he is up to? All I am trying to do is find out his intentions toward you so he doesn't end up hurting you or taking advantage of you."

Before Sierra could respond Greg replied, "What are you, some kind of priest, some kind of moral authority who thinks he has the right to mix in other people's affairs just because you might not like what's going on? You know, if you give me the benefit of the doubt and don't insult me with your antics, you might just find that my intentions are honorable."

"Honey, stay out of this and quit arguing in a futile cause," said Sierra. "I'll handle this."

Jorge looked at Greg straight in the eye and said, "When it comes to my daughter's wellbeing, I will always have the moral authority. You are the one who insults me by the way you act with my daughter and the way you treat me after I invite you into my home. It is probably a good thing that you are leaving because I don't think you have enough respect for women or their families. I guess that is what happens when you abandon your own family. I don't think you are worthy of my daughter."

Greg looked around and saw that everybody was looking at him and instead of being gracious his anger got the best of him. He looked at Sierra then looked at her father and said, "I've always tried to be forgiving of the undeserving things parents can do to their children. But you...you demonstrate to me the lack of faith some parents have in their children. This tells me that since you cannot respect the private life of your daughter, then you don't love her enough, you're just lying when you say you love her."

Greg turned to Sierra and said, "I'm leaving now since I'm not welcome here anymore. "If you're coming with me, I'll be by the car. If not, I'll see you later." With that said, he walked away from the crowd and the house.

Jorge, in front of all his guests that were looking at him now, said to Sierra, "What kind of man is he, that he would come into my home an insult me like that? I was only trying to find out what his intentions were toward you."

Sierra, showing her anger, said, "No, you were only antagonizing him just like you do with anybody you don't like, and when you don't understand what's going on. I love you, but you are a bastard sometimes. Greg is right; what's between us is none of your business. That is something you have never understood about my private life since I became and adult when my mother died."

She turned around and walked out, not giving him a chance to say anything. She walked past Raul on her way out and told him she was going with Greg, and that he should tell everyone she was leaving.

Raul responded, "I will, and don't worry, everything is going to be all right; I'll even try and talk to dad." Then, trying to lighten things up a bit, he said, "Well I guess you just can't bring any guy around here; some things never change. You really care about this one don't you?"

Sierra didn't say anything to him, but just smiled at her brother. Sierra walked outside and saw Greg standing by his car. As she was about say something, Greg looked at her angrily. "Is this what you wanted from me meeting your father today, an exchange of insults and tempers flaring?" he asked.

"I'm sorry about what happened, and I should have warned you about how he can be. He can get very hostile towards people he hasn't met, especially after he has been drinking a little."

Greg laughed and replied, "So he does this with all strangers? If I didn't know better, I'd say he was provoking me and trying to turn us against each other. You know, I do know a little bit about people provoking other people just to start a fight or turn people against one another. My father was really good at it, especially when he started to drink."

"Look, I'm not condoning his actions. It's my fault that he doesn't know that much about us. I haven't been around lately for my own personal reasons, and some of them have to do with him, so I haven't done a good job about trying to make him understand what you and I are to each other. Although he was wrong to treat you so badly, you have to understand that my family and the people here are very traditional. Us living together means that we are about to be married, and by not seeking his permission to marry me it is an insult."

Greg calmed down a little. "So what if this summer romance of ours if turning into a marriage proposal? He still has no right to interfere with us. I don't care if he doesn't understand what's going on between us. You're an adult now and your personal life is none of his business. And since we're on this subject, what exactly did your father mean that this wasn't the first time you've done this with guys?"

Sierra replied, "What you're saying is true, and yes you're not the first summer romance I've had. I've made no attempt to hide the romances I've had with other men and the fact that I did not tell my father about them."

Greg asked again, "So you're telling me that there have been some that have lived with you for a while, and then you just ended it with them?"

Sierra replied, "Yes, I've had a few other men in past years live with me, and it wasn't very serious, except for one. This is part of what my father doesn't understand, and why we have fought."

"I do want to know the details and how serious it was," said Greg.

Sierra touched him in a way that soothed him and said, "I told you when we first met that there have been others that I have known that came to La Pesca searching for something and there was one that I got really serious with to the point that we almost got married. And yes, I did not tell my father about him, the fact that he was living with me, and that we almost got married because he would not have understood."

Greg was mad and he looked at her with rage in his eyes, but he tried the best he could to hide it and talk to her with an understanding tone. He was not very good at it, and responded to her with a chilly tone, "You know, at this point I don't know what we are and I thought I knew by now. But the truth is, I can't figure out whether I'm just another summer fling or you actually do care about me."

"I was going to ask you something later this evening after we got home," he continued. "I was going to ask if you would come back to Boston with me because I didn't want to live without you. And just maybe marriage might be a possibility, but I don't know now, especially after dealing with all this."

Sierra began to get emotional. "I don't want you to go," she said, half sobbing. "I like having you around. That much I have figured out in the few months we have been together, and I was hoping more could be a possibility."

Greg finally smiled and said, "Then let's forget about all of this and be spontaneous. Let's just drive away right now and live out our lives together."

Sierra looked at him and said, "As much I as want to be with you and don't like my father interfering with my life, I still live by certain traditions. I couldn't do this without my father's blessing, and even if he doesn't like it I need him to accept this. I still love him and respect him."

"Look, I don't think he will accept us, especially after tonight, but we don't have to let that ruin our lives. We can still be together if you want me as much as I want you."

"You're probably right about my father. He may never accept us, but I still can't go any further without his blessing or at least him coming to some understanding of all this."

Greg, suddenly dead serious, said, "If you agree with me, go in there and make him understand and accept us."

"I can't do that to a man who is as stubborn and traditional as he is. Only God can change his heart, and I can only pray for that. After all, he won't listen to me until he's ready, but nonetheless all I can do is wait until he does."

Greg laughed and said, "Well, if you don't have much faith in him then maybe I don't either, but if that's true then there is nothing more to talk about."

Greg started the car and waited for Sierra to get in before he drove away like a reckless teenager. The two of them didn't say a word to each other on the way home, and the drive was filled with loneliness and the chilly night air. When they got home, Greg started to gather his things and load them in his car with Sierra watching him in shock. She finally asked him what he was doing and where he was going. The only thing he could say was going to spend the night in a hotel before going back to Boston.

"You don't have to just leave here before you go," she said. "You're welcome to stay for as long as you like. Besides, I thought you weren't going back for at least another week."

Trying not to start another argument he carefully responded, "I just don't see the point in staying around here anymore. I have a long drive ahead of me anyway, so I will probably leave early."

"That's just an excuse to leave, and don't tell me there isn't any reason to stay."

"I have fallen in love with you; I'm positive about that. I want you to come with me because there's a chance for us. If you feel the same then come with me. Let's just forget who we are here and be with each other somewhere else."

Sierra's eyes started to well up and she replied, "The person you are in love with as you say you are is here, and I cannot abandon that. If I leave like this, then I abandon all that I am and that includes my family, even though I may not always agree with them. It also means that I abandon all the things that I've learned and

I disrespect the traditions I still believe are sacred and right. If I do all that, I'm not who I am anymore, and I don't think one can ask that of someone they love. I couldn't do that of you if I truly love you."

As Greg stood in the doorway he looked at her with a somber, but understanding look and replied, "Perhaps you're right." Then he walked out without looking back. That was the last time she was to see him for the rest of his stay in La Pesca.

Greg stayed the night in the only hotel in town and the next day he got his things together so he could leave Mexico for good. Before he left he had one more meal in the only café he dared to eat at, a place he became strangely fond of since he didn't like Mexican food all that much. He was sitting quietly in his favorite spot when a familiar face walked in. It was Raul, Sierra's oldest brother. Even after what had happened the day before, he was still a welcome site.

Raul walked over to the table to where Greg sat down and asked if he could sit down. After he sat down he said to Greg, "I was hoping I could catch you before you left town, before you walked away for good."

"Look, it's good to see you, but if your sister sent you then I don't have anything more to say," said Greg.

"No, she didn't send me. I came on my own because I was hoping to have a few words with you."

"Well I guess even after all that's happened I could hear you out, but do me the credit of not trying to change my mind."

"I wouldn't do that. I think there has been enough interference by outside parties. But you should know that my sister went and saw our father last night. If nothing else, I wanted you to know that, because she is still too stubborn to come and tell you what happened."

"Whatever happened, I hope everything is okay with them now."

"I think everything is going to be okay with them," said Raul. "She talked to him about her life and made him understand what he needed to understand. I talked to her last night as well and she said she had a real good talk with him. She basically told him that her life was her own and if he really loved her then he will have enough faith in her to live by what she has been taught, but no matter what that she had to live her life her own way."

"How did he take it?" asked Greg, curious.

"He wasn't pleased at first by what she said, but then Sierra reminded him of the way our mother was and why he fell in love with her. After that, he really didn't have anything to argue about."

This peeked a curiosity in Greg, for he had not heard that much about Sierra's mother, so he asked Raul, "What was your mother like?"

"She was very beautiful and very full of life. Our mother lived for the joy of life and always found something to inspire her in this crazy world. And if it called for it she would throw all tradition to the side for the sake of passion, for she thought not to be happy was the most immoral thing in world. It was that passionate spirit of hers that made my father love her more than anything. Sierra is very much like our mother, but she does have a sense of tradition, and the fact that she is almost a mirror of our mother makes my father have to remember what he lost."

Sierra hardly spoke at all about her mother, so all of what Raul was saying was very new to him. Greg was beginning to see a bigger picture of something, more than what he was allowed to see during the past few months.

"How long has it been since your mother passed away?"

"Our mother died when we were just teenagers, so it has been awhile, but no one has truly gotten over it. Sierra had a very tough time when she died because they were very close. It was also about that time Sierra really changed and started to live her life to the extreme and live for what she called passion; after all, she saw how fragile life was."

"I can see why she hasn't spoken about her mother and why she lives her life the way she does. I guess everybody has their own way of dealing with death."

"I am not a shrink," said Raul, "but I tend to think my father is the way he is because Sierra reminds him of her, and that causes him serious pain. And what he wanted so desperately to do was to hold onto his children, the most valuable thing he had left. Also, our father is a very traditional man and his way of thinking comes from many generations of beliefs and ways of doing things. And since Sierra insists on living her life to the very fullest, it is why she and father have clashed so much since then."

"The thing I really wanted to tell you," Raul continued, "was that you have to understand something more than anything, we live by certain traditions and no matter how extreme Sierra lives her life she is not going to abandon that; there are things that she will not give up. You know we are all that way about certain things that we cling to because we regard them as being very important to us. I don't know what kind of family you came from or all that happened with your father and your reasons for walking away from him; I'm sure you were probably right in what you did. The thing is, nobody who truly loves you can tell you what you should have done, but just respect your choice. That is something that's hard for all of us to do because we are human."

"I hope that wasn't all that came to tell me, because I've been wrestling with this issue for a while and I don't need somebody to preach to me about what to do."

"No, I'm not going to tell you what you should do or keep preaching on what you already know. I just wanted to make sure that you already knew. The only other thing I wanted to say is if you decide to stay for another day then why don't you come out to the house tomorrow night. It would probably do you good to talk with my father again, but if you decide that the best thing to do is go back to Boston, then have a good trip."

Raul shook Greg's hand and walked out of the café. As Greg was finishing his meal, he couldn't help but think about Sierra and all that Raul had said. It wasn't too long before Greg went back to the hotel to get a room for another night. He thought to himself that he should at least make his peace with Sierra's father even if nothing else ever came from it. There should at least be one father he should make peace with, even if it wasn't his own.

The next day after walking around La Pesca for what he thought would be the last time, he stopped at the highest point of the city to look out over the sea. He didn't know what he was looking for, or maybe he did, but he didn't want to admit it yet. He did know that there was one thing that he had found there even if it didn't make sense. He stood there for the longest time, looking like a philosopher trying to understand all the mysteries the sea would teach and then try to make sense of them within himself.

After a while he drove to the place of Sierra's birth to talk with the one man who could give him a future or take it away. He thought to himself that it was the longest drive that he had ever taken, perhaps like a prisoner walking to the executioner. It was late afternoon when he arrived, and there were many children running around playing in the streets without a care in the world, and Greg couldn't help but laugh to himself about the innocence before his eyes or wonder if he ever had it himself at one time. He knocked on the door and it was Jorge that answered it. For a long time both men just stood there before Greg finally spoke.

"Hello Mr. Leon. I think there are a few things that we should talk about before I leave Mexico."

"Yes, I think you're right. Jorge led him through the house to the back part where the patio was so they could talk alone.

The kitchen was busy with dinner being prepared for the few guests that were coming over so Jorge grabbed a couple of Cervezas and walked out to the patio and handed Greg one.

"Sir, I'm sorry for insulting you the other night," said Greg, "but I think it's best to be completely honest about a few things. I love Sierra more than anything, and believe me, I've had plenty of time to think about this."

"I figured you probably loved her, or else you wouldn't have come here tonight. I was wrong in how I treated you the other night. You will have to excuse me, I am very protective of my children. This is probably the only time I am going to admit that so I hope you heard me."

Greg smiled and replied, "Well, I guess you know what I am probably going to ask now."

"I think I do," said Jorge, also smiling, "and I hope you will ask it, but first there is something I need to say before and then maybe you will understand."

Greg sat down with his drink in the chair next to Jorge, the same place he had been a few nights ago. This time he hoped as well as Jorge that the results would be different. Jorge humbly continued his narrative. "I had a long talk with my daughter, one that we needed to have had for a long time, and I know that she does love you very much. I learned with her mother that there is no time limit on love and there is only one moment that you will just know that you love someone. That was the way it was with her mother; I knew the very moment we danced together for the first time that I wanted to spend the rest of my life with her."

Greg smiled, for the same truth had become known to him and it seemed that things made more sense to him.

“Perhaps Sierra is right,” Jorge continued, “I have not understood how her life is or who she is, then again maybe I have just forgotten because she is very much like her mother. I know my daughter has to live her own life and all I can do is hope that she takes with her all that she has learned from the members of her family. I am proud of her and the person she has become because if she is anything like her mother then she is great."

Greg smiled and replied, "She’s a very wonderful person and has enriched my life more than anything, including music. I am definitely better off having known her."

"Her mother was the same way with anybody who was around her. She made me a better person and Sierra got that from her. The only other thing I wanted you to know is I can't judge you for what I have no control over, because we never have control over what our family is like. I guess it would be hard to understand all the traditions that might go behind a family if you never really had one. Considering all that, you’re an okay guy, and hopefully one day you can be as fortunate as me to have a great family around you. And sometimes it takes a few days of being angry to finally come to your senses and say the things that really need to be said, so you’ll excuse me for not getting around to this sooner.”

Greg smiled and said, "Hopefully you’re right, and I’m sorry for all that has happened. I don’t mean any disrespect toward you. I should have said all the things I’m telling you now sooner, but anger is a great delay. I would like to ask for your daughter's hand in marriage if she will have me, and I would like your blessing.”

Jorge leaned back in his chair and replied "I have just one thing to ask: do you truly love her, and are you willing to sacrifice anything for her?"

"Yes, and no matter what I have to give up I will spend the rest of my life trying to make her happy."

"That is all I can ask of you, so I give you my blessing. If she will have you, then let this be your family."

They shook hands and Jorge invited him to dinner like an old friend. Jorge looked at him again and asked, "I've been wondering if you hated your father so much, then why do you still have the car he left you? I would think you would have sold it."

"The only reason I haven't gotten rid of it is because as a kid I used to go riding in that car with him, just him and me. I even learned as kid how to drive in that car, and it's the one time in my life that I can remember my dad being my father to me, it's the one piece of innocence from my childhood that I have. My dad will always be a son of a bitch, but I can't lose those moments when he wasn't. Besides, it's a Cadillac. On my salary I could never afford to buy one, so it's my one bragging right."

Both men laughed and had their first decent moment together. "You know," said Jorge, "the more a parent tends to love their children the more opportunities will arise to show how much of a son of bitch they can be, and that is the only thing that can happen when a parent tries too hard."

Greg just smiled at him for his sincerity. After that Greg tried to excuse himself so he could go and find Sierra, but Jorge told him to stay because she would be coming there for dinner and it would be a nice surprise for her. Greg made the rounds and said hello to Raul and Alex and Jorge's parents as dinner was being finished up. Not too long after that, Jorge heard the front door open and went to catch Sierra before she walked into the dining room.

Jorge hugged her and said, "I am glad that you could make it tonight. So how are you?"

"I'm fine, and you seem to be in a good mood. Is there something going on?"

"Can't I just be happy for a little while after yesterday? I think it's time I start being happier around you."

Jorge escorted her into the dining room and then she saw one of the most surprising things she had ever seen. Greg got up from his chair with a smile to meet the surprised, but joyous look Sierra had on her face as she looked at him.

"We had a long talk about you and other things so I invited him to dinner," said Jorge.

Sierra hugged her father from the side and walked over to Greg and asked him as she gave him a hug, "What are you doing here?"

"I came to talk to your father about us," he replied. "Because I love you and because you make me believe. You make me believe in love, in you, and in us; you make me believe in family and tradition. And you make me believe in finding that joy of life, because for me being happy in this life is being with you."

"You're just saying that."

"No, I'm not. I don't want to live another moment without you, so I came to ask your father's blessing in marriage if you'll have me."

"I love you. Of course I'll have you, but what about Boston?"

"I don't need Boston to be happy, I just need you in whatever place that has you. I haven't found everything I was looking for in La Pesca, but I found the most important thing. All I need is someone who'll keep making me believe, someone that will hold on to me when I'm falling, and someone who I can do the same for."

With tears in her eyes, Sierra hugged and kissed him for what seemed like an eternity, and then everybody sat down to dinner and to celebrate a new union.

Eventually, Greg and Sierra settled in San Antonio and another generation was started. In the end, there would always be one place they could call home and be completely lost in. A paradise on earth; an earthly city by the sea, and it would always be like something out of a dream.

As the plane landed at the San Antonio airport, the lonely passenger from Boston woke up from his deep sleep. He seemed confused about where he was and what was actually real. The dream he had been having was very vivid and it was almost like he was living it. The one thing he knew for sure was that it was a good dream; it was a calming relief to the reason he had come back to this place after fourteen years.

About two days before Greg had received the call that his father had passed away, and since he was the only living relative still alive, Greg had to settle his father's estate. He knew one day he would have to come back home and put things to rest, but in the back of his mind there was a small part of his past that he could just as well leave alone.

He took a cab to the office of the attorney that was handling his father's will so he could finally get done what he had come home to do. It didn't take him long to reach the office and there wasn't even much to go over in his father's will.

Since Greg was the only living relative, he had received everything his father had left behind, although he could not understand why at the time since they hadn't spoken to each other in fourteen years.

The attorney read the will to Greg and told him that his father's new house was his now, as well as about ten thousand dollars that was in his father's saving account. Greg was in shock about the money, and then the attorney told him about the car his father had left to him in the will, which became even more of a shock.

The attorney led Greg down the stairs to the back parking lot while asking all sorts of questions about Greg, his father, and the car that was left behind.

"So are you surprised about your father leaving his car behind?" the attorney asked with curiosity.

Greg looked at the attorney as they approached the door and said to him, "If you must know, I'm really surprised he left the car to me, because all the time I was growing up it was his pride and joy, even more than me."

The attorney answered, "Well, after seeing the condition of the car it must have been a real joy to him while he was alive. He really took care of it."

They finally reached the parking lot and both men stared at a beautiful 1966 Cadillac Seville Convertible with the amazement and satisfaction of staring at a beautiful Greek sculpture. Greg peered over at the attorney and asked even though he already knew the answer, "Is that the car? If that's it then I have to hand it to my father for taking pride in something and preserving it till the end of time."

Greg stood there for a few minutes admiring the artistic expression that was in the form of a car and he thought to himself that he might still be in a dream, but then he touched the car, running his hand along the side to remind him that he was not in a dream. The caddie was more than just a car, it was part of his life. He had learned to drive in it and drove his prom date in it.

The only time he and his father were at peace with one another was when they were driving down the open road together in the car. Greg was always sure that his father loved the car more than him and maybe his own wife, too, but after something like this car being left to him he began to question his own notions about what kind of man his father really was. He thought that when his father finally died it would be out of spite that he would leave everything he owned to his neighbor or something of that nature, and at first Greg didn't even really want any of it.

After finding out all that had been left to him, he began to wonder a lot of things about his father, things he hadn't thought about in a very long time.

Greg and the Lawyer shook hands and then he drove off in his red chariot. Greg went to Mexico not knowing why, but he went while escaping to a paradise that had always brought him peace in his youth. It was some place near the open sea where dreams and visions disappeared and became reality.

It was a place that one became lost in and it beckoned the soul while the question of why this happened could never be answered. Greg was seeking an escape from all that he known up to that point in his life, so he journeyed into a place where most had never returned, or at least if they did they were forever changed.

After a couple of hours of driving beneath the bright sun with the top down, he crossed into Mexico and immediately felt better since returning to this part of the world. He still didn't know where he was going, but he drove in the direction of the water like he was searching for something that was not meant to be found, but something that he was inspired to find anyway.

Sometime in the afternoon Greg entered a little coastal town called La Pesca that was more or less a small fishing village, or at least that's what it looked like to him. It also looked as if the modern world hadn't found this place yet, but it carried a beauty within it that could only be found in simple serenities. He entered slowly into the town trying to take in all that he could from such a mysterious place that he knew nothing about, and it was this place by the sea that he seemed to be drawn to. Although he couldn't begin to say why this little fishing village beckoned to him, he approached within its celestial borders without fear and without any form of logic.

Greg hadn't eaten since early that morning so he decided to stop and see what he could find in the way of a restaurant. He turned onto a little side road that looked like it had a bunch of shops and cafés from a road that seemed to be Main Street. He drove slowly down the little road, not paying much of attention to the people that surrounded it. All of a sudden he stopped to avoid hitting some people that were crossing in the middle of the road. As soon as he stopped an old Buick crashed into the back of his car.

It was obvious to the passenger of the Buick that Greg was not very angry about being in a car accident, but this was an unusual place for Greg and not the kind of unusual that provoked fear. Both cars pulled in-front of a little grocery store that was surrounded by more produce stands than Greg had ever seen in his life.

For Greg it was a place away from all common places and one that was rich in timeless treasures. He looked over at the passenger of the car that had hit him and saw for the first time that it was a young woman.

To his surprise, the very sight of her made him forget all that had happened so far in the day, for she was like a goddess that he had only read about and never believed could be real. He thought to himself that she probably was the most beautiful woman he had ever seen, something that was truly made by God's own hand.

She looked as if she was a soft crystal-like snowflake that dances with the cold winter wind and never knows sorrow. He walked over to her car and spoke in a soft tone hoping to calm the anger that showed on her face,

"I'm sorry about having to stop all of a sudden; I was trying to avoid those people over there. Are you okay? You're not hurt or anything, are you?"

She looked at him and paused for a moment as the anger disappeared off her face then she casually smiled at him. She replied, "No, everything's okay and I'm not hurt, just mad that I crashed my brother's car. I figured you would be screaming at me right now for following too closely behind you and hitting your Cadillac."

Greg smiled and said, "I'm not mad since this whole thing is my fault anyway.

Greg paused to just look at the woman. He stared into her and looked inside of her. Greg asked, "If you don't mind me asking, I would really like to know something. It's kind of important. Do you believe in dreams telling you about things that are going to change your life even if you don't know it yet?"

The woman replied, "Yes I do, and sometimes they lead to places you need to escape in order to be lost. Lost places are the places that change your life for the best. You look like you have experienced something like that before."

"I think I'm beginning to or I already have," said Greg. "I had this really vivid dream and I think it led me here. I know this will sound crazy or like some really bad pick-up line, but I think I was meant to come here."

The woman looked at him and said, "It's not that crazy; maybe you were meant to come here. Anyway, I don't think it's that crazy because like I said I do believe in that kind of stuff. By the way my name is Sierra Isabel Leon." She stuck out her hand to shake Greg's and a beautiful smile was on her face.

Greg took her hand and smiled, which was something he had not done in a long time. He looked at her long and looked deep into her eyes, which he began to be lost in and then he said to her, "I know."

THE END OF THE LETTER

It was a dark and stormy night. Actually, no, that would be too common for something like this and this story is everything uncommon.

It was a slow paced rainy night filled with the stalking of death. Death for me was a hungry monster hunting its next prey so it could be fed while waiting behind its own nightmarish memories. The rain slowly fell in small, but sonorous drumbeats on top of the ambulance as it whizzed carefully through the rain soaked streets of the city. Although I was fading in and out of consciousness inside of the vehicle, time seemed to slow down, but perhaps it was always this way as death approached.

After what seemed like an eternity the ambulance drove up to the hospital and the crew that drove me there with the purpose of stopping this monster rushed me through the hallways of the hospital. Each flashing light above me was a flashing memory of all those that I had killed and all those that I loved. But the persistence of my memory only brought back that single important memory of her and all the good that she had brought to my life.

I was wheeled into the emergency room and her memory faded away while the only things that loomed were the scattering of nurses and flashing lights from the hospital machines.

I could feel the blood and the insides from my lower body pouring over the bed onto the floors and then suddenly all sounds went away except the dripping of my blood on the floor like the slow drip of a leaky kitchen faucet. Then a soothing and sorrowful voice from somewhere above me saying,

"I guess death and life for you will start and end with a letter."

It had been a long night so far and the whiskey wasn't making it any easier. It was another one of those days for me as I sat and stared at the piece of paper on the wall. The TV was blaring low muffled sounds in the background; just the right level to push me back into my trance as I tried to push away my contempt for this world and my own life. I found myself wondering if I had eaten that day, or if it had been another liquid diet for me.

Suddenly I jumped up to the phone ringing, hoping that maybe my waiting was finally over. I answered it and immediately recognized her voice.

"Hi John," she said.

"Hi back kiddo," I replied.

"It's been awhile, hasn't it?" she whispered.

"Yes, it's been too long," I said to her, feeling my pulse begin to race.

"I want to see you, can you meet me?" she asked.

"Where do you want to meet?"

"How about the place?" she replied.

With a smile on my face I said, "Our place, you got it."

I slammed the phone down with excitement and rushed to grab my keys and coat, knocking over a tray of magazines in the process. I was in a hurry because I was going to see my Annabeth. I was so excited that it didn't register in my head that she was dead and it couldn't be her. I saw her die. Could I have been mistaken? Could the doctors have been wrong?

Maybe it was all an illusion. Maybe she was hiding, waiting for the right moment when it was time for her to come back again and that time had finally arrived.

Whatever might have been true or false I had to see her and find out what had happened and why my life was the way it was now. She had always made sense out of things and brought peace to the simplest of moments. I needed her to do that again.

That's why I drove fast and didn't care about the dangers that could hinder me on my way to the place. I arrived at the diner where we had first met and it was a place very familiar, not only because of her, but because I had spent so much time in it with her. It was a place that we would meet each other for coffee and breakfast quite often, so it wasn't surprising that she would want to meet me there.

I went inside the diner to see if she was there, waiting in our usual place. She wasn't there, but it could just be that I arrived before she did. I sat down in our usual booth and the waitress who had worked that same shift and that same section got me a cup of coffee. I seemed to know her well and she didn't even have to ask what to get me to drink. She instinctively knew what I wanted and what I always yearned for.

It was beginning to rain hard outside now, and it had already been a long time since I arrived. I was worried, more so because maybe this could all be a dream. She wasn't here and I thought for the first time that night that I didn't hear her on the phone, but then again, I could hear her. I could hear her as plain as the wind whistling through the trees in the midst of the storm. Her voice was ringing in my head, echoing the memory of that night, a night that would change our lives for the worst.

It seemed like that she haunted me in every sense, but it wasn't a bad thing because it was the only thing keeping me going. As silly as it might sound, it was my only reason for living. After all, hope like irony had the strangest sense of humor. I sat there in the same place that I always sat when waiting for her when she was running late, and where we would sit together telling each other how our day was over a nice cup of coffee.

Most times I wouldn't have to wait very long for her, but this time the wait became longer and longer. I always seemed to be waiting for nothing or everything. It was always my hope to be waiting for everything and that's what my Annabeth was: my everything.

The manager came out from the back of the diner. He was burly man, worn down by the 17 hour shifts he worked and the stale coffee he served. He was friendly though, at least as friendly as anyone could be when spending such long hours with the decaying growth of society, people like me, or at least what I had become.

He walked over to the waitress who had been serving me all night and it became apparent for the first time as I overheard the words coming out of his mouth the truth that had eluded me for so long and I effused to accept.

The burly man sighed and said, "He's here again, I thought you were going to tell him not to come in here anymore; I thought you were going to finally tell him the truth."

"I can't do that. Can't you see that he's hurting and that me telling him to go or that I don't care anymore could be the one thing that pushes him over the edge? I can't do that to him."

"Somebody has to. He'll never learn to get on with his life if he doesn't hear it, and it might as well come from you since you seem to be part of the cause."

"Look, I just can't do it, it wouldn't be right," she said.

"Fine, either you do it now, or I will. I don't want to see him agonizing over a stupid memory and wasting what life he has left in my diner."

"It's not stupid. It's his hope, and if it keeps him living in one capacity or another then let him keep living," she replied.

"It's only stupid if it's not true. Now do it; it's time to put an end to this," the manager said.

The waitress walked over to where I was and sat down. This was unusual because she always wanted to stand up and keep her distance. She looked at me hard and very truthfully.

"John I think we finally have to talk. I've wanted to talk to you about this for a long time," she said.

"What is it Kate? I hope I'm not keeping you from your other customers," I said.

"Look, although I do like seeing you almost every day, you need to quit coming here and waiting for her. She's not coming back; she's finally gone and there is nothing that can bring her back," said Kate.

"Hey, she's just late as usual," I said to her.

"Damnit John, you need to let her go. She's dead."

"I know she's just putting you up to this and that she spares no expense to pull a joke on me," I replied.

"John, she was my daughter and I loved her very much. Seeing you two together made me very happy for you both, but she's gone, and although you come here almost every night expecting her to walk through those doors and kiss you hello, it isn't going to happen. You have to accept that and get on with your life," Kate said, almost yelling.

"She's not dead! I heard her on the phone saying she was going to meet me here tonight so we could catch up with one another since we haven't seen each other for a long time. I know she'll be here!" I yelled.

"John, don't keep doing this to yourself. You remember what happened, don't you?" Kate asked.

"I remember something that seems like a nightmare, but it's not real and she will come back when she's ready. I know it's a dream, it couldn't be real," I replied.

"You remember the wreck don't you? You were entering the diner together when a truck slid on the wet street and drove through the front door and hit you both. You were hurt very badly, but she received the brunt of the impact and was killed instantly," Kate explained to me.

"Yes, but it was all a dream, and one that I must have explained to you in detail, wasn't it?" I asked her with a questioning look. I didn't like where this was going one bit.

"John, if it was a dream then where did you get all that scarring on your side, and why do we have a new paint and plaster job around the front entrance?" Kate asked.

I leaned over and lifted my shirt up to feel the scaring on my side. It was like lightning striking the memory of the truck hitting me and Annabeth. All the pain came rushing back in a New York minute. I could see the truck as plain as the rain falling outside coming through the old building and hitting us both. I jumped out of my seat and rushed to the door.

I slowly ran my hands over the new plaster and new paint that was the same color as the paint job in the diner, but had more clarity than the old age colored paint throughout the rest of the place. I had to feel it for a long time to find out if it was real or not, and then suddenly the flashing memories of that horrific night knocked me over onto the floor.

The memory was so intense it was like I was living it again and again, over and over until I, too, was dead. I couldn't stop the revelation, and then the tears came for my Annabeth. They were replaced by anger and sorrow mixed up together, something that was as lethal as a bullet piercing the head.

"No, this can't be. I won't believe it to be true. It can't be the truth. I won't let it, I won't let this be true with me, and she will come back," I shouted.

I ran out of the diner into the rain soaked streets without even looking to see if it was clear. As I looked over my right shoulder a pair of head lights came out of nowhere, rushing the death that was stalking me. My whole body froze as if to wait for the inevitable and I stood there staring down the lights at the end of the tunnel as they came closer and closer, and then it happened.

My body was hit and it flew through the air into the windshield of a parked car. I wasn't dead, but I was cut very badly and very deep from the waist up. My blood was beginning to pour out and be washed by the rain until the street below was covered by the stain of water mixed with blood.

I laid on the bed in the emergency room and my last thoughts were about how I ended up here. I thought about all the events that led to this moment and the twisted irony of how I should suffer the same fate as my Annabeth. As my blood poured out and the pain pushed me into my eternal sleep, I pulled out the letter that I had been carrying with me every day since that night when I truly died, the night that my Annabeth was taken from me and my life was shattered.

I wasn't the same man after that, but it was all over now. I closed my eyes for the last time and this sleep would now be my salvation. The letter dropped to the ground and a nurse picked it up to hand to the doctor standing over me. The nurse just looked at the blood soaked letter and the dying man on the hospital bed with the strangest of looks, but she had already begun to figure out what the doctor had meant by the man's life beginning and ending with a letter.

"Dr. Gray can you take over while I get Dr. Stone out of here. It looks like you won't have to do much since the patient is already dead," the nurse said.

"Sure thing Joan. Time of death 11:18 pm" Dr. Gray replied

Dr. Stone began to cry as he heard those words spoken by Dr. Gray which was unusual for this strong man of science, but this time he couldn't help it. He held the letter tight because it was the only thing left that could make sense out of everything.

It was a thick letter and it was one that words were being added to for it was never finished until death would come and claim it's writer. The Doctor cried more at the moment of his brother's death than he had in the last twenty years and part of his sorrow was for the fact that the letter he held would never tell the complete story of all that happened.

"Dr. Stone, are you alright?" asked the nurse. She'd never seen him break down over the death of a patient before.

"Yes, it's just..."

" It's just what?" asked the nurse.

"He's my brother, and I think his torture is finally over so I'm happy and sad in a strange way," he replied.

"I'm sorry Dr. Stone. I'm sorry that you have to be here for this. If you don't mind me asking, what happened with your brother that would drive him to this?"

Dr. Stone in a somber tone began to answer her question, "About a year ago his fiancé died in a horrific car accident and it nearly killed him, too. The day it happened he was going to propose to her and make it official by giving her a ring. Anyway he has never gotten over it and he has tortured himself over it ever since then, thinking that she is still alive and claiming that on more than one occasion he could hear her voice over the phone when he received a phone call. He just hasn't been the same since then because he won't let it go and I knew that a physical death for him would be very soon. It's just hard for me to accept that it's here now and I won't ever see him again."

The nurse replied "Again I'm sorry for your loss, and if there's anything you need don't hesitate to give me a call."

"Thank you. and thank you for giving me this letter that fell from his coat pocket. I can finally put this to rest now as this letter is truly his end. Now if you'll excuse me, I need to go and call our parents to tell them that John is finally dead, and his torture is over," he replied.

He walked down the hall to his office as the nurse gave him a confused look, not knowing what he meant. He entered his cluttered office and sat down by the phone. He pulled out the letter that John carried with him. It was a love letter that he wrote Annaneth asking her to marry him and saying everything he felt when it came to being with her.

He told her in the letter that he loved her very much and that his life truly began when he met her and that was when he began to write this letter even if it was only in memory at the time. He had said before to her on many occasions how his life truly began when he met her, but he wanted a record for her to know how his life was changed by her. This was the purpose of the letter.

He remembered when John told him about the letter and what was in it, and how he poured out his heart into the words on the paper, since he was not a man of words or much of a writer. After the tragedy the letter continued and was added to by his grieving brother.

The last parts of the letter were filled with rage and regret, and an anger towards God for taking Annabeth away. It was his cry for help and his own way of dealing with the pain, but towards the end of the letter he was released from his pain in a strange way.

Stone read through all of the letter, but it was the last lines of the letter that caught the doctor's attention most of all, and as he read it he began to cry for his brother and the love that was taken from him, and putting him on the path of the slow stalking death that waits for us all. The last line read,

"Annabeth I love you and not even death will make me stop. If you become lost and are taken from me, even though death I will come and find you, for nothing will keep us apart. Even through death I will follow because I love you that much and this is how much I need you in my life."

He picked up the phone and called his parents.

"Mom, Dad, it's about John. His torture is finally over and the letter has its end." He talked to his parents for almost thirty minutes and then quietly put the phone back on the cradle.

He closed his eyes for a long and somber moment and then opened them looking up at the window in his office door. He saw the faces of Annabeth and John and they smiled at him like so many times before while waiting for him to come and have dinner with them. He couldn't believe it and closed his eyes just to make sure, but Annabeth and John were still there. He got up to open the door and suddenly the images were gone as if to have an end to the letter.

Dr. Stone would write to Kate, Annabeth's mother, explaining all that had happened and how the grief of loved ones would never let any of this truly end.

"It's going to be worse than that," I said.

"Well, I know that the city will be destroyed, but they can rebuild it," she said.

"That's not what I was talking about," I said.

"What do you mean that it'll be worse?"

"A part of our culture is being washed away with this hurricane, and a part of my youth that was very special to me is disappearing."

"I'm sorry. I didn't know New Orleans meant that much to you," she replied.

I didn't know how to explain it to her. I didn't know how tell her how much this city meant to me. We had been married for a few years now and she had told me all about the time she had spent in Paris. We had spent countless hours talking about how much being in Paris had changed her life like something out of a Hemmingway Novel or Audrey Hepburn movie, but I had never told her about the time I had spent in New Orleans.

I knew my wife very well by the stories she would tell of how Paris changed her as a person, but I had never allowed her to really know me and how music became so much a part of my life because I had lived in New Orleans for a while. As I watched my favorite city and the place that brought me into adulthood being destroyed on the television I found the courage to finally tell her about this point in my life.

"I've never told you about the better part of a year that I spent in New Orleans and how I finally grew up while being there?" I asked her already knowing the answer.

"You've never said anything about that to me," she said. "How did New Orleans change you?

"In the same way Paris changed your life," I said, "New Orleans changed mine. It's where I truly learned what music was."

"I thought you learned to play the piano as a child and by studying it in college. Isn't that where you also learned how to be a professional musician?"

"Sure, that's all true, but through all that I didn't truly learn music," I said. "I learned the true art of music in New Orleans over the eight months I spent there trying to be a professional musician."

"Well, I think it's time I finally hear this story, don't you think?" she asked.

I just smiled at her, got up to get us a drink and replied, "It may take a while, but yes, it's time. You know how sometimes you'll say you don't know me at all when it comes to me playing the piano because I enter a different world?" With a surprised look she responded with a nod and then I told her, "After this story you will, and you'll finally have a part of my soul."

My wife and I didn't talk a lot because I didn't have a lot to say to her. It was easier for me say what I felt in music. This story was hard for me to tell because for so long it was the one part of me that nobody had a piece of and I always knew that the people close to me couldn't understand it.

I didn't know for sure if I could trust my wife to understand and not hold it against me, but I also knew that if we were going to have a future and a strong relationship, then I had to give more of myself to her. So I finally began my story of why New Orleans was so special to me.

When I was about 19 or 20 years old I took my first trip to New Orleans. I was going to college in Texas on a football scholarship and bartending on the weekends at some little college joint called Dixie's. It was spring break and some of the girls I worked with at this bar thought it would be fun to go to New Orleans for a couple of days.

One of the girls I worked with was from there and wanted to show those of us that had never been one of the "best places on this damn earth", as she called it. So there I was on my way with two girls I hardly knew driving down to New Orleans, about to enter a world that I had only read about in books, but not very nice books.

When we got there we found one of the last rooms available and it was in the most luxurious hotels in New Orleans, the Omni Royal Orleans hotel. Somehow we got a good price and I assume it had something to do with the girl from New Orleans knowing somebody there, but that's how one usually gets things in a city like this. It was a beautiful hotel right in the heart of the French Quarter; we were only a ten minute ride on the trolley from where the action was on Bourbon Street. Now when you're young there's only one thing you want to do in New Orleans and that's party. That we did, for about two days straight in a town that really never sleeps, where the music is always playing from the dingy jazz halls to the street corner musicians.

The partying was fun and even making love to two beautiful women in a big comfortable bed while being serenaded by jazz musician on the street corner down below was nice, but it wasn't the thing that made me fall in love with this city.

The music I heard in every joint we visited and the songs from every street corner musician I passed were like heaven's sound mixed with exotic lust where you couldn't help but give into temptation without the worry of your falling soul. I don't think the girls I went with were that keen on the music we heard compared to the liquor we had every night, but as for me, my soul was lost to the music and I knew I would never return.

We only stayed for two days and I only got to see the French Quarter while we were there, but that's all it took for me to be hooked. I knew I had to be a part of it, a part of this "no need for words" music scene, especially after the first night we were there and I got to jam on the piano with some jazz musicians in one of the joints we had visited. Now this feeling I had could have been from the standing ovation I got for my playing and the owner offering me another chance to play, but when I was on stage I felt that I had just been born and that was what it was like to be alive.

I went back to the Texas town I was living in at the time, but not after leaving part of my soul to be stored as a keepsake in the Soul Kitchen of America.

Home and college for me wasn't the same after this trip because I felt like a part of me was missing and I knew I had to find it. However, unlike many who lose a part of themselves and then spend a lifetime trying to find it, I knew where I had left myself. I wasn't back too long, maybe a few days, before I felt like I had to go back to New Orleans.

At the time I had nothing holding me back, not even my college education. There was nothing to keep me in Texas, so I packed some of my things, moved out of the house I was living in with some roommates, and drove south to a place called The Big Easy.

I didn't have a plan. I had no sense of what it truly meant to struggle as a musician and I had no idea of the true nature of New Orleans. I didn't know how this city could claim a man's soul while at the same time destroying him from the inside out and then remaking him into a true human being with passion and soul; the two things that give us the means to really, really live.

When I arrived I stopped to breathe the air, to breath in the beginning a new life, and a chance for a remodel in who I was. I was here to try my hand at being a professional musician.

The first place I stopped at was the little joint where I first played music in New Orleans, The Blue Nile Club. It was a little dingy place with old dirty wooden floors that creaked a soft melody of experienced jazz and was filled with the smell of smoke and cheap bourbon. It was the best place for true music, the music made from true human experience and sorrow, the music of life.

It wasn't the most glamorous of joints, but it was real and it was the best place to learn the very nature of music. The stage was in the furthest corner of the place, but it was the very underbelly and soul of The Blue Nile Club.

I walked in, and as I tried to take in all that the place had to offer, the bartender came over to me and said in kind of an annoyed tone,

"Are you lost, can I help you find your way?"

"Perhaps you can," I said. "I played piano here about a week ago in some open mike night with a bunch of local jazz musicians and I was looking for the owner of the place to see if I could get some other gigs."

"Well we get a lot of piano players here; you'll have to be more specific," he said, obviously still annoyed.

"I played with some guys that hang out here a lot, I think one of them is called Sam and I got a standing ovation the night I played."

"That doesn't really help me, but if you played with Sam then you might actually be good. Let me get Dave, the owner."

The bartender went to the back to get the owner and the both of them walked out together. Dave seemed to recognize me as he walked toward me, but it was apparent he didn't remember my name. He shook my hand and said,

"Well it's the piano kid who got a standing ovation about a week ago. I was wondering if you were ever going to show back up at my place again."

"I'm here and I'm looking for work as a piano player," I said.

"I don't have anything for just a piano player; we mainly get jazz bands to play at The Blue Nile."

"Oh, well I need to find some kind of work as a musician, I just moved down here to see if I could make as a professional musician."

"Hold on there, kid, it takes time to get to that level and you have to pay your dues. I already know you haven't done any of that yet or I would have heard of you long before last week."

"I'm willing to start somewhere. Hell, even you said I was good enough to do this business after playing that night and the standing ovation I got."

"You're good, I'll give you that, but I don't know if you should've moved down here and given up on college to try and pursue this. If you're willing to start somewhere then maybe we can accommodate you in some way."

"Thanks, I'll start anywhere I have to."

"Well I hear Sam needs a piano player in his little jazz band since his other one died from old age. If he'll take you on then you can start playing with his band here about three or four nights a week."

"Hey, I'll take anything I can get."

"Good, because it's about the only thing you're going to get as a musician around here. Musicians are like bums and drunks in New Orleans: they're everywhere you turn. "

About an hour later Dave had located Sam and his band to see if they might be interested in me. I was nervous; the only thing I'd had to eat was some complimentary gumbo at The Blue Nile to which I couldn't begin to describe the contents of. It was tasty, but like most Cajun food it was good because I didn't know what was in it.

Sam gave me an informal audition and after about three songs and jamming with his band I had the job. However, just because I had a job didn't mean I was good enough to be there, but this is where my true education would begin.

Sam was an old jazz musician who had been playing in cathouses throughout New Orleans since he was about ten years old, and he still had the lungs of a young boy to blow a trumpet. He was well traveled and had been a part of many jazz ensembles from the west coast to the east coast, even jamming once or twice with Miles Davis.

He never knew for sure if he had played with him one or two nights because he was too drunk to remember, but not drunk enough to play music from his very soul with one of the greats. He had settled back in New Orleans after spending about 25 years on the road and decided to dedicate himself to producing young jazz talent that could have the stuff to make it. He had formed and broke up about a dozen bands since he settled back here, always looking for the perfect mix of music and soul in a group of musicians to play what he called "the real thing".

Now he had five other members of his band. There was Jonesy, a cross eyed drummer with glasses thicker than a microscope, but he never missed a beat. He was the quiet one who only expressed himself with the soft beat of the drums.

There was Rick the bass player who never quite felt comfortable with an electric bass and had hands that stretched the entire handle reaching down to find the deep notes of the song and the soul. There was Marc the trombone player, who was never seen without a smile on his face or a joke to tell anybody who would listen. He had one hell of a sweet melody when it came to jazz. Then there was Jerone the saxophone player whose talent could rival Coltrane himself.

It's bold to say such things, but it's true, and he was also the smart ass of the group. As much of a jackass as he could be, you couldn't help but like him, but there was always one problem that consumed him. He was a heroin addict, and it was just as much a part of him as jazz. All of these guys were street musicians who had been playing all their lives. They were thrown together as one of Sam's last creations, with a sweet melody that could reach deep inside someone and find the purest form of love. As good as all of them were, Jerone was probably the one musician who could make it and become a legend.

This was the group I was thrown in with and would learn from; I would learn much more than music, I would learn many different shades of life that I had only heard about as if it were legend. So there I was, a part of this little jazz band within a day of moving down to New Orleans, and the next night I had my first gig with them at The Blue Nile. I can't say I was that good, but I had a place to learn and some of the best musicians to learn from.

Being part of a jazz band isn't like jamming with some local musicians in a garage somewhere, where the only thing you do is just play music. When you're in a jazz band there's more than just playing the music, there's finding the perfect balance of rhythm and harmony, the basics of living life.

You have to be in sync with every member of the group to create the perfect harmony, the perfect wave of tempo. Jazz is about feeling, it's about living the songs that are being played because they are part of your very soul. This is what I was taught when it came to jazz and the road to this understanding was just part of the education I would receive while in New Orleans. This was the real education I got from Sam.

I can't remember if the jazz band I played with had a name or not; for the most part we were just referred to as Sam's Jazz Band because everybody knew Sam throughout the clubs in the French Quarter. We would play about three nights a week at The Blue Nile and there were also other places that would give us a gig.

All in all, we played five or six nights a week and sometimes in the afternoons on the streets throughout the French Quarter, depending on what kinds of events were on the calendar for the tourists. There was music on every street corner and music in the parks was a big thing for the city. As professional musicians we played anywhere we could, and anywhere we were offered money.

After every gig there was usually time for drinking and other things, which was a pastime for professional musicians. I had never known this, so after the gig we played I would be inducted by ritual to the musicians great past time of unwinding. I wasn't old enough to drink legally, but that didn't matter in the French Quarter; if you could see the bar then you were old enough to drink. I wasn't too big of a drinker either, but I would be initiated by good southern whiskey. Sitting around, drinking, and just hanging with one another could last for hours even past closing time.

Everybody in The Blue Nile was like family so I don't remember ever really paying for a drink; we would just sit around as if we had known each other all our lives and this could go on till dawn. I have never felt more at home in an unfamiliar place than I did at The Blue Nile.

As all the other guys would sit with their drinks and jawjack with one another while flirting with the women parading through the club, some local and some doing the tourist thing, I would mainly sit around and just listen. I really didn't know that much at that time in my life so the best thing for me was to sit and listen.

I hadn't really lived life up to that point and college is just a small part of life. You have to get out there into the world to see every aspect of it to really know what life is, to really be educated in things. Sam knew that this wasn't me and that's why he always referred to me as the rookie. So after my first gig with the band he got me a girl, which really is like a rite of passage for passing into manhood in a strange sort of way.

"Until you've done it with a working girl," Sam told me, "you don't know what the sweet lowdown really is." That's where you find that things can be sweeter in the bottomed out hollows of life because they're more real and they never hide behind masks. Sleeping with a prostitute and not having to pay, especially one that can teach you a few things, is just one of those things.

You might not believe me, but the best education a man can receive in life is being taught how to be a great lover, because we are never born with some great erotic instinct. Talent in the bedroom has to be taught and the best time for this is when a man is young so he can be taught by an older woman who has been around and will never fail to tell you the truth. Unfortunately young girls still have the problem of extreme exaggeration, and yes this is just one more thing that Sam would teach me about life.

The girl Sam found for me and the one that would teach me talent in the bedroom was a local working girl named Melanie. She was regular at some of the less classier strip joints who offered more than just dancing topless. She was in her thirties, although no one knew her real age and was one of the most beautiful women I had ever seen. She was the type of woman that had experienced almost anything imaginable; there wasn't anything that really shocked her. To look at her you wouldn't think she was very smart, but she was very keen about life and there was an artistic side to her that was never seen behind her great physical assets.

She just used what she had to make money, which was more than art can do for you sometimes, although as she would say, sex was just a different kind of art. Looking back, I think it was her artistic side and her dry sarcastic sense of humor that made her beautiful. That's what I loved about her more than anything.

Melanie was the perfect example of someone who hid behind a mask, and you had to go behind it to find out who they really were. She wasn't just a working girl using sex to make money; she was a beautiful artistic soul full of life. Like most working girls in New Orleans, there was more to her than her physical assets, and she was just as full of shit as anyone else; she was normal.

She helped me pass into manhood that night. I wasn't a virgin, but young and immature girls never open your eyes to the truth of the world that's hidden behind the mask of youth. Melanie removed my mask that night and I began to see the word anew; someone who sees it more cynical and with realistic eyes. It was the night of my first gig in New Orleans that the world turned for me, and I was reborn, never to be the same again. I put the childish things away and grew up overnight.

I don't remember a lot of the nights I spent in New Orleans, but no matter how much whiskey I'd had that night, I could never forget the events of my first night there.

All total I would spend about eight months in New Orleans before finally coming home. My nights were spent the same way; music, drinks and lively conversation about the real human philosophy, the experience of truly being alive.

I would stay up almost all night, every night hanging out with the band and the half dead inhabitants that would come and see us play. While this went on I was getting to know a different class of people. They were people I had only read about from books of the Beat writers or a Faulkner novel, real people trying to find something to sustain them in their sheepish lives, like soulful music or smooth whiskey.

During the days I saw New Orleans and the heart of the city. I visited the usual places like the cemeteries, the Garden District with houses that were built in the Civil War era, all of the French Quarter, and even the Voodoo Museum. I saw every historical site there was in New Orleans, but the real substance of the city came from visiting the places that aren't found on maps.

They're the places that we don't want to know exist because they're the ugly side of life. It's that place where pimps, prostitutes, gamblers, junkies, and people who have nothing left to lose hang out; there in the back alleys and dark buildings where most tourists never stray. I even ventured to those kinds of places just to see with my own eyes what they were really about and hopefully come out with a better understanding of life's darker side.

I saw more than I probably should have, and whatever innocence I had left after those moments vanished with a whisper. One day on my exploration into those places I saw Jerone there getting his fix to feed the monkey that had been on his back for so long. He had a desperate look on his face as he dealt over the money to his dealer. It was as if he was trying to say without words that it was this which was the only thing keeping him alive, and he would do anything to have it.

I had only been there about two months when I saw this, and Jerone never knew that I had seen him that day. Up to that point, I hadn't realized how much of a problem he really had, but you would never know it by the way he played. The heroin never affected his genius on the sax and it was the only thing that it didn't affect.

I tried to get to know Jerone while I was playing in the band, but he never let me, and I think it's because he never liked me. Maybe it was because I was white and just a young cocky kid posing as a musician. However, it seemed he was always in a bad mood and was mad at the world. There were moments when he was pleasant to be around, and after sharing those rare moments with him I like to think it was the drugs that affected his mood. Everybody in the band would cling to that notion.

I tried to get to know everybody in the band while I was there, but most of them were hard to know. The only two people I really did get to know were Sam and Marc. Sam would talk to me a lot because he had a lot of knowledge to pass on to me.

He knew right off that his role in my life would be as a teacher, so we would spend a lot of time talking about music and spending time on the road. Marc, on the other hand, as seasoned as he was in playing jazz just simply loved people and loved talking to people. It was hard to shut him up, but as I look back he was an absolute delight to talk to because he was always talking about something funny. I don't remember not ever laughing when I was around him. Looking back, I don't feel like I really knew any of them at all, but maybe I knew enough, and that's all that really matters.

I got to know these men as jazz players, as artists, and as fellow musicians. This is how it is with musicians; we never know the people we play with as the people they really are. We know them by their sound and the music they play, and that's enough.

I don't remember most of the time I spent in New Orleans because most of it is just a blur of smoke and whiskey; my time there was just like a dream. I do remember seeing the city and many of the most interesting parts of it, even the dark underbelly of it. I can remember the smell and look of every club we played in even if I couldn't remember every night that we played.

Each place had its own distinctive look, but they all smelled of smoke and cheap bourbon. It's a smell that has never left me and one that I still love today. I wonder if every jazz or blues joint smells that way; it would be nice because it's the smell of something real. Out of all the things I could remember and couldn't remember there are two moments that stand out in my memory more than anything and they are the two that changed my life the most. The first one would be the one that would make me leave and finally come home.

After being there for about eight months, the band that I played with came to an end. We were getting pretty well known throughout the clubs and getting some good recognition outside New Orleans on the jazz circuit. I guess it doesn't hurt when you get to jam with Wynton Marsalis for a night.

He had come home for a few days and like any musician, you're never home unless you're in a club. We happened to be one of the acts at Tipitina's on a beautiful cool fall night and there he was in the club like a god among mortals. Since we were playing at the time and he liked the sound and wanted to know if he could jam with us for a while, but as I later found out he and Sam knew each other.

They had crossed paths on more than one occasion and they were friends on the only level that musicians can be. They had complete respect for one another and the craft they have. After having a brief conversation with him I can honestly say that I have never met anybody more humbling, nicer, and worthy to be envied.

As our band gained more and more fame and the disbelief started to be stripped away that a white boy could play true jazz on the piano, we became more and more destructive. Our sound was still there and Jerone was still just as much of a master on the saxophone as he ever was despite having more and more problems with the monkey that constantly stayed on his back.

However, that was the thing, his heroin problem was becoming more and more of a problem and he was taking Rick down the same demented path he was on. No matter how high or comatose he became, he could still play and he never missed a note. Even then one could still get lost in his music, his soulful notes, and his true art.

The band members would fight constantly with each at the end of our eight month stay with one another. Jerone would bicker amongst everybody and the only attitude he had toward Sam was one of contempt, just like a teenage child has towards a parent.

Sam would spend more time babysitting everybody towards the end instead of composing and helping fine tune our sound so hopefully one day we could play for more than just New Orleans audiences, but it would never happen. I tried to stay out of most fights because I was still for the most part an outsider, but there were a lot of times that I wasn't at least a little bit drunk so I even had to get in the middle of it sometimes, which just made everybody hate me more except for Marc and Sam.

Sam would constantly say that he was too old for any of this and he was going break up the band because everybody kept acting like children. He never did it because of the sound we had. By the end of our run we had a perfect sound and we were in perfect sync with one another. When that happens everything else takes a back seat because it's very rare when something like that happens.

However, it would never last, because like most great things they eventually pass away into a cold unforgiving night. Sometime in the fall we were back at The Blue Nile after being on the music circuit in New Orleans for a few months. We toured just about every place you could think of where music was allowed to be played in New Orleans and then we finally came home to where I started.

On the night we played I noticed Jerone being even more agitating than usual to everyone in the band. He didn't look well at all, even more so than usual. Rick didn't look good either, and as we started into our set I knew that the both of them had taken a really big hit of the juice, but it never affected our sound that night. We were still good that night and they were still masters of their sound.

After our set was done and we started to clear the stage Jerone, rushed back stage just in time before he collapsed. He hit the floor hard and shook violently. He was overdosing and this time there was no going back or coming out of it.

I was the first one to reach him so I propped him up off the dusty floor trying to get him to stop shaking, but nothing I did helped him. The other members of the band rushed back stage to help, as well as Dave the owner, but nobody knew what to do except Sam. He just told us to hold him still and wait for an ambulance. He had seen this before.

Years of being on the road playing with drug addicts had taught him that the only thing that could be done was to wait for a medic. A shot of adrenalin was the only thing that could save him if the medics could get there in time, but this was the Big Easy and time wasn't something of importance.

All of us just watched in horror as Jerone shook violently while he overdosed, slowly drifting away into restful sleep. He died just as the medics arrived at the club, and all that time I held him slightly off the ground. Jerone died right there in my arms even though he would be pronounced dead a few minutes later after the medics tried vainly to revive him.

They had to try because it was their job, but we all knew he was dead before the medics could try anything. None of us cried except Rick; we just stood there and stared in disbelief, even though we all knew that one day the juice would get the better of him. Today was that day and I can't say for sure if Rick cried out of sorrow or out of some misplaced guilt because he let his friend take too much of a hit that would eventually kill him.

All I know is that he ran out of the club that night as the medics loaded Jerone's body into the ambulance and we never saw him again. Rumor has it that he suffered the same fate in some dark back alley of the French Quarter, but those are just rumors.

Although, fate sometimes has a very sick and ironic sense of humor. And now as I remember back to the two of them arguing with one another before our set I like to think that they argued over the amount of heroin they took and Rick couldn't live with the guilt of his friend dying after taking too much.

I had never seen anybody die before, much less have someone die in my arms, but this event has never left me. Watching Jerone, a true artist and gifted musician, overdose on heroin and die made me look at life in a different way. I have never been careless with my life since then, and I knew that if I was ever going to make it as a musician, I couldn't carry anything with me as to be completely free to flow in the music.

None of us in the band went to the burial service, which just consisted of two grave diggers putting his body in a hollow grave that nobody would ever know the location of. He didn't have any family except fellow musicians and as a musician you can never remember someone being buried; you remember them on a stage playing their music, living their art. That's how I remember Jerone, because that was the only way that I knew him and I can never forget his sound.

As for the band, we never played again, and except for Sam and Marc I never saw anybody else from the band again after that night. To tell you the truth, I never heard about them again either.

The next day I saw Sam at The Blue Nile. He was reading a newspaper at the end of the bar while Marc was cleaning his instrument on stage. They were like two people waiting for a musician to walk in and the show to begin, but that day would be reserved for goodbyes. I knew the band was over and I also knew that I couldn't keep going on like nothing happened.

It had affected me too much and it would be awhile before I would get over it. I had truly grown up in New Orleans, but I still wanted to hold on to some of my innocence in youth and that couldn't happen in the Big Easy.

Sam just looked at me and smiled when I walked over. He knew I was looking for some clarity over what had happened the night before so he offered me a simple philosophy of life wrapped in a few kind words.

He said to me "Pull up a seat my young friend and I'll give you something you need to know."

"What makes you think I need to know anything about last night?"

"Because the lack of understanding is written all over your face, and being as you are, I know that you need to hear some encouragement so you can get on with the rest of your life."

"I've been trying to make sense of what happened, but I just don't get how things can change so fast from one day to the next. I mean, we were going along great then this happened."

"Welcome to the life of a musician," said Sam. "Life is like the notes we play. It's up and down; you never where they can take you. You've never seen someone die before have you?"

"No," I said, "it was the first time I'd ever seen something like that. I've never done any drugs before or seen somebody do them. If that's what it's like seeing somebody die from an overdose then I don't want see it again."

"It understandable, but you've woken up to what the world is really like and how such a gifted artist can be struck down by their own misdeeds. Now you know what true tragedy really is."

"Does it get any easier after something like this?" I asked.

"No, I wish I could tell you it does, but life is full of disappointments and misery. All we do is learn to cope with it and then try to find something not quite so bad that we can call happiness."

The bartender brought us a couple of drinks and some lunch. Sam and I just sat there for a moment sipping on our bourbon while Marc smiled and hummed a sweet Charlie Parker tune in the middle of cleaning his instrument on stage. After a long pause and the burning sensation of the drink had numbed my throat I asked Sam,

"So what now, what do I do?"

"I can't tell you that, you have to figure that on your own, but that's the joy of youth. It's getting to figure it out on your own and make all sorts of mistakes while clinging to the notion that you actually know something."

"Are you going to continue with the band and add new members?" I asked.

"Probably not, but I'll never quit playing. There will always be a song for me to play and a stage somewhere for me to stand on. I just gotta find where that is in due time."

"I guess I could always go on the road and try and make it."

"If you do you won't find anything easier than any of this. Its tough out there and you can end up just like Jerone or Rick."

"I think I'm smarter than that."

"That's got nothing to do with it, we can all fall and when we do we fall hard. That's what the road is. It may seem glorious and romantic, but it's even more dark and brutal to the human body."

"I guess I could always go back to school."

"And you'll be better at it because you've grown up now, your life has been changed while being down here, and probably for the better."

"You think that's what I should do?"

Sam just smiled and let out a light chuckle; then he sat there for a long moment. I thought at first he wasn't going to answer me and he probably didn't want to. However, like a teacher to an eager student you can't help but pass on some kind of knowledge or advice.

Finally he spoke up and said "Alright. You want advice then I'll tell you this: you have to live life like you play your music, with caution, passion, intensity, and vulnerability. True music is about playing how you live and it's with everything you are; that's why you live the music. If you do that the song will never leave you and there will always be a stage for you to play on. Now I can't tell you where you should go or what to do, but you have to live your music and you have to let the music be in you."

That's all he said to me, that was his only advice. Sam was my friend, but he was my teacher more than anything else and he told me all that I needed to know. I knew I was going to go home and Sam knew it, too. He knew what I later figured out; my life was more than the road.

I had more to offer than life on the road could provide me and Sam, being a true mentor, pointed me in the direction to finding that out with simple and profound words. They were words to live by and they are the words that I've carried with me every day. I shook his hand, and then said goodbye to Marc. He hugged me and made me laugh one more time and that was it with the Big Easy for me.

I left New Orleans that day and came home. I hadn't seen my family in eight months and when I came home they knew as I did that I wasn't the same, but it was in a good way. Before I left, I made one last stop to see Melanie.

She didn't say anything and didn't have to, because I was a changed man and in no small way she had a hand in that. All she did was kiss me and give and me a hug then she turned around and I never saw her again. No matter what though, I have never forgotten her and especially one of the most exciting, sexy, erotic moments I ever experienced, posing nude while she painted me.

That experience was the one thing that made me realize, to truly know someone is to go with them behind the mask they hide under. The last thing I did was make a stop at the Mississippi River and throw my spare change in the river as if I were making a wish or paying the boatman not to take me across just yet.

I never saw anybody that I knew down there ever again, even though I visited a few times since then. When I first moved to Chicago I got a postcard in the mail from New Orleans letting me know that Sam had passed away and there was going to be a service for him. The card came in care of The Blue Nile Club and I could only assume that Dave had tracked down as many musicians as he could that Sam had played with to let them know about the service.

I didn't make it, but I had flowers sent for the gravesite. It wasn't a proper tribute, but I like to think Sam knew he had a profound impact on me and for somebody like him it was the perfect gift.

"I came home a changed man," I told my wife as she sat there with a sorrowful look on her face. "And as I said before, I don't remember a lot of the time I spent there, but I do remember Jerone's death and Sam's words. They have never left me and they are the two things that really changed me. I still remember them as if they happened yesterday and it's been ten years since all this happened."

My wife finally spoke up after hearing this tale and said "Why didn't you ever tell me any of this? I mean, this is the one of the most profound parts of your life and something that completely changed you."

"I don't know, I guess I thought you wouldn't understand."

"Maybe not all of it, but your sense of finding the right sound makes perfect sense after hearing this story. Were you ever going to tell me about living in New Orleans?"

"I figured someday I would take you down there and show you, but since there really isn't a city anymore I thought I should tell you about the New Orleans I knew."

"I'm glad you did and I would have liked to see what you saw."

"You know, everybody has their one special place that really changes them: Hemmingway had Paris, Armstrong had New York, but I had New Orleans and now it's gone."

"They can always rebuild when this tragedy is over and what you had will never be gone because you have it in memory and you have it in your music."

"I guess you're right, but I feel like a home of mine is gone and I can never get it back."

"You may be surprised, you know they will rebuild because the spirit of the Big Easy as you described can't be taken away. I have a feeling that there are too many people like you who feel the same way about that city."

"What do you think is the best way to remember it, through song?" I asked.

"You could do that, but I think when they start rebuilding in the months to come we should go down there and help. You can show me what you took with you that made New Orleans so special."

Months later when the rebuilding process started, I took my wife to New Orleans and we volunteered through the Red Cross. I wanted to show her what this city really was, what I saw in it, and what I learned from it. It was a place more free than other places, where great music and a darker sense of life collide to bring a perfect balance of humanity; the true beauty of the world.

The Big Easy is the true melting pot of America where whites, creoles, and negroes are stewed in thick, sticky, gumbo like stew found below sea level. But what comes out of all that besides a little bit of tragic circumstances is a natural cuisine of true people. From those true people comes a creative expression that we live by and is inside of us, and that we dub jazz. All of this made me a better person, made me more humane, and the least I could was to help rebuild this Soul Kitchen.

The first day that we arrived and started working with other Red Cross and Habitat for Humanity members I saw one of the most extraordinary things. The best example of survival, the best example of true human passion which is what will make this city survive through this tragedy.

What I saw was a wide smiled trombone player standing on a street corner in the French Quarter talking with the crowd of relief workers and making them laugh. Then he started playing a familiar jazz tune from my youth so he could entertain us just a little bit. He was the epitome of Jazz, he was true music, and he was a living art.

MOMENT OF TRUTH

Reality Check! The time had finally come. My moment of truth where all chances fade away, leaving us with last minute decisions. I couldn't take it anymore in a city that never sleeps. The skyline was fading to black. I had seen it coming for a long time, but like most of us we don't want to admit it could happen to us. We tell ourselves that we're not insane or depressed That's what I had been telling myself while drowning away in a sea of pointless sex, trying to forget about the one I truly loved. There was no amount of alcohol or small piles of cocaine that would make me forget. That was my punishment and my blessing. I guess God has fucked up sense of humor.

She was gone now. She was dead and never coming back and in no small way, I had something to do with that. It had been the best of times once, but nobody had told me so I looked away, always, waiting for the other shoe to drop until it finally did. The one thing I realized is that over the last few years since that tragic event, time keeps ticking away even when we don't notice anymore. Perhaps it's pretty selfish of me to think that time could stop just for me, but somewhere in the past I used to be a big deal. No matter how many times they told me I was great or I saw my name in headlines I was still nobody. They told me I was an Inspiration, what a crock of shit – it was some lonely desperate soul's way of justifying why they fell in love with my work. I guess there had been more than one us snorting the coke that's handed to us by a masked stranger.

So here I was, years later, holding in my hands the last memory I had of them. My family – the family that slipped away...the family that I had pushed away until it was too late. They drifted away until I didn't know them anymore and yes, I could have saved it. But I was too busy with my own life, trying to make myself important, somebody destined for high society even though I couldn't see the truth about who I really was. What's the purpose of having a mirror if we're not going to look into it to see ourselves for who we really are? Ugh.

Eventually time slips away and our reality turns into our dreams and then when we least expect it our dreams turn into our reality. Sometimes it's good and sometimes it's the worst thing for us because then it happens, reality check. It's when we've finally hit rock bottom and there are no more hiding places from the truth that has plagued us for so long. It's the truth that we try to snort or drink away and there I go again letting the booze and the drugs do my thinking once again. I can't remember how I got to this point, but if I think really hard I can go back and see how it started. And maybe then I can change what happened. I've learned my lesson and God's a fair guy. Even a sinner like me can get a second chance or is that too much to ask for in this pitiful and disgusting charade that we call life.

As I stand there holding my memory I think back and there I am at the beginning. I see her once again, how she used to be. She had long dirty blond hair with those razor sharp blue eyes and that stubborn attitude that just made you want to be around her so you could learn to be an individual, not just one of the mere drones that walk blindly into a boring life. She was exciting, she was intoxicating, and I just wanted to be a part of it. I had seen her many times on the elevator in the building that we worked in. Always the same time, always the same smile, always the same smell for that was her. I didn't have to see her in order to know her – those little things always told me.

Months went by and I finally worked up the courage to talk to her. Of course I embarrassed myself when I did, but it was a foregone conclusion that I would. Although I hate to be a foregone conclusion this time it was alright because I was talking with her. So that's how it started, a simple question of do you want to have a cup of coffee with me as much of a cliché as it is. It worked and we started dating. She had enough bad relationships in the past so of course she didn't want to date; she just wanted to be friends. Most men would take that as a dagger in the heart, the great excuse of why you're not good enough to be with, but I was not most men, at least I didn't think I was. That was alright with me because just being around her was enough.

She even gave up sex, which I guess works for some, but we can't live without it no matter how much we try. It takes a special person to be a monk –to give up on that idea of love and most of us never have it in us. Also don't be fooled, don't let some stupid Christian tell you that sex isn't part of love and that intimacy can survive without it. Anybody who tells you that has never dared to enjoy that part of life and they're just setting you up for disappointment. What a shame for them. Now it worked for her, but only for a while.

This goes on for about two years until it's realized that there's more here than you thought and that you care more for one another than you want to admit. You even have that discussion – you know the one where you try and decide whether you can be soul mates, the one, meant for each other or whatever convincing cliché you want to come up with. Then in a moment of drunken haze when things have never been clearer you find your answer. Loving each other is the best thing you have going for one another. Loving each other is right, it makes sense, and it makes you forget all the bad things you've done to each other because you're true to one another and that means hurting each other more than anyone else ever has.

So there we are finally admitting that we're in love with one another. Is it Time to move forward? I would say so – the dream has become reality with one more added wrinkle. You finally say it- the one thing that can save you or destroy you. One night while making dinner and after a nice bottle of wine has been opened. She finally says it.

"I love you, you know that right?"

"I know, "you reply in your less than cool Han Solonesque tone. "You know I love you, right?"

"I know."

"It's the first time we've said it before."

"Yeah how about that."

It's over now, you've fallen and fallen hard. There is no turning back. All of what you once knew is a blur and that's okay. The only thing that matters is what you feel and know from now on. She's the one - you've taken a chance and you've never done that before. But just when you've gotten used to the first wrinkle another one comes along, actually it comes along nine months later. You're scared and you know that life has really changed for you. You will never be the same person again, but again that's okay. You've accepted the fate and it's a good one. You have a family now and your precious baby girl that looks just like her beautiful mother makes you see the world in a whole new way.

All your life you've been looking for some kind of answer. Religion never did it for you. Love sort of did, but now being a father makes the answer seem more real, seem more truthful. However it's only a hint to what is really to come. It's the ultimate truth, the truth that can only be seen in love and loss. The Greeks loved tragedy and with good reason because it was more truth – more importantly it was real, based on life itself. So now comes the tragedy, are you ready? You started on the journey of going back and now you have to complete it. You have to remember what got you here in the first place. It was your own selfish delight wrapped up in the blind devotion to material things.

Remember how you got that promotion in your career. You made more money, you could buy the finer things – a better car, a bigger house, fancy clothes and let's not forget the gold, but the for the sake of this story we will call it jewelry. You became famous and people hung on your every word because you sounded interesting. You had access to other women, to more pussy than you could have ever imagined. You could fuck up and it didn't matter because you were untouchable, after all you were famous and people would remember your name. Promotions are good, being praised for your God-given talent and being recognized by people who could never do it themselves but made you their inspiration. It's a great thing, but at what cost.

You lie awake at night asking yourself that very question, but there are no answers when all of your life's pursuits are to forget about the good things you really have. You have a beautiful family and where are they most nights, alone without you because it's easier to forget them than to face the truth- you're not the man you've led them to believe. All the money and all the fame hasn't made you happy and you've become the person you swore you never would be. Reality check, how about breakdown, it's the answer you may not have been looking for, but it's the one you've found. And it smacks you right in the face. After all the years since the promotion, since your big status change in life, and since all the fame made you somebody different you finally know. The hard truth, you are your own worst enemy. If somebody gave you a gun you would pull the trigger yourself.

So after a few years when happy days become nightmarish moments eating away at your very soul and when you're daughter is barely old enough to start school the curtain is lifted to show that true man of OZ. You say the one thing you never thought you would say – it's the perfect lie that sounds like the most magnificent truth. After all the pointless sex and being praised by everyone for your talent you turn to the love of your life and you tell her what you know is not true. You tell her those hateful lies and because you swore you would never lie to her even though you end up doing it anyway you tell her the awful truth. You've been unfaithful and you've done this sinful deed in more ways than one. Then you tell her that you don't love her and maybe you never did.

Of course you know it's a lie, but your blinded and your prefer it that way because it's easy and it seems real. What happens? It's what always happens – the family you struggled for and sacrificed for is pushed away like a cheap meaningless strange. They leave and walk out on you, mother and daughter, and it's the right thing to do. You pushed them away and you did it for your own selfish pursuits. You may not see it at the time, but it will be the biggest regret you'll ever have. That's when it happens; tragedy will strike in a split second when mother and daughter are struggling to get their things into a taxi cab. Bam! They never knew what hit them and just like with a snap of the fingers it's over – they're gone. You could have stopped it, but you didn't and now you have to live with it.

So here you are a year later, alone and grief stricken, holding their memories in your hands. It's a constant reminder of you and what you did because you are to blame, at least a little bit. If you had never said that one thing to make them leave and if they had never walked out the door they would still be here. You would be more than a guy whose family just walked out on them. And they would be more than just a memory, they would be real. But of course they're dead and gone; only a memory left behind.

Now all you can do is walk around in this city that never sleeps like a hooker with cheap red eye shadow that will suck you off for only a few dollar bills. It's a cheap thrill, but not enough to keep living. Many nights of wandering around below the bright shining lights of this wakeful city have left you wondering – why are you here, what possible answers can you find. Redemption, forgiveness, happiness – there's no chance for you, not anymore. It's a sad story, but it's your story, – it's the story of us all. It's one more sad tale of pimping out our true happiness for some cheap exciting thrills. Only then at the end can we see what we've always known, but never had the courage do anything about. What are you left with- a giant "fuck you" to the world, which you blame for your own stupid indiscretions. What do you do now, where do you go from here, and finally that's all you have left. You are left with those lingering questions to which there are no answers.

So there you are, in the middle of the night, holding their memories in your hands, wondering what do next. You're still asking the questions, is life worth living now, are there second chances for people like me. You're hurting, you want it to stop, drugs and alcohol couldn't make it stop, and you don't know what to do. You look off in the distance and here the horn in the background. You're at the edge of the tracks, at the end of your rope looking for the next big answer and there in the distance you see the bright shining light. All you want is the hurt to stop, to forget the regret, and to finally put it all to an end. But do we really get second chances, can we really go back and change things? That's when your dream becomes reality and your reality becomes the dream. It may not make sense, but what does when you're hurting and refuse to face the truth. You stand at the edge, no answers are left, waiting for your moment of truth. Here is comes. Are you ready? All you have to do is take that one step towards redemption or certain death.

So her you go....the choice is yours.

POETRY

Let Us Go Exploring!

Let Us Go Exploring
And see the world in new and amazing ways
Let Us Explore with a sense of wonder
And Childlike innocence
Remembering those days without strife and sadness
When we were not burdened by the mundane and the madness

Let Us Go exploring
With our Eyes Wide Open
For there is Magic in everyday life
Waiting to be discovered
If we go where others dare not through ceaseless exploration
It will lead us to most wonderful places locked away within our imagination

Let Us Go exploring
And let our true passions take flight
To find the Greatest of adventures
Where all good things never end
Come, my friend, take my hand, it starts with leaving
Stepping into that spectacular now, for we shall go exploring

Kissing is Everything

Kissing is where it starts
Where true passion arises within our hearts
For if love can make our soul sing
Then the instrument we play is kissing which is everything

Kissing tells no secrets or lies
Just like the glory of the flower beneath the sun that will rise
A kiss is pure and last forever in a day
And is the only thing that while standing still can take your breath away

What kind of world would we have without the kiss
Ah, but the tragedy of all the love we could miss
For it is only in the soft brush of your lips upon me
That awakens the joy inside for all to see

Let me kiss you again and again
To be reborn and for this love to never end
Let me taste heaven and hear their bells ring
And have you touch my soul with your kiss that is everything.

To Live

You should live as if you are young
And see the world through wide open eyes
You should dream as if there is a tomorrow
And laugh as if there is an abundance of joy
For when you are finally too old and death approaches
Go, knowing that you have lived enough for many
lifetimes

To Know Love

When the poet was asked what he knew of love, he said.
I know only of words filled with my heart's expression
Accompanied by all that I feel inside and seen through quiet reflection.
For not even heartfelt words allow us to truly know
The unbounded nature of love that is found all around, above, and below
Love is a mystery
Surrounded with good and bad history.
Love cannot be expressed by definition, only by feeling.
Sending all of our senses all of our logic reeling.
Love should never be complicated and always simple
Sending shock waves through time and causing a ripple
Love should be expressed through a tender touch and a soft kiss
Leaving nothing to chance or something we miss.
We don't love because it's right
We simply love and it feels as natural as warm sunlight
Perhaps about love there are no perfect words or expressions
For its perfection can only be seen in love's confession.

Angel's Bliss

To feel alive at the sight.
To smell a sweet aroma is in the air.
Not carrying if my feelings are right,
She stands before me anywhere.

The chambers of my soul are touched
By an intoxicating sense of light.
Guiding me to a warm hope,
A forever presence of day over night

Grace, dignity, and elegant composure
Are the very least of her surreal being.
A sense of self that is mature.
And compassion that is more commanding than knowing.

Yet foolish I may very well be.
Things with her are unseen
They are still more beautiful that this sight I see.
The first sight of her serene.

She forever haunts me.
Like the sounds of Angel's Bliss
Giving way to the endless possibilities.
Of her and me that I don't want to miss.

Go Down As You Live

If there is one certainty about life
It has a beginning and it has an end
But everything in between is uncertain
And we can choose to go down as we live

We were not meant to go through life half hearted
Nor face the end with fear and indecision
And if all our strength and courage of old should disappear
We would still arrive at the end with eyes looking forward

But I say to all of you that it is not too late to seek new adventures
To journey beyond the places that only reside in our imagination
For this place, the in between, is still here
And the rode is long and wide and unwritten

Not all of us will experience everything this life has to give
Too afraid to live in between our many lives
For we are what we will be
Baptized by time and fate, tested to our very core

Let us look onward to the horizon for a new journey
And if we should look back then we should smile with pride
At that heroic spirit which lead us to this place, which we have not often traveled enough
The place inside that keeps us moving beyond the dim light of the sunset.

And if we go down with a fervent heart and an unburdened soul
Then this life will have meaning and not be forgotten

These Words

I am more than words on a page
And I live beyond the here and now
I am not defined by a four letter word
And can only exist in a world without limits

With each word I have life
And they will be here long after we are gone
Each one can lift the soul from the depths of despair
And when spoken, find perfect harmony

Come with me
Go beyond your walls
For these words are electric
And will light the way

Let these words set us free
To play in this world without limits
To Be Angels or Devils
To be who we truly are, you and me

The Death of a Sailor

May a soft breeze catch your sail
May the Wind always be at your back
And lead you in the right direction
May there always be a glass of whisky at your fingertips
To keep you warm on a long sea voyage
And make your journey smooth in rough waters
For even though you will not pass this way again
We will remember our time with you
No matter how long or short it may have been
We will remember the wisdom you imparted.
And the laughter you generously gave to us
We will know that our lives were made whole
For the time we spent in your company
And when other sailors make port here
They will know through the many stories we will tell
About the person we simply called our friend

Who You Have Always Been

You are more than the sum of one feeling
You are more than a hundred tragic moments
You will feel sadness
You will feel joy
And at times the distance between the two seem a lifetime
But every day is a blank canvas
A chance to create something new
And as long as your heart is true
What you write, compose, paint or create
Will continue to inspire after you're gone

The Poet's Words

Beware you villainous souls
Whose tyranny towards choice and free thought will not be forgotten.
There is nothing more dangerous than the poet's words that will live on forever
And whose written history has an unforgiving memory.

My Dearest Friend

My Heart is filled with song.
A song found deep within the bitterroot.
Where the grass is high
And dances with the butterfly.
Where the wind like a lover's
First night becomes impatient,
And a song is found within the joy of simple things.
Where a child plays on knowing not
When the days have ended.
Or the flowers that bloom
At the end of winter's fair.
And to the thought of you my dearest friend,
My heart fills with song.

It seems like a dream,
But a dream where I am truly free.
A place where the only thing known
Is a certain peace and serenity.
Where the stars shine extra bright
On a cold and lifeless night.
Not often do I travel this merry road.
Where the truest of comforts I find
Is being held by a friend like you.
Of all the nightmares,
And sorrow that pass my way.
I am reminded of a dream.
A dream with my dearest friend,
And again my heart fills with song.

Our Life's Reality

Life is giving and life is taking.
The sun will rest upon the weary,
And the winter beast will descend upon the depressed.

Where spring brings hope,
The morning bird sings to the waking.
Filling the dreary with song and only a song found
within its soul.

We live our life by the human heart and its emotions.
Our fears will sometimes become us.
Or the harsh realities of this life we partake of.

But if life is giving and life is taking
Then we take with it all its joys and all its pains.
Why, for they are ours and part of the adventure
worth living for.

Anonymous Being

For we are not always what we seem;
We strive, we seek out, we find.
We remain hidden behind shadows,
That shaded light that covers the fading soul.

We are always searching for truth.
It is the truth which looks forward.
It is the truth which remains behind.
It travels on a perpetual journey that will
never cease to be.

From the still breath of a cold black night
Our demons within are shown.
The impulses of that which is disregarded
Becomes clearer and finally to our eyes are
known.

Dangling before us is Adam's sweet scented
fruit.
With all our temptations and those thoughts
that linger behind.
Almost without uncertainty they travel down
the same path as us.
Their time always stalking and their escape
always sought.

Like the hunting predator the conflict is not
far behind.
Increasing so slightly as the day passes,
It pushes us to the mountain's edge.
With a voice that shouts to stand or fade away
to our last.

Two faces emerge from the shadow become my own,
They create a deathly war for the truest of rewards.
Fighting for all that I am, all that I become.
Finding all that will become lost and all that can be won

There is hope left standing in the end.
A faith found to keep searching for my truth.
A truth that is buried deep within,
And only the essence of one still standing in this place

I will always carry with me what is inside,
I will carry that curiosity that looms within the shadow.
But only becomes an afterthought that brings the black widow.
No matter what may come it shall remain behind.

There are some things that are not to be known.
And joyous mystery still remains.
Always it is at play with our truth.
And if the truth cannot be found it will still be here.

The end approaches in time,
It is followed slowly by my own regret.
The importance of life is too high,
And I should not forget to just live

To the endless journey where escape is none;
I will always look within to see the healing begun.

The Musical Harmony of the Street

When I walk down the blackened path of the cobbled street
The dim fluorescent lights that shade it dance with rhythm.
The rhythm that matches my beating heart.
And a beat that keeps pace with the sensation inside my soul.

There are numerous sounds that fill the streets.
Each one just one part of the playful symphony.
Every corner that I turn another troubadour plays the notes.
To complete a song that find its way inside me as I walk down the cobbled street.

No currency has influence over what I feel about this musical harmony.
My reward is to hear the music play.
For in every instrument the words and sounds play the symphony.
The Symphony is us and it is ours never replacing this truth.

Everywhere , every day, life exists and I hear the music.
The Music is full of life, it is never false.
I feel it, I breathe it, and I consume it,
With every fiber of my being so all that I am is reborn.

Perhaps if you walk down those rhythmic streets you can see what I see.
And you can be swallowed up by the sweet sound of a musicians dream.
Only to be reborn in a paradise never known before,
Then live again with the sweet symphony of a life that becomes forever more.

If there was ever a place for me it is here,
In the harmony of the symphonic sound that will make me be.

A Child's Day

I remember those childhood days;
Those times of carefree innocence.
Of timeless play till the sun's end;
With those truthful attitudes of the world around us.

I remember the weeping willow out back
And trying to climb to its peak every time.
So I could touch the heavens or the stars that shined so bright.
I remember those joyous days that were always mine.

Does every child have a place like that?
A place where way leads onto a springs descent,
Or a place where strife and the cold harshness of this world does not prevail.
And only a world with joyful play can be a child's world.

Although it is not possible to travel back in time to those childhood days.
Perhaps we can still relive that wonderful dream as constant time.
And to always live in those childhood days,
Where our innocence and worry free days become our joyful play.

Something Within

The things that come from deep within
Are not of lies or sin
They are the things that speak what is true
Emotions that spring forth life of what we always knew

The world is filled with accidental chance,
But none are found within the human heart.
Life may be our own wonderful or destructive dream,
But all that is found between birth and death are ruled from what is deep within.

A Lover's Journey

Through boundless circles of time
Love stretches out and echoes the eternity.
For two people caught between circumstance,
The road runs through all its twists and turns never letting them meet.

Always searching but never finding
That love that we leave behind.
The raging sea with all its schemes
In balance with a journey that is our time.

I am longing for a time remembered.
Not of days that were lost or wasted away.
For days lived through youthful innocence.
And for times of misguided love but finding only one that is true.

What is first shall be last and what is last shall be first.
It was said by he who is called I am.
Perhaps it must be true of love if it is eternal.
While it stays within that infinite circle that connects love torn souls.

In anticipation the heart fills with song at the chance that spring will bring forth a flower.
Not just any of the Indian's paintbrush or a Lilly from a grassy meadow.
They too are touched by God's own hand.
It is a flower from the toil and play of Venus.

Too often not we are undecided.
Never knowing what brings joy in the realm of love.
It seems that without that our truth is reveled.
And what is said of truth becomes that which is known.

We have timeless searches and the never finding.
It seems too cruel even for Antigone.
Even fate has its own scheming.
But is it true for those who dare to love unconditionally.

There are two wandering roads that never meet.
It is where ill-fated lovers are caught between raging and senseless storms.
If the seasons can come and go through brilliant change,
Then the sun if only once can radiate to calm the raging sea for a pair of crossing lovers.

The Tree Surrounded Road

A long and winding path of celestial colors
That compliment a time forbidden journey.
I hold a notion of being caught in nature's play.
Only to find that logical time has slipped away

Looking ahead to a heavenly unknown,
A delight not often seen in a contemptuous world.
Looking back to see the leaves dancing with a soft breeze
Only to find such simple pleasures in the most sacred of places.

I am surrounded by godlike wonders.
Even though it is true they disappear in the short seasons of time.
They are here now, in this place, for the purest form of enjoyment,
And for some lucky soul who happens to wonder down this wooded path

I am in constant amazement with a place like this,
And how we can be so fortunate to travel such perfect roads.

The Two Sides of Sight

I sit and look out beyond.
Trying to see further than what can be seen.
Hoping for what may be hopeless.
Never ceasing to believe in the illumination of chance.

As we go there is a threshold of being that we cross through.
Losing an identity as we pass through the heart of it.
Can we truly be made again,
In that perfect creation set from the beginning?

There are those that live as if is it not true.
Faithless in their endeavors of what can be.
Life it seems is not lived by those kind.
They know only of their own tortured souls where joy does not exist.

Perhaps we live two different lives in the journey that we travel.
One life is the one we dream with, the other life is the one we learn with.
Two lives in one to make the same mistakes with;
Two lives that cannot survive without the other

Our Journey is not as fun without its duel nature
Only our duality can give us true insight.
Is it that insight that makes our direction.
For what is a journey without at least an idea of where we should go.

While on this journey I will always look ahead.
Sometimes in silence or with a shout to the beyond.
I see all that is around me with a heavy heart.
For this is why I will continue to sit and look beyond.

At Love's End

It has been a long time since I last talked to you.
I know that I am not the first person you tell when something is great anymore.
Maybe it was once that way and now you have completely forgotten me.
Or perhaps all you see is the lie that became of me, an illusion to what could be.

Did you know that there is a comfort in remembering the best of times?
Times when anger or sorrow would not dare travel our way,
Or days when the joyous sound of your laughter was at play.
Instead of those times being sad and ignorant to what was truly happening.

These are the times that need to remain in thought.
To remember that hope is still alive and never dies.
That with each other was once good and can be again even if it be with someone else.
And that love cannot destroy, but only breathe life.

For me I have to cling to those discouraging memories.
In those memories is the student that learned well.
From a patient teacher all that was needed to know about love.
And what still remains is the place where I was born again.

It would be nice to take back all the wrongs we made to one another.
And maybe when the world is just right and the heavens open up.
We can escape and disappear only to come back again as if nothing happened.
But it is more likely to happen in the forgiveness of regretful individuals.

The anger that once consumed me is replaced by the silence of regretful tears.
And so I cannot forget all that was good within you.
Maybe when all that has been said passes away,
You will remember me in the best light of the day.

Perhaps when the wanting and fantastic delusions cease to be,
It will finally be as it should have been for you and me

What Can Make Us Free

Through the child like dreams of the faceless beast
I am in fear of those nightmarish things that cannot be seen.
Pulling me in the direction I do not want to go
And making me see those things that I don't want to see.

There is no escape from this thing that follows.
No road, or path, or even journey that can out run this thing that will come to pass.
Only myself and the pity that is mine lives in its hollows.
My pain and utter contempt will only prove to be my compass.

It is that thing that will become known.
No matter if it is here, there, or the place that is everywhere.
At that instant, faster than traveling light.
Our eyes become open to the reflective realization that we have always known.

At the instant all will cease to be as we become aware
So we might truly be free.

A Sense of Hope

Hope is often defined within the meanings of words
As something to cherish or desire with anticipation.
Or the expectation of fulfillment or success.
Or even better to expect with complete confidence.

Although there is worth in the speaking of these words.
Hope cannot be defined by mere words.
It is living and breathing inside of us,
It will show us who we truly are.

It knows not prejudice or social constraint.
It knows not ill will or death.
It is a faith warmed and rekindled.
And like love it is the most perfect of prayers.

Sometimes it is hard to find in the dark.
Sometimes it is hidden while we travel this road.
Truth be told it is always found when needed most.
And when everything has slipped away, hope is the one thing that cannot be taken away.

The Mother's Gift

From our beginning we hear a soft voice.
A calming voice telling us that the world is not as bad as seems.
We feel a deep hearted touch, a nurturing hand that only a mother has.
Guiding us into days on end with a soothing smile and a knowing eye,
That says nothing can truly harm us as long as we have a mother's love.

To this I am filled with a song to the glad refrain.
That in world filled with tormented souls and possible pain.
I am fortunate enough to have this glorious gift from above known as a mother.
Is there anymore we can ask for during childhood days when we are beginning to know our world?
There is, but not nearly important as this maternal gift.

As days pass before the sunset's eyes.
With forecasted troubles making way into our lives.
We can find solace from the one whose answers are known deep inside even when uncertainty comes our way.
Although our work is never done the best answer still comes when she says everything will be okay.

When she has long since gone we will still mourn and remember with a pain that will never go away.
We are better for having had her in our life and having been completed in no small way by this guiding hand.
Yet our heart will rejoice for this human gift sent to us from above with her virtue to instill.
To the one who puts forth this spiritual gift within her and knows best how to make us who we are.

Sunday Kind of Love-
Unconditional Torture

It's the piercing eyes that see deep within.
It's the softest touch that calms a restless sleep.
It's a whispered breath on the neck brushing a peace across this divide.
It's a knowing glance that pierces two souls filled with love.

It's a slow tight squeeze of a warm embrace during a peaceful slumber.
It's the unsaid words saying all that we need to hear from a lover.
It's the laughter of complete joy.
It's a serene smile conveying all that we feel about the other.

What does it all mean, what is it all for?
Why do we yearn for it so much?
Knowing that it will push us over the edge,
What is this torture that eats away slowly?

These questions are always recurring.
They are never fully answered, but somehow known deep inside.
To the greatest question comes the most important answer.
The answer is what will truly make us alive.

The Answer is, we are here to love.
We are meant to be in love from the beginning.
We are meant to reach down into the abyss and find something more.
We are meant to find something that can only be seen by loving someone more than our self.

From the words of heavenly poets: and the greatest of these is love.
We have to ask ourselves what is the best kind?
To my knowledge there is only one kind of love.
It's what is simple, serene, and the most perfect moments of the Sunday Kind of Love.

It's the time when we are most peaceful.
The time when the touch of the person lying next to us,
Or the small simple smile from the other across the table,
That will let out all of our anger and all of our strife hidden within so we can be renewed.

The Sunday Kind of Love is what we truly yearn for.
It's a love that is the light at the end of the cold, dark, whirlwind of a ravaged life.
The love of a smoldering, intense, and unashamed passion for the person that makes us complete.
It's the true love that we only find once in a lifetime.

It's not a love we have because it's right.
It's not a love that we put conditions upon.
For that kind of love has to be unconditional and nothing else,
And it is a love where we find our unconditional torture.

The unconditional torture will push us beyond madness.
With it we stumble over the edge beyond any normal range of sane thought.
Within this torture, within the clearing of the madness we find our Sunday Kind of Love.
It's the kind of love that cannot be without the torture, the agony, and that which we cannot be without.

For both the Unconditional Torture and Sunday Kind of Love are one in the same in this great life changing adventure

System Failure

To the drunken word, to the drunken sound.
All I hear is the whiskey song.
The splashing of Irish over perfect squared ice in a clear glass.
To the screaming rant of the heart felt sorrow.
The screams of the inner demons clawing their way out.
I can feel the break down, I can feel the overload.
Its time, it's finally over.
I have lost all sense of self.
All I know is the system failure.
It's shrouded with mystery
Knowing is lost with the sense of time.
I am spiraling to the deep inward abyss.
My voice is fading with each sip I take.
Some say its poison, but those who don't try can never truly know.
Poison comes from losing our self.
It comes from keeping silent when we should shout out loud.
For me the passive is the way to Hades.
All I know is the system failure.
The beating of the drum is silence.
My generation's word is fading.
Right becomes wrong, morality is blurred.
All I can do is sit and wonder, what if.
Tomorrow is gone, today not far behind.
The dreaming of possibility is lost in sleep.
The echoes of the past slightly whisper.
Inspired again we can become tomorrow.
For today all I know is the system failure.

Morning Water Dance

In the waking morning I hear the tiny beats of a
hundred water dances.
Piercing and soothing me to an endless
consciousness.
They calm me to that relaxing slumber within myself.
They hold me to a stillness not often found in a
normal day.

Are these water dances the tears of heaven
As myth might have us to believe?
Are they water from the hands of God washing away
all that is unclean?
Or are they the mere taker or giver of live?

Sonorous Beats on the concrete ground.
Soulful Drops that become no more.
To those water dances I see and hear.
Can your soothing dance and sounds return me to
myself?

A Thousand

There are a thousand ways I can say you're beautiful.
A thousand ways to say your kind.
A thousand ways to describe you grace.
And perhaps more than a thousand ways to say how I am inspired by you.

There are a thousand definitions that mean the same thing, you.
A thousand words that tell of the good within you.
A thousand ways to show how I feel when near you.
And perhaps a thousand more to say what I would do for you.

There are a thousand stars that shine extra bright because of you.
A thousand ways the heavens pour their wonder to show the possibility within you.
A thousand different things that can bring out the radiance of you.
And more than a thousand ways that this world would not better without you in it.

Of all the different ways to reflect upon you and show my high regard
All I can truly say is that I am mesmerized by you.

The Trueness of Me

I am a writer of the word.
Not the one of sanctimonious religious belief ,
But of the word that only comes from life.
From the pain and the sorrow,
For the search of a better tomorrow.
From the joy that comes from simple moments.
From the finding of complete happiness.
I will write of the tears that are shed from my sadness.
I can only write what I see.
I can only write what I have come to know.
A truth from experience that never comes fast, but slow.
In this my world will open up and there is a face I see.
The face is me, a mirror to someone who has lived.
Someone who has lived the pain, the joy, and of someone who will always have to relive
For the writer will know no boundaries.
And the truth we find never has limited means.
The illusion that it does is only what it seems.
I am a writer and pour out the words from my soul.
The truth from what I see and what I know makes me whole.
From deep within my identity, my soul fills me till I over flow.
Inspiration comes and the words from that deep place feed my writing.
And I become a Writer of the word.

The Dead Town

It's a nameless face.
It's a motionless race.
A quiet merry go round of lifeless people.
They never break a desperate routine to see even the simple things.

Young unbridled heroes they once were.
Now only a slow limping shadow of what they try to be.
All they can do is trudge desperately down the fleeting road.
They go to the place of the invisible people.

Praise to the misfits they have become.
Joyous contempt for what cannot be seen.
To the seasons that have waned without notice.
While life passes without new invention.

Time is an unfriendly stranger to those in the dead town.
It will rob them blind while your back is turned.
Time will lead past that which they chose to ignore,
It will wake everyone to the eternity that is nonexistent.

Why does this kind of town exist if there is no life in it?
Should we even notice this place if it is nonexistent?
We must see this town for what it is; a lesson.
For us not to live by fear, the fear of what can be.

The Only Thing I know

So it seems in the grand scheme of the world,
That I should only know very little.
We are granted, but few gifts in this life we live.
Mine are to only know very well what I do know.

I know only from experience,
The true education for worldly men.
I know from only what I see,
The cautious examination of life that is lived.

I know that the love for someone is by faith,
Faith in that someone to do right, to be the best they can be.
I know that true love can only come from giving,
The giving of that love which we most desire.

I know that good is done by self-sacrifice,
To do away with our selfish wants and do for someone else.
I know that we are all capable of evil,
And that evil comes from the disregard of mankind.

I know that we are born, suffer, and die,
Although there are moments of complete joy.
I know that in the areas of none choice,
We still have the choice to live life how we see fit.

I know that my life is for me to live without interruption,
And not to live well is an insult to that which is given.

Hidden by Sunsets

There are words hidden behind that dying ball of fire.
They are the words of the eternal, the words that are not often spoken.
They are words only spoken in deep somber glances from those who watch the sun's rest.

The sunset reminds us of the end.
It also reminds us that the end cannot last,
That time is always evolving and words will never remain hidden.

The Red Crimson in the sky fades to the inspiring.
It is an untouched mark of perfection by the hand of God.
It is the inspiring knowledge of simple truths.

Too often we never do what we know is right
We are quiet when we should shout, we sit when we should stand.
That the real truth comes from what is unspoken

Sunsets speak only what is true.
That truth is usually found in simplistic things.
And that one simple moment is the real priceless treasure we seek.

To the words hidden behind sunsets,
The words of the unspoken glance that will lead me home.

IRISH TOASTS

That Time of Year Again!

It is that time again
And if you all have Guinness, let us begin
The best holiday is St. Patrick's Day
Because the drinks are so much better than on the 5th of May
We should be glad to be here with family and friends
Who with we never have to make amends.
By the end of this night
Hopefully our laughter will still be cheery and bright
And although there will be many stories of us
A few, I'm sure filled with Lust
We will remember our toasts with pride
And not our misdeeds that we will choose to hide
So raise your glass and let us toast this night
And try to be good with all of our might!

It's Halfway to St. Patrick's

Lift your glasses of beer
And be full of good cheer.
It is halfway to St. Patrick's Day
For six months is not that far away.
So let the 2nd best party of the year begin
And if we make it through this night, then let it be considered a win
Let us drink good beers and great whiskeys soon
As we sing a fine Irish Tune
Tonight begins our training for the best party of next year
And it's great that all of you can join us tonight right here.

Why I Drink

Yes, there are some that drink to forget
I do not, for with me there's not even one regret.
Can't say that I am truly good, but definitely not bad
Just a stubborn lad
So when I was told to stop drinking
I got to thinking
Who Me, I am not crazy enough to do that
For that would be worse than being a rat
I drink because it feels great
And those that think it is wrong must be full of hate
Now an apple a day may keep the doctor away
But 4 pints of Guinness keep the voices in my head at bay!

A Girl Who Drinks Guinness Beer

I know a lot of pretty girls
Some with long beautiful hair and some with curls
And if I have a chance to steal a kiss
It's something I certainly won't miss.
Now I do believe that a pretty girl is a gift from God
And better than anything I've got
But God's greatest gift is a girl who drinks Guinness Beer
And if she's Irish then I will definitely be full of good cheer
If I should meet her, I will have a big smile
But If I don't keep an eye out, after awhile
My Guinness will probably disappear
And if that happens, oh well, I will still love a girl who drinks Guinness Beer.

Three Great Things in Life

There are three great things in life
And they will take away any strife
The first is a woman's love
And on this list there is nothing above
The second are great friends
For whom with you will never have to make amends
The third is a Guinness in a very tall glass
Served to you by a pretty young lass

The Prettiest Girl

She was the prettiest girl I'd ever seen
With a sassy mouth that made her mean.
But she had a good side too
When she poured a Guinness, there were always two
She always had one for her and one for me
And it opened my eyes so I could see
There was a lot more to her than good looks
And she was better than any woman found in books
With me she liked to drink Guinness Beer
And despite being mean, that will always bring me good cheer!

He Came to Dallas

There was a lad who came to Dallas
Who was known to be quite restless
He came from a windy city known as Chicago
In what has become a long time ago
He came to find the perfect beer
And an Irish Pub full of good cheer
But the best is what he found at Trinity Hall
Instead of sitting at home waiting for some girl to call.
He found the perfect beer, the perfect friends
All within this hallowed Hall.

I Drank a Pint of Guinness

I've drank Guinness at the Londoner
And I've drank Guinness at The Dubliner
I've had it poured right and poured wrong
But it's always best drunk during Irish Song
So I now drink Guinness in this place
Where the girls still wear stockings and lace
And you will hear "I want my Guinness with a Big Head"
For after all, that's what she said!

A Fine Glass of Whisky

Tis no better thing than a fine glass of whiskey
A taste of heaven that makes us do things which are risky
Two fingers worth can make it a wonderful night
And make the worst day alright
But in case you're wondering there is something better
You may think of it as a fine whiskey's love letter
The best whiskey is poured by a pretty Irish lass
And if I'm lucky, she'll still be with me at morning mass

Oh Thy Pub

Oh Thy Pub, there is no better place to be
Where smiles and greetings have the most sincerity
On days like this where the air is bitter and cold
And the wind pierces our bones and makes us feel old
Oh, they Pub, fill my glass of whisky high
For that golden smoky nectar does not lie
It is best served after a very long week
And will always fair better than a kiss on the cheek.
Oh Thy Pub, where love can happen every night
And the kiss from a pretty girl feels oh so right
But if tonight my glass of whisky is my one and all
It's still a great night in thy pub, also known as thy Hallowed Hall

Gather Old Friends

Gather ye old friends to this hallowed place.
Where the Guinness is smooth like satin and lace
It is time to leave your worries at the door.
And drink, and sing, and dance upon the floor.
Where else would we be on this perfect night
But only a place that serves whiskey and Guinness right.
For in this great pub there is no better place to be at
Since it was the seat next to mine where this pretty Irish lass sat.
And if I be the luckiest man tonight
That which shines upon her would be the morning light.

This Time Next Year

Raise a glass to another year gone by
Through all its triumphs and tragedies it should end on a high
Looking back is something we shall not do
The next journey is always forward for me and you
And if I can find joy in a simple thing
It is that which can make my heart sing
That this year all those whom I love
Will find great fortune from above
And this time next year
It will end with us all full of good cheer.

PLAYS

The Music of Life

Characters

Rick – The piano player at *The Blue's Note;* former point guard for the De Paul University basketball team.

Liz – An artist and Rick's girlfriend

Charlie – One of Rick's best friends from childhood. He is the sarcastic friend

Chad – Charlie's little brother and Rick's other best friend from childhood. He is the innocent and funny friend.

Bud - Owner of *The Blue's Note* and is the father figure in Rick's life. Has known Rick since childhood.

Susan – A cocktail waitress at *The Blue's Note;* one of Rick's best friends and the promiscuous friend.

Old Man Henderson – A drunk and a regular patron of the club; he is the clubs "Norm."

The Judge – The local Municipal Court Judge who has known Chad and Charlie since childhood because their mother use to be a clerk in his office.

Lee Wayne Johnson – Famous blues musician who started out playing at *The Blue's Note* and grew up in the same neighborhood as Rick.

Mary – Liz's mother and is very submissive to Edward.

Edward – Liz's father and doesn't like Rick. He still wants to control his daughter's life.

Amanda - An acquaintance of Liz's and director of the Chicago Chapter of PETA.

Michelle - An acquaintance of Liz's

Clara – An acquaintance of Liz's

Officer 1 – A Chicago Police Officer

Officer 2 – A Chicago Police Officer

Gus Davis – Old man and jazz musician who taught Rick how to play , but he is just a stock character. He has one scene and is only mentioned by name

There are scenes where other stock characters can be added to show club patrons and make a crowd in *The Blue's Note*, but I will leave this up the director's discretion. I think extra people in the club scenes will make those scenes more realistic. The scenes that have a band will require extra people to stand in as musicians; this can be people from the tech. crew. However I do leave some things to a director's vision for I am just the writer. There is a bit of an accent on the characters since they are from Chicago so some words will be misused and pronounced differently.

Act 1

Scene One

The first scene is inside a little blues club called *The Blue's Note* and the piano player, Rick is sitting at the piano staring at a picture that came with a letter from an old girlfriend. The club isn't open yet and the only two people inside are Rick and the other owner, Bud. The club is located just a few streets over from De Paul University and is a favorite to many of the University's students as well as local musicians. It has been that way for years, but it's never been quite as entertaining since Rick started playing piano there many years before. The same crowd graces the place almost every night except for a few new faces from the University and surrounding neighborhoods; like most clubs that's how it usually is at *The Blue's Note*. Every spring and fall always brings new faces to the little club and there are always some that leave, forever changed by its magic. To some, as strange as it might sound, this is family to Rick and they always bring out the best in him and his art.

Bud comes walking out from the cellar carrying some wine and sees Rick reading a letter at the piano.

Bud: So did you get another letter from her today?

Rick: Yeah I did, and this time she sent a picture of herself in front of a French Jazz club. I guess she wanted to let me know that Paris had good music and she wasn't being deprived of it.

Bud: Well how is she doing?

Rick: (in kind of a solemn tone) She seems to be doing fine; according to her letter she's having a blast living out her dream.

Bud: Uh oh, I know that tone.

Rick: (laughs to himself) What tone?

Bud: It's your "sorrow filled regretful tone". You always get it every time she sends you a letter or someone mentions her name. It's that tone that says "I'm not sure if I made the right decision".

Rick: Look, I've told you before Bud. It was the right thing to do. As much as I wanted her to stay or she wanted me to go with her to Paris, I had to let her go. She wouldn't have been happy if she stayed, and I wouldn't have been happy leaving even if it was with her. It just wasn't time for us to be together so no matter how regretful I might sound; I still think I made the right decision, but that won't ever stop me from reflecting back. ***(Rick takes a drink of whiskey from his glass sitting on the piano)***

Bud: Hey, you're the only one that has to convince yourself of that. ***(He walks off stage as to show walking out the room)***

Rick: (while staring at the picture on the piano) Yeah, there's nothing like reflecting back on the past to find your inspiration.

The lights fade to end the scene

End of Act One, Scene One

Scene Two

The next scene is one year earlier inside *The Blue's Note* and the piano player has just finished his first set. The club is starting to get busy as groups of customers are walking in. There's a pretty good crowd sitting around the bar while the bartender and the cocktail waitress are busy. The piano player, Rick, puts up his music and then walks off stage to help with customers from behind the bar. The regular crowd is seated around the bar having their usual philosophical conversations about life.

Rick walks behind the bar to get himself a drink and greet the usual crowd that's sitting around the bar before walking into a conversation his two best friends are having with Bud. His two best friends Chad and Charlie that he has known since childhood were having one of their usual philosophical discussions that really had to do with nothing. But no matter what, they were entertaining and always kept anybody who was willing to listen laughing. Conversations like that were not uncommon in this little club, but it was usually welcomed from anything that could be seriously talked about. Rick walks to the corner of the bar where they were sitting just as Chad is talking

Chad: (in a sarcastic and commanding tone): You know what's really wrong with the world today, the problem is isms, and you know I don't wanna have anything to do with them.

Charlie: (in his usual cynical tone): So let me get this straight you're now saying that everything wrong with the world has to do with isms. Yesterday you said that everything would be O.K. in the world if everybody was Catholic and the Catholic Church was the only church in the world.

Chad: Well everything would be okay in the world if everybody was Catholic, but also there's the problem of isms.

Bud: (starts laughing as he says): I am almost afraid to ask, but what is the problem with the world and isms?

Chad: Well I'm glad you asked because the problem is that everything has got one and that means everything has to be categorized. And we all know that when things get categorized they become bad. Do you realize that to succeed in life you have to be in the right category? Why does everything have to be organized anyway...why can't we leave things just the way they are, you know a little chaos or anarchy and a few nut jobs never hurt anybody and it helps keep the balance in life.

Charlie: Is there anything resembling normal discussion on the planet you're from? Do you realize most of these philosophical questions of yours never make any real sense? There is no scientist that could even begin to figure how your mind works or how you think of stuff like this.

Chad: It's probably something that will never be figured out and if it weren't for people like me thinking of things like this then we would all be living in an X-Files episode. Just think about it.

Rick: (rolls his eyes and replies in a sarcastic tone): Well I think that you have a long way to go before you find the truth that's out there. Also I think this theory of yours is just your way of trying to justify the way you make your living.

Chad: (looks shocked and is expressed in his tone): There is nothing wrong with how I earn my way in this categorized world. Besides, Charlie and me, we supply the things that other people can't get anywhere else.

Rick: Let's see, you rip off flea markets convincing the people who own them that they're selling worthless crap just so you can sell the same stuff out of your van at a very much inflated price. Plus you also scalp tickets which are sold at a very inflated price. Don't you think that's a little dishonest and scrupulous?

Chad: (in a commanding tone): We only take the stuff that other flea markets are going to throw out anyway and sell tickets to those who weren't lucky enough to get them at other places, somebody in this world has to do it.

Rick: The world in some weird way wouldn't be better off if there weren't people like you, and I do mean that.

Charlie: You know there are people in this world who are suppliers, some people who are producers and some people who are just buyers; me and Chad we're just suppliers. At least that's what Father O' Brian told me the other day when he asked us to get him *Phantom of the Opera* tickets.

Rick: (gives a sarcastic smile as he replies): I bet drug dealers consider themselves suppliers as well, what do you think?

Charlie: Maybe, but we don't supply anything that kills anybody therefore we don't break any commandments. You're the one that is selling stuff to people that will eventually kill them so you're worse than I am.

Rick: Yeah, but we do it legally and it's really the government's fault for allowing us to sell stuff that might kill people so whose fault is that?

Both men just laughed as they usually did when they found a moral loophole for the things they did. It was just part of the game that they played every weekend that had to do with "anything goes in a bar." As they all continued their conversation Chad looks up and sees four women walk in together and makes all his friends take notice by tapping them and pointing at the women walking in. None of the women looked familiar so it becomes obvious that it was their first time at the bar.

Rick, Chad, Charlie, and Bud know just about everybody that walks in, so they quickly recognize new customers. The four women take a seat at a table near the stage as all the guys watch in curiosity.

Chad: (with excitement in his voice): Cool we've got some lesbians here tonight; it's not often that we get lesbians here for us to watch.

Charlie: Look you big giant pervert do you think gay women are some feature attraction at a porn theater for us to get our jollies off at? Just cool off there peewee hormone, it's not that much to get excited about.

Rick: How do you know that they're lesbians? You can't tell if a woman is a lesbian by the way she looks! Besides we probably get them in here all the time and you never notice.

Charlie: Hey what about Cindy Williams you can definitely tell she's gay by the way she looks.

Rick: Okay that's because she looks more like a man than both you and me so it's easy to assume that she likes women, and frankly that assumption just happens to be right about her.

Chad: Trust me I know a lesbian when I see one and when four women walk in together without a man they have to be gay.

Rick: Chad, you really are just a simple minded creature aren't you?

Chad just smiles and winks at Rick and then gets up to go talk to the four women.

Rick: Great, it looks like I'm going to have to stop him from making a fool out of himself and driving our customers away again.

Charlie: And how's that different from any other night?

Rick: He's your brother, you should know how to stop him when he gets this way.

Charlie: I've been trying for nearly thirty years and the only conclusion that I have come up with is that there is no cure; we just have to wait for his species to become extinct.

Chad walks up to the table checking his hair like an inept cool guy. All four women look at him at the same time with the same surprised look as he begins to give his ultra -cool opening line that is sure to make them fall in love him.

Chad: (with suave tone): So how are you chicks doing, can I get you something to drink even though I'm not the right type for you?

Amanda: (with a discontented tone and look): Sir we don't know what you're implying, but we didn't come here to be harassed by some local that thinks of himself as a real ladies man...

Chad: Hey it's okay I'm not trying to pick you up or anything. You know I had a cousin that was a lesbian and she was cool as hell; I loved hanging out with her.

Amanda: Congratulations on your cousin, but you're not assuming that we're lesbians are you?

Chad: Well the four of you came walking in together without a man and you're sitting pretty close to one another. Besides, some of you have short haircuts, so doesn't that mean you're gay?

Clara: You have got to be kidding! You think that just because four women are together and some have short haircuts they're gay?

Chad: Hey it's okay; if you're cool with it then I am certainly cool with it. It just so happens I'm a lesbian, I mean I love chicks and sometimes they even like me. I just wanted to buy you a drink since I happen to know the owner of the place and also I wanted to see if you wanted to have some fun.

One of the women at the table begins to laugh quietly ***(Liz)*** as the other three with horrified looks try to find something to throw at him. Before they can find anything and respond to his remark, Rick walks up to the table. He looks at the one laughing to herself and begins to speak.

Rick: Ladies I'm sorry if he's bothering you; I'll make him go sit back in the corner again while he finishes his time-out. I don't want you to think that this sort of thing happens here all the time, and since I'm a person in charge around here let me know if there is anything I can do to make your stay more enjoyable.

Michelle: Well I don't suppose you could shoot him for us, but you probably wouldn't do that since it looks like he's a friend of yours.

Rick: Ma'am we have similar thoughts about him almost every night and yes, he is a friend, but that's just because he ignores the restraining order we have out against him so there isn't anything else we can do except sort of be his friend. Hey, everybody needs a friend I guess. All jokes aside though, I will make sure he won't bother you again and I'll get a round of drinks for you on the house. ***(To Chad)*** Chad, it's time for you to go back to the bar now, they're not interested in you.

Chad: I don't see why not; I'm a gorgeous guy. I don't see what they have to be mad about.

Rick: I'm sure it was the lesbian remark considering they're not really gay. The other thing is when you flirt with women it comes off pretty sleazy.

Chad: I didn't say anything that wasn't true, but you see it just goes to show that you can't call a chick a babe anymore.

Rick: Go sit down before I have to hit you.

All four ladies thank him as he directs Chad back to his seat at the bar. Rick makes them their drinks and looks at Chad saying to him:

Rick: Alright, I just got you out of trouble again and don't bother them anymore or any other guest. If you keep this up I will revoke your talking privileges for the night again.

Before Chad could say anything Charlie speaks up saying to him:

Charlie: You see, this is why I can't bring women over to our place. You can't keep your mouth shut and you're a constant embarrassment. ***(Pauses while Chad gives him a dirty look and then to the other club patrons)*** So anyone want to bet he loses his talking privileges tonight like last week?

Within a matter of seconds, people sitting around the bar start placing their bets with Charlie and all Rick can do is laugh.

Bud: You know there are some things that never change around here, and before you started playing here years ago this would have seemed strange ***(as he walks past Rick patting him on the back).***

Rick walks back to the table that the four women are sitting at with their drinks, never taking his eye off the one who was laughing to herself while the others were getting angry earlier.

Rick: (as he puts the drinks on the table and passes them out) My name is Rick and I usually provide the entertainment around here. I can't say that I have ever seen you in here before.

Liz answers him back before anybody at the table can as she and Rick keep eyeing each other.

Liz: It's nice to meet you. My name is Liz and this is Clara, Michelle, and Amanda; Amanda is the director of the Chicago office for PETA. Are you a supporter of PETA Rick?

Rick: (with a sarcastic look and tone): I never gave much thought about it because we don't get any abused animals around here unless you count Chad, but that's only because we abuse him being one of our regular customers and all.

Amanda: (in an angry tone): You think that's funny? PETA is a very serious organization, and what we do for the ethical treatment of animals is no laughing matter. I hope you're not like your friend over there.

Rick: (with kind of a disdained look): Well I'm not, and I thought I was pretty funny, but talking with you has made realize that I'm not and there is a very serious issue of abused animals, especially here in Chicago bars.

Liz starts laughing at him while the other three all give him dirty looks for his remarks.

Rick: I'm sorry for being too sarcastic. I've had fun talking with you, but I do have to do my next set since I am the piano player. Please come back again and I hope you do enjoy the music.

Rick walks off towards the stage and takes a seat behind the piano to do his next set of music. The music will play from a recording and the entire song should be played in this scene. Only one song will be played in this scene even though Rick is supposed to be a playing a set.

Amanda: I can't believe him and his insensitive remarks; he is just as bad as the other guy. I heard this place was supposed to be fun and one of the best places for good music and drinks on the North Side.

Liz: Well it certainly is entertaining here and you can't blame that guy Rick, he was just trying to be funny and help liven up the somber mood you three created. I'm sure he didn't mean anything by his remarks.

Michelle: He's the exact type of guy you would fall for; I still can't see why you think sarcasm is a great quality in a guy.

Liz: (as she is looking at Rick on the stage): Well when you have a good sense of humor then you'll understand.

Michelle gives Liz a dirty look as the music starts and all four of them stop in the middle of their conversation to listen. When Rick is done he walks back to the bar to help out.

Charlie: You played *The Way You Look Tonight;* there must be a woman in the bar that peaked your interest.

Rick: Charlie you know that's one of my favorite songs and it's just been awhile since I have played it so don't start getting suspicious.

Chad: Yeah, but you don't usually play that song unless it's a request or there's somebody in the audience you're secretly trying to impress. I bet it is one of those four lesbians over there, but I don't know why because it's not like you actually have a chance with them.

Rick: Hey, here's a concept maybe not familiar with; they're really not lesbians, but just ultra-liberal feminists that don't like you.

Chad: No we don't usually get those around here, they have to be lesbians. Besides, who could resist a guy like me or least a guy that would buy someone a free drink? Women love me because I'm happy and handsome.

Rick: Hey Chad, you just keep telling yourself that and you won't have to worry about over-populating this world.

Just as Rick finished his sentence the four women get up to leave. Liz starts to walk towards the bar while everybody sitting around the bar takes notice. She walks up to the bar with confidence and with a smile while staring at Rick every step of the way. At the same time,

Rick cannot take his eyes off her as she walks up to the bar.

Liz: (she extends her hand to shake Rick's): I just wanted to thank you for the drinks and tell you that at least one of us had a good time tonight.

Rick: That's good; hopefully that person will come back. Also, I'm sorry if the sarcasm was a little much, but it tends to be that way around here; it's a bar and anything goes.

Liz: That's okay. You're not that insincere as my so-called friends tried to point out, and you did make up for it by playing one of my favorite songs.

Rick: (with a charming smile) Which song was that?

Liz: The song was *The Way You Look Tonight* by Sinatra; my grandmother used to play it on the piano for my grandfather so it became one of my favorite songs because of them.

Rick: Well it's always been one of my favorites too; maybe I can play another song for you sometime if you are willing to come back.

Liz: Who knows, stranger things have happened so I guess we'll see what happens.

After that she walks away to leave, turning around just once on her way out to look at Rick again before she walks out the door.

Rick: (turns to face his friends and say in a sarcastic tone): Nobody say a damn word and I'll even get you a free drink if you can refrain from your comments.

Lights fade to end the scene

End of Act One, Scene Two

Scene Three

It's the next day at *The Blue's Note* and the scene is almost exactly the same. The bar is starting to get busy and the same faces are sitting around the bar carrying on their conversations. Rick is on the stage helping set up equipment for the live band that the bar sometimes has. The jazz musicians are people from the neighborhood who have been playing together for years and people that Rick grew up with as well as learning how to play music with. As the band is ready to play its first set, the lights slowly dim to give an "ambience" in the club. The jazz band begins to play, and as they start Liz walks through the door and takes a seat at the bar not too far from where the regular crowd is sitting. The regulars that usually sit together all look up with amazement and watch her as she sits down.

Chad taps his brother Charlie on the shoulder and points at Liz smiling with a cocky look as if to say that she is in the bar to see him.

Charlie: (looking at Chad) Don't get too excited, I don't think that she's here for you. Something tells me Rick has already got the victory when it comes to getting this girl.

Chad: You don't know that, maybe my charm overwhelmed her last night and she came back in to see me.

Charlie: You're right little brother and that's why she's staring at Rick and hasn't come over here to say hi yet.

Chad: She's just playing hard to get.

Charlie: You know, mom was right about you; you're just a lost cause when it comes to women and that's also why she always said that she wouldn't be surprised if you turned out gay.

Chad: Hey, I am not gay and just because I got caught wearing a dress one time, which I might add was for a Halloween costume because I wanted to look like a member of *Twisted Sister,* doesn't make me a gay.

Bud walks over in the middle of this conversation and he over-hears everything that has been said.

Bud: Well I don't know any straight guys who wear dresses around here do you Charlie?

Charlie: No, can't say that I know any, and besides Chad, we're not judging you in any way. If you want to be gay, that's cool. You'll still be my brother; just my really, really gay brother who likes to wear women's clothes and who is going to hell according to the church.

Rick walks over to the bar after finishing his last set for the evening and hears the last part of the conversation.

Rick: Is Chad trying to prove again that he is not a closet case? You know you should just finally admit that you're gay and quit using the excuse that you have no luck with women.

Everybody starts laughing.

Chad: All of you can just kiss my ass and I don't have any luck with women around here because none of them understand me.

Rick: You know, I'm just going to leave that one alone because it's just too easy. Also Chad, you should be left to your own delusion.

Rick looks over and sees Liz sitting alone with her drink and walks over to talk to her.

Rick: Well I thought yesterday would be the last time we would ever see you after my friend harassed you and your friends.

Liz: Oh, he was harmless and I'm sure he's not that bad of a person despite what my so called friend said about him after we left.

Rick: Those people you were with were not really your friends were they?

Liz: No, there more like acquaintances; my real friends actually have a sense of humor. The only reason I was with them last night is because I was helping out with their little rally yesterday. I like to help out where I can, especially if it's an organization I can believe in. Anyway I believe in giving people a second chance, and I mean all people.

Rick: (looking directly into her eyes; smiling with a confident look) Why, thank you; we all deserve a second chance I guess.

Liz: (with a little nervousness in her voice from the way Rick was staring at her) Oh I was referring to your friend Chad.

Rick: **(confidently smiles at her)** So was I; I was just thanking you on his behalf.

Charlie: Hey Rick not to break up this nice little moment with you two as you cut through all the sexual tension, but don't you think you should quit being rude and properly introduce everybody?

Rick: I don't really think you feel all that bad about trying to ruin the mood, but since you are my friend I will indulge you and make the proper introductions. ***(Pointing at each of them)*** Liz, this is Charlie, Chad whom you have unfortunately met last night, and the owner of the bar, Bud.

She shakes each of their hands while the cocktail waitress walks up to all of them.

Susan: Now Rick, you're not going to forget me are you? ***(gives him a little shove behind the bar)*** You know I would never let you live it down, or I could just ruin this nice moment you have right now by telling her your dirty little past with other women who've come in here.

Rick: (shakes his head with and with a sarcastic look on his face) Damn, the bitch in you comes out at the most inappropriate times. Liz, this is Susan who has very sharp claws that she likes to dig into anything good when it comes to both men and women, so watch out. ***(Looking at Liz)*** You probably wouldn't find it too surprising that she is going to Law School.

Old Man Henderson: (sitting at the other end of the bar and with a musky voice) Hey what about me Rick, I'm in here every day and practically watched you grow up. Aren't you going to introduce me to your new dame?

Rick: Oh yeah that's Old Man Henderson and he's our "Norm" at this club.

Liz: Does he have a first name or do you just call him Old Man Henderson?

Rick: We really don't know what his first name is or if he actually has one. As long as anyone has known him he has been called Old Man Henderson and he has been coming to this bar every day since even before Bud became the owner. Apparently He went to an AA meeting across the street over thirty years ago, stayed five minutes, decided he didn't like it, and then came here. Since then he has never really left.

Liz: Is that a true story or are you just making that up?

Rick: I don't know if that true or not, buts it's a funny story regardless and consequently enough the Alcoholics Anonymous chapter across the street has been trying to shut us down ever since. Although they have forgotten one thing.

Liz: And what's that?

Rick: People love to drink around here and as long as we are selling the last legal drug that can kill you, people are going to come here like its water in a desert.

Liz: So is there anybody else in the bar I should meet?

Rick: Well, everybody else is just a regular, and once you've been coming here for a certain period of time, then you just become a regular and names are unimportant. It's kind of like a family I guess.

Liz: Well you definitely have an assortment of interesting characters here. I knew this would be a place I could like as soon as I first walked in the door, unlike those women I was with yesterday.

Rick: If that's the case, then would you like to stay and have a cup of coffee with me after everybody else leaves?

Liz: I would like that.

It's about closing time and Rick tells Bud that he will finish closing up. Bud says alright and announces that everybody has to finish their drinks and leave. Bud then gathers the money out of the cash register and goes to the office to count it while Rick makes a fresh pot of coffee and washes the last of the glasses. Susan is busy gathering the last of the glasses around the bar for Rick. The remaining crowd that's left in the bar is leaving.

Chad: (pulls something out his pocket and hands across the bar to Rick) Hey Rick, here's something you might need.

Rick: Damn it Chad, it's not like that and I don't need those.

Charlie: **(grabs his brother and pulls him away towards the door**) Chad, you really have no idea what tact is do you? For crying out loud you don't give a guy condoms in front of a woman; it just makes him look like a perv. How many times do we have to go through this?

Chad: What, I was just trying to help the guy out. I didn't mean anything by it.

Charlie: You never do; that's you're problem.

Liz is just laughing to herself the whole time.

Rick: My friends… they're always looking out for me.

Liz: That's what they're supposed to do even if it is at the wrong time.

Susan leaves, saying goodbye to both of them and it's now just Rick and Liz in the bar. Rick is behind the bar washing glasses and Liz is sitting in front of him on the other side of the bar.

Liz: Ever since I met you last night I have been racking my brain trying to figure out where I have seen you. I know you from somewhere.

Rick: Well I'm known throughout this neighborhood and this part of town since I play piano here almost every night and I grew up around here. I'm also known around campus because we get a lot of college kids in here. Some of them work part time, but most of them just come to drink.

Liz: Actually that's not it. I did ask one of my professors about this place. After I asked her she asked me if I got a chance to meet the piano player and I'm quoting "He is really good and shouldn't be playing in a place like this, but more like Las Vegas or Hollywood." She also told me that you were a student and played Basketball at De Paul. When I went to find out about you I ran into the Coach Graves, the head coach of the basketball team and he told me all about you.

Rick: Yeah, it's true I used play basketball at De Paul University and that's another reason I'm still known around campus.

Liz: Coach Graves told me that you were an All-American and you were going to play professional basketball. He also said you were going to be the next Larry Bird.

Rick: I don't know about the next Larry Bird, but everything else is true. I was really good and had a chance to go into the NBA. You did a lot of detective work just to find out about me. Why? What is it about me that's so interesting?

Liz: When I am curious about something, I want to know everything there is to know about it. After Coach Graves told me about you I remembered that I saw you play one time when I was a junior in High School. My father is a huge basketball fan and loves De Paul; he took me and a girlfriend of mine to the Conference Championship that year where you hit that winning three pointer to win the game with only one second left on the clock. Honestly, I just want to know why a guy with so much potential is in a place like this.

Rick: I bet you think that I ended up in this place by accident, but maybe I ended up here on purpose. Besides, I don't really know you well enough to tell you the story. I'm not really sure you would understand.

Liz: Everybody has a story they think other people won't understand. Even I have a story that you might not understand, but I'll tell you mine if you tell me yours.

Rick: Well I guess that's fair, but maybe I don't want to tell you my story. It is a little too personal for a first date.

Liz: Is that what this is, a first date? I don't know if I would call this a date. Maybe dinner and movie would qualify as a date instead of sitting in a bar having a cup of coffee with someone who can't answer any of my questions. I not trying to find out about you as if this were an interview, I just want to get to know you a little better.

Rick: Liz, all first dates are interviews and if you can conceive that this might be a first date with the possibility of a second date tomorrow, then I *will* tell you want you want to know.

Liz: You're not going to make this easy are you?

Rick: No, but when is anything between Men and Women easy, especially when they first meet each other?

Liz: I can see I have my work cut for me here, but I'll bite. We can call this a first date if you answer my question.

Rick: I just wanted to make this seem like a first date, so if I actually ask you out for dinner and movie then the awkwardness of a first date would be behind us and we can move right into "dating bliss."

Liz: That's very nice and well thought out Sherlock, but you're still stalling.

Rick: You don't cut anyone any slack do you? So just to put you out of your misery, I'll tell you what you want to know, but for some details there will have to be some friendly torture.

Liz: So what you're saying is you like to be dominated? That doesn't happen on the first date for me, but the sky's the limit on the second if you have the nerve to ask me out for real.

Rick: We'll see ***(smiling);*** Any way I grew up in this neighborhood. There were two things I learned how to do very well: play the piano and play basketball, and for whatever reason those were the two gifts that God "granted" me. Most of my formal education on the piano came from local jazz musicians who've been playing music for most of their lives in this part of Chicago. Well, I was so good at basketball, too, that when I graduated high school I was recruited by every major college in the nation. It didn't hurt that my high school won two state championships and I was mentioned in Sports Illustrated. Even Coach Graves took a shot at trying to get me to come to De Paul, even though he would later admit he knew he probably never had a chance at getting me to come. When my mother died that year, Coach Graves was the only coach to come to the funeral and he told me he would help me in any way he could even if I never played ball at De Paul.

Liz: Is that what made you decide to stay here and play basketball at De Paul?

Rick: Yeah, and I knew he would be someone that would do me right. Also, when it really came down to it, I didn't want to leave home.

Liz: So what happened at De Paul that got you here?

Rick: I ended up in the starting lineup halfway through my freshman year and it's been put to me many times that I became the heart and soul of the team for three and half years. I played on some really good teams at De Paul, so good that we went to the NCAA tournament three years in a row, and made it to the final four my junior year before we lost to Duke. Duke ended up winning the championship that year. I had a lot of NBA teams that wanted to draft me my junior and senior year, but it didn't quite happen that way.

Liz: Why didn't you go the NBA?

Rick: I tore two major ligaments in my right knee diving for a loose ball in our first round game during the tournament my senior year. After two surgeries, I was told by my doctors that I would be lucky to ever walk normally again, so my chance at professional basketball sort of bounced away with that loose ball. It would've been really nice if De Paul would have at least won the first round without me, but they didn't and my basketball career was over just like that ***(snaps his fingers).*** If you really want to know, diving for loose balls like that at is also one of the reasons I have been compared to Larry Bird. I could shoot like he did and very rarely missed, and I also would go diving for the ball like he did, which ironically ended my career.

Liz: So you became a piano player slash bartender because you couldn't play basketball anymore? Please tell me there's more to this story than just that.

Rick: Oh, my story is not that boring and unoriginal. There's a combination of things that got me here, but what you should know is that this place saved me in more ways than one. I found a saving grace in my "Hub in the Universe."

Liz: Your "Hub in the Universe," what do you mean by that?

Rick: You never heard that before?

Liz shakes her head no with a sarcastic look on her face.

Rick: Your "Hub in the Universe" is that one place where you can retreat to so you can feel totally happy and at peace. It can be anything, and the variables of that place will be different for everybody. My place just happens to be a dingy blues and jazz bar with a piano in the corner. Not too surprising now that you know me a little bit better, huh?

Liz: I guess I shouldn't be too surprised, but I don't quite understand why this kind of place is so special; maybe I just need to get to know you better first.

Rick: It may take that before you know the answer, but if you do figure it out let me know, because even I don't fully understand why this kind of place would be my "Hub in the Universe."

Liz: You still haven't answered my question on how you ended up here. Do I get to know the answer or do I have to see you again to find out?

Rick: What the hell, I'll tell you, but you still have to see me again tomorrow. Deal?

Liz: Okay, deal. So what happened?

Rick: After I got injured and couldn't play anymore I was a total wreck and didn't see the point of living anymore. I'm sure we've all felt that way before at some point. So I started drinking, quit going to class, and didn't do what I needed to in order to graduate. My girlfriend of seven years left me for one of my teammates who did go into the NBA, and I basically ended up here most days playing piano for the crowd. I gave up on life, my friends, school, and pretty much anything that mattered. The only thing that saved me was being here and playing music. This place was the only place I really felt happy, so I became the regular piano player again like I was in High School and a permanent bartender. I eventually became a partner with Bud in this little club and so I never really left. Besides, the only family I have left is here. From the best friends I've ever had, to the musicians that I learned music from that live around here, and a partner that has been like father to me. I can honestly say I have found my total happiness here.

Liz: So all the depression you had disappeared because you were in this place? I don't think I've ever heard of that before and I don't know if I can quite believe it.

Rick: When you find your "Hub in the Universe", you'll also find that it also has magical powers that can take away any sadness or depression. I found that here and that's probably why I never left; and as you saw yesterday, it's never a dull moment around here. So now that I've answered your questions, tell me about you and what brings you here.

Liz: There is not much to tell except I'm going into my seventh year at De Paul University. My family is Rich because my Dad invested in Microsoft and Intel back in the eighties, as well as starting his own technology company. I'll graduate from De Paul with three degrees this year and I have no idea what I really want to do, but my father's plan is for me to come and work for him.

Rick: Wow, three degrees, and yet you don't know what you really want to do with your life. I figure three areas of study should give you some options, but then again maybe it's not enough and you should try every department before you decide what you really want to do. Oh, wait, as a college student you do get to do that. It's called general education requirements, designed to make you a more well-rounded individual, or perhaps it's just called junior college, or perhaps even high school.

Liz: Not all of us can be a philosophical piano player slash bartender who has it all figured out when it comes to the meaning of life and uses what few lines he actually remembered from philosophy 101 to hit on women in a bar.

Rick: I may be philosophical, but even I can concede that I don't have it all figured out when it comes to the meaning of life. I think Monty Python has the answers to that more than I do, but I do know that a little philosophy is a good tool to use when hitting on women. See, it works because you did come ***(with a big sarcastic smile)***. So what are your degrees in?

Liz: My first degree is in Business and Marketing which is the one my father said I had to get if he was going to pay for my education. He made this deal with me when I was 16. I could go to any school I wanted to for my college education and he would pay for it, but I had to study business. He also told me that I could study anything else I wanted to as well, but I had to get a degree in business first. So I did my course study in business first and got done with it in three years. The other two degrees are in Astronomy and Art. I've always loved Art and really didn't want to study anything else ever since I was a kid. That is where my main passion is, but it's hard to be successful in that area unless you're a Picasso and dead. I had a roommate who got me interested in the stars so I studied Astronomy as well until I realized last year that I actually had enough credits for a degree in Astronomy.

Rick: So are you going to actually do anything with your art degree since art is your passion, or are you doomed to work for your father's company?

Liz: As far as I am concerned, I'm not doomed to work for my father; the business degree was just an easy compromise so I could study what I wanted. I've applied to some art schools in Paris that I think would be really fun to study at, and if you're going to do any graduate work in Art there's probably not any better schools to do it in, so we'll see if that works out. The great thing about these schools is that there are scholarships that I could get so my father doesn't have to pay for it, and therefore he couldn't tell me that I'm wasting my time.

Rick: Well there is still hope for you even if you don't get to go to Paris. You did discover this place, and no matter if you keep coming back or not, you'll always find something to laugh at even if it's the most mindless conversation you have ever heard. All I can tell you is that there is something magical about a place like this, and it's the people in it that give it its character. I'm sure your friends from last night would disagree, but people with no sense of humor usually do.

Bud walks out of the office after having finished counting the money and doing the daily paperwork for the bar.

Bud: Don't forget to lock up tonight Romeo, and I don't want to be cleaning any disgusting messes on top of my bar from things going too far between you two.

Rick: Hey I'm not Susan; I can control who I have sex with and where I do it. But if anything does happen we'll just make her clean it up just to get her back for the last time.

Bud: How about nothing happens so my bar keeps clean and sanitary? I don't know why you young kids just can't get a bed or wait to find a room somewhere. A sign that says bar doesn't mean have sex here.

Rick: Apparently it does in Susan's book, but hey we love her anyway and that's only because the Bible says we have to. I know you love her as if she was your own daughter, but you have to make her clean up her own messes. I mean, you would make me clean my mess wouldn't you?

Bud: Don't start with me Rick; I'm not worried about her tonight as long she shows up to work tomorrow. It's you I'm not too sure about because after all, you're the piano player.

Rick: Nobody trusts the piano player anymore, especially since we're the one person in a bar you should trust.

Liz: You're also a bartender, so you do have that going against you. So what happened with Susan?

Rick: She closed up one night and her two week boyfriend at the time stopped by to see her while she was cleaning up. Well, one thing lead to another, and she left a bigger mess than the one she was cleaning up, and most of it was on top of the bar. Bud wasn't too happy when he discovered it, and ever since that incident, whoever she is dating is not allowed here at the bar after hours.

Liz: I can see why he would be mad, but what about you? Is there reason for him to be suspicious of you?

Rick: I don't really know what he means by that; he's probably just getting paranoid in his old age. Besides, I'm completely innocent ***(he has a sarcastic smile).***

Liz: Somehow I doubt that. Every piano player I've ever met has had some skeletons in their closet. And I really doubt that there is any innocence behind you having me stay behind tonight to have a cup of coffee with you while you clean up.

Rick: Ah, you have foiled my secret plan because after all "do you want to have a cup of coffee with me" really means "do you want to have sex with me."

Liz: Thank you for proving my point, and I didn't know that about "do you want to have a cup of coffee with me," but maybe that's only in this bar.

Rick: Perhaps, but if that's true and you don't ever come here again, then it will mean you don't like having sex, and I don't know anybody who hates sex.

Liz: Maybe I just don't want to have sex with anybody in this bar. Chicago is a big place and there are lots of other bars where I might find someone I like.

Rick: No, I'm going with my answer on this one because there has to be at least one person that you want to have sex with in this bar; it probably won't be any of my friends, but there is someone in here that you would like. Oh, and by the way, you don't have to worry about anything. My innocence will get thrown right out the door if I ask you out for breakfast tonight.

Liz: Why don't we just start with dinner tomorrow before we get into the whole breakfast issue; I don't know if I can completely trust you yet.

Rick: Hey, I told you, you can always trust the piano player. But needless to say, this is going to get interesting don't you think?

Liz: You're right, this is going to get interesting, but I still don't trust you yet.

Rick: Hey, where's the faith? I mean, come on, this is not the best way to start getting to know somebody.

Liz: (with a stunned look) You're pretty perceptive if you already knew what I was going to ask or what I was thinking, but in response to "where's my faith" have you seen any of the guys around here? Some of them are your friends!

Rick: Yes some of them are my friends, and because of them it makes me look a whole lot better. So I guess I'll meet you here at eight and we'll see how interesting this can really get.

Liz: Okay tomorrow at eight then.

Lights fade to end the scene

End of Act One, Scene Three

Act 2

Scene One

It's one month later on a Tuesday afternoon at the club and Rick is behind the bar cutting fruit while Chad and Charlie are sitting at a small table next to the bar playing dominoes. An elderly man walks through the door. He is a local Municipal Judge and is a regular at the club. He has known everybody at the bar since they were kids and has known Bud since he first bought the bar. Rick and Liz have been seeing each other for about a month now.

Rick: Hey judge, how are you doing today?

Judge: (walking toward the table where Chad and Charlie are sitting) I'm old and one more day closer to death, so you can imagine the mood I'm in today. By the way, I hear you have a new love in your life and you've been seeing her for more than two weeks this time.

Rick: I didn't know that my love life had reached the inner sanctums of the municipal court. I wonder who I have to thank for that one.

Judge: Actually my bailiff told me this time. Apparently, he met her not too long ago in here, but it was Chad who dispensed with all the details.

Chad: All I told him was that you were seeing someone again and you were happy again.

Rick: But how much did you embellish in your tale? That's what I'm worried about. I wish everybody around here would quit thinking of me as the Sam Malone of the bar. I just happen to know most of the women that come in here and occasionally I ask one of them out.

Charlie: Yeah, but how well you know all of them is the point we're making.

Rick: Those are just mere rumors and you have no proof of anything. That's the story I am sticking to.

The judge sits down to play dominos with Chad and Charlie.

Judge: Well, are you two ready for me to kick your ass in dominos? If you two let me win this time, the next time I find you in my court I'll actually throw you in jail instead of just making you pay a fine.

Charlie: We never let you win. You're really that good at dominos, and we wouldn't just say that to make an old man feel good.

Judge: Or to make me go easy on you every time you end up in my court. Don't patronize me. I know you two professional criminals are better at these kinds of games than you let on. Remember, I'm a judge. I see criminals every day, and I know how you think.

Chad: Now judge, you know I'm not that good at dominos. Checkers is my game, but there isn't any money in it.

Rick: Judge, don't let him fool you. The game he's really good at is "gay chicken." I've never seen anybody play it better.

Charlie starts laughing out loud and the judge sits at the table with a bewildered look.

Chad: Come on, Rick. You know I've only won one game, but it doesn't mean anything. The guy I beat didn't even know what the game was, so that was the only reason I won.

Judge: What in the hell is "gay chicken"? Is that some weird sex game that you young people are into now? It sounds disgusting to me.

Rick: "Gay chicken" is where someone dares you to try and kiss another guy, and just like an old fashioned game of chicken, whoever breaks first is the loser, but as the winner it isn't saying much if you're straight. Oh, and Chad is the only one who lost to a real gay man who thought he was trying to hit on him.

Judge: Is this true Chad? Are you trying to tell us something about yourself, because you don't need to hide in a closet all your life. There is no judgment on our part if your lifestyle is a little bit different than everybody else's. Your mother would be disappointed in you of course, but *we* wouldn't judge.

Chad: I want everybody to know for the last time I am not gay, and I can't believe you would actually think that about me. Can't anybody see how much I love women, even though I have no success with them and they don't understand me?

Chad sits at the table to play dominoes with an angry look upon his face. As soon as he is done talking, Liz walks in and gives Rick a kiss.

Liz: Hey guys, how's everybody doing today? (looks at Chad the looking at Rick) What's wrong with him?

Rick: Oh he's mad because we told the judge here about the game that he's really, really good at.

Liz: Oh, you mean "gay chicken".

Everybody starts laughing

Chad: You guys are *not* funny; I think every one of you are trying to start rumors because you think it's funny.

Charlie: Actually, it is pretty funny whether it's a rumor or not. It's funny because even though it's not a big deal, you get mad for everybody thinking you're gay.

Rick: Liz, I haven't introduced you to the judge yet; he's one of our regulars from the neighborhood. He hasn't been in for a while, so you haven't had a chance to meet. (Pointing to the judge) Liz, this is the judge; judge, this is Liz, the woman I've been dating.

Liz: It's nice to meet you.

Judge: It's nice to finally meet the person that I keep hearing is making Rick so happy. Let me get a good look at you and see why he likes you. (***He takes a long look eying her up and down)***. I can see why he likes you and why you made such an impression on him.

Liz: I don't think I quite understand the basis of approval, but I guess I just got a really good compliment.

Judge: You can say that; I've known Rick for a long time, and I also know what kind of woman it will take to make him fall again, so I just wanted to see if you fit the bill.

Liz: What do you mean make Rick fall again?

Rick: Look, before the rumors of my past love life come out and you start adding to those rumors, why don't you get back to your game and I'll see about getting you a free drink?

Liz looks a little confused because of the way Rick is acting, and the judge gives the sign of O.K. then sits down.

Liz: Rick, I came by to tell you that I can't make it tonight. I have to help out at the concert tonight on campus. A friend of mine said she needed some help at the last minute so I said yes.

Rick: Don't worry about it. We'll do it again some other time. By the way, who's in concert tonight?

Liz: It's a blues singer who's apparently from Chicago. His name is Lee Wayne Johnson, but I've never heard of him before. He went to De Paul years ago, so he's doing a concert there tonight.

Chad: Wait a minute, there's a Lee Wayne Johnson concert tonight at the University?

Liz: You've heard of him?

Rick: Yeah, we all know him because he grew up in the neighborhood, and he also used to play here before he made it big. I actually got to jam with him a few times here when I was in high school. He's now a famous blues artist along the same lines as Stevie Ray Vaughn.

Liz: Well that's good, because I had some extra tickets for all of you.

Charlie: (with a sarcastic tone and a big smile) Just how many tickets did you get girlfriend, if you don't mind me asking?

Chad: Yeah, because if you have any extra tickets you don't need, we can sure use them.

Liz: I only have four, so you boys will have to divide them amongst yourselves (***She takes them out of her bag and hands them to Rick).***

Rick: Hey thanks Liz, but guys, if I give you two tickets, then you can't scalp them. The fourth one is for Bud.

Chad: Hey, what do you take us for? We actually want to go to this concert! And not everything we do is about making money, either.

Charlie: My poor pathetic excuse for a brother is actually right. We're not the materialistic weasels that you think we're are; we don't always think about money.

The Judge shakes his head and clears his throat so as to remind Chad and Charlie that they have been in his court many times for scalping tickets and other criminal activities.

Rick: I mean it guys, don't be scalping tickets at the university. The last time you got caught there, I stuck up for you and nearly lost my scholarship because I almost got kicked off the team . If you get caught again I'm not bailing you two out of jail.

Charlie: (with a sarcastic tone) After all these years Rick, I thought you would have thought better of us. I guess I was wrong about you.

Rick: No, it's because I know you too well. (yelling towards the back office) Bud!

Bud: (comes out of the office) What is it Rick? I'm actually trying to do some work.

Rick: Liz got us tickets to the Lee Wayne Johnson concert and there's one for you.

Bud: Lee Wayne Johnson is playing in concert? Sure I love to see a local boy play in concert. It's definitely been a while since we've seen him. Where's he playing tonight?

Rick: He's playing at the university tonight, one night only.

Bud: I guess we're closing early tonight, but hell, it's worth it to see that boy. ***(He turns around and walks back into the office).***

Liz: So I guess I'll see you there?

Rick: You can count on it, and since you got us the tickets I guess I'll have to be nice and take you to one of my favorite places on campus.

Liz: It's not one of those kinky places I'm always hearing about, is it? If it is, then you're getting a little too presumptuous when it comes to properly thanking me for the tickets.

Rick: (with a sarcastic smile) You really have to quit listening to rumors about me in this bar.

Liz: I'll see you tonight (***She kisses him and then turns around to leave).***

Rick: See you tonight.

Lights fade to end the scene

End of Act Two, Scene One

Scene Two

Outside the theater at the end of the concert, Bud and Rick are standing outside waiting for Chad and Charlie. Rick is also waiting for Liz to finish helping her friend at the box office.

Bud: Where are those SOB'S? If they're in trouble again and got arrested then I'm definitely not bailing them out this time.

Rick: Who knows where they went this time? I should've known that as soon as we got here they would disappear and probably start doing something illegal. Sometimes they're just like children who never listen.

Bud: Well, I'm not waiting for them anymore, and if you see them tell 'em they owe me breakfast just like they promised.

Rick: How many times have they really lived up to their promises? Hey, they're my friends, but let's be honest here.

Bud: You're right, and I don't know why I give them the benefit of the doubt, but we'll see how they like it when they can't get free beer anymore. Anyway, I'm off.

Rick: I'll see you tomorrow.

Bud turns around and leaves off stage. Liz comes onto the stage and greets Rick

Liz: Well how was it, were the tickets pretty close?

Rick: Yeah, you certainly out did yourself with these tickets, which means that I'm going to have to be really nice to you for a while.

Liz: Oh, you're going to have to be more than just nice; something along the lines of being treated like a queen comes to mind.

Rick: Yeah, you're not much different than any other woman I've met.

Liz: Probably, but I'm more fun. So was Lee Wayne Johnson just as good as you remember him playing in the club?

Rick: Yeah, he still has the stuff. Say, you want to meet him? After all, I might as well use this back stage pass you gave me.

Liz: Sure, I've never met a real blues musician before and it will be nice to see what he has to say about you since you two know each other.

Lights go down to end the scene

End of Act Two, Scene Two

Scene Three

Liz and Rick walk back stage to see Lee Wayne Johnson. The stage changes just a little bit to reflect the dressing rooms of the theater and back area of the theater. Lee Wayne Johnson is sitting on couch talking with another man and a woman. An Attendant lets Rick and Liz into the room to see Lee Wayne Johnson. They come from off stage.

Lee: (he gets up to greet Rick) Hey Rick, haven't seen you in as long time. What are you doing here?

Rick: I was given some free tickets to your concert so I thought I better come out and see if you've actually developed any talent.

Lee: What, are you saying I'm not good enough to for you to buy tickets to see?

Rick: Do you really want me to answer that? Hey, if I can get free tickets to something I'm definitely there.

Lee: I see why you really came to my concert. So what are you doing these days?

Rick: I'm still playing at *The Blue's Note* and helping Bud with the place.

Lee: So how's Bud? I bet he hasn't changed a bit.

Rick: Well he still isn't dead, and he's still grouchy as ever. I'm sure that will never change

Lee: You're probably right. So, still doing what you love the most, uh?

Rick: That's right, couldn't imagine anything better. By the way, this is Liz, she's a student here and she's actually the one who got the tickets for me.

Lee: Don't you know this guy has to be charged double when he comes to my concert? If he's told you any bad things about me from my club days, then I'll go ahead and tell you that they're all true except for my musical ability; despite him, I actually have some.

Rick: This guy is the main reason there are a lot of rumors about me at the club. After all, you know how those blues artists can be' just a lot of made up stories about other people's pain and stupid mistakes.

Liz: If your theory is correct then I really can't trust anything you've said to me so far. Is trying to show off in front of a music star your way of showing your manhood?

Lee: You know its love when she can put you in your place and have you figured out to a tee. Just for putting him in his place, you're always welcome at any one of my concerts as one of my personal guests.

They all laugh as Rick just smiles at Liz for her perfect comments.

Rick: The concert was great. If you're still around tomorrow you should stop by the club and have a beer on us. I think I should get out of here before Liz really shows me up and I can still have some of my manhood left.

Liz: You know you like it.

Rick: Sure, we can say that if it makes you feel better.

Liz: That's not what you were saying last night.

Rick gives her a weird look, but not one that shows any anger

Lee: Oh, not even Linda could make you have that kind of look; it definitely must be love for you.

Liz looks a little surprised by Lee's comment.

Rick: (he laughs and extends his hand to shake Lee's) She is something isn't she? It was good to see you again, but I'm going to get out of here before any more bad memories come rushing to the surface.

Lee: It was good to see you; and Liz, it was very nice to meet you.

Liz: It was very nice to meet you and I'll try not to give in to his bullshit. So thank you for warning me about him.

Lee: Anytime.

Rick: We better leave before my so called bad reputation gets any bigger.

The lights go down to end the scene.

End of Act Two Scene Three

Scene Four

The scene begins on a park bench in the middle of campus where buildings and trees surround the open meadow with the park bench.

Liz: This is your favorite spot on campus, a park bench?

Rick: Yeah, this is it. It's very simple and right in the center of things on the campus. There's no mystery behind my favorite spot if that's what you're looking for. ***(With a smile)*** I just like the simple life.

Liz: I was looking for something a little kinky since I've heard all these interesting things about you.

Rick: They're just stories; it doesn't mean that they're true. Although. if you have your doubts, then I guess you'll just have to find out yourself.

Liz: I can just imagine what you have in mind, which brings up the subject. I want to know what Lee Wayne Johnson meant by "Linda couldn't even do that to you." I'm not one to ask about past lovers, but I'm curious about what effect she had on you to make you be the way you are. I know you had a career ending injury and that changed you in a way, but her leaving must have had some serious effect on you.

Rick: I think anybody you love when they're gone affects you in some profound way, and if you want to know the truth, yes she had an effect on me, especially when she left.

Liz: Well you haven't talked much in the month that we have known each other about what happened with you and her, or why you've come to believe what you believe. I want to know what happened.

Rick: Do you really want to know, or do you just want to know if the rumors you've heard about me are really true?

Liz: I don't care about the rumors, I'm just curious about her and how you got to this point.

Rick: Okay I'll tell you, but you have to tell me about your ex as well, and I do have a serious question for you.

Liz: Okay, go ahead. I'll let you ask yours first.

Rick: Why have you waited so long to ask me something like this? I would've thought that this is something you would have asked me a couple of weeks ago.

Liz: I wanted to get to know you a little bit better before I asked this kind of question. You told me a little the second time I talked to you, and it's made me really curious, but I think there's a certain point in relationships when you can ask these kinds of serious questions.

Rick: See, that just proves my theory about people; when you start out dating you should just hand out a dating resume to each other so you don't have to wait to get certain questions answered. The dating resume could have things like: I dated this many people, been in love this many times, these women have had this kind of effect on me, and just for added bonus to bypass the really embarrassing question that we all want to ask, but are too afraid because of the answer, how many people have you had sex with?

Liz: You're right that would probably help, but it would take all the fun out of having these kinds of conversations on a park bench with such a romantic setting. You never know what might happen in a place like this.

Rick: I knew you were a tease, but most women are and I should know because I am a bartender/piano player. We do know a lot and we do see how women can really be.

Liz: And I'm sure the alcohol in your place has no effect whatsoever on how women act. But enough of being a sexist, please just answer my question.

Rick: Do you really want to hear about ex-girlfriends? I mean, somehow it just seems wrong to talk about an ex. You know that no matter what I say you won't like it because you'll think I'm just comparing you to her.

Liz: Quit stalling and just tell me; I'll decide if I want to get mad or not.

Rick: (smiling) Okay. The reason you hear a lot of references to Linda and I is because as much as we tried to have somewhat of a private life, everybody at the bar and in the neighborhood were a part of our lives, so they knew us and the affect she had me. Linda was from the neighborhood and we grew up together. We actually started dating in high school and she ended going to De Paul as well, probably because of me. We had planned on getting married, and to give you an idea of how we were together, we were just like one of those perfect couples in the movies who have a fairy tale relationship. So when she left, everybody knew what happened and my time of being mad at the world wasn't a very private thing either. This is why everybody knows about her and makes a lot of jokes about her and the affect she had on me.

Liz: That doesn't really answer my question, because you didn't tell me how she really affected you or what she meant to you.

Rick: You noticed that, did you? Maybe I'm kind of skirting the issue. I haven't talked about this in a very long time. I was very much in love with her and she had a tremendous effect on me. It felt in a lot of ways that she defined me and helped make who I was. I know now a person can't make you who you are, but she came pretty damn close. She was there when I needed her most after my mother died, she could do the best thing in the world, which was to make me laugh, and she didn't seem to mind that this was home. Although I found out the hard way that the last part was more of a delusion. If you really want to know, the hardest thing about her leaving was finding out that she didn't want to stay here in this place that we called home and a place that I really never wanted to leave. That probably doesn't make any sense, but it's the truth. So there's my one piece of honesty for the evening. Now, what's your story? I want to know about this former love of your life since I've told you all about mine.

Liz: I guess it's only fair that I tell you about him since you've been honest with me. But I do think that this is the last time we should talk about ex-lovers, and for your information, I'm not worried about being compared to Linda. What do you think; no more talk about former lovers?

Rick: That's music to my ears! Besides, we don't want to be like those sad and pathetic souls who dwell on the past and usually sit in my bar night after night nursing their regrets with a stiff drink.

Liz: I'd like to think that were better people than that, but like Charlie said once, sometimes our delusions get the best of us.

Rick: But sometimes our delusions tend to be better than our own reality, and if that's the case, no one can really judge you about your delusions. Now you quit stalling and tell me about this ex-lover of yours.

Liz: If you must know, I met him my first year of college and he was a few years older than me. We really didn't have anything in common, but I had love in my eyes when I first saw him so I immediately became infatuated with him. When you're looking hard for love, even the wrong person will seem right. He was smart and funny and knew all about the world, but most importantly my father didn't approve, so it made the relationship even better on some level.

Rick: So you're saying that you're not any different than other young girls in wanting to piss your father off with dating men that he will never approve of?

Liz: No, not really, and when I was eighteen and nineteen I was hell bent on making my father mad at anything I did. The thing is, I really did like Scott and I think with him I learned how to love. He graduated and moved to New York so he could pursue a career in politics. He would call and send letters, but they became less and less. After a while I never heard from him again, and then I heard he got married. My story isn't very original, but that's what happened. My father on the other hand was very glad he left, and proceeded to tell me a very big "I told you so."

Rick: I would venture a guess that your father really didn't like Scott because he was a Democrat, and your father, being a lifelong Republican, just couldn't have a Democrat spreading his demon seed upon his daughter.

Liz: That was the main reason why he hated Scott, but the truth is that my father is just a big asshole and doesn't like anybody who isn't the mirror image of him, especially when it comes to his kind of politics.

Rick: Ah, one of those. I can tell your dad and I will be the best of friends.

Liz: Well I don't know how well Jesus and the anti-Christ would get along before things came to blows, but I'm pretty sure it would be something like that with you and my dad.

Rick: Perhaps, but I like to think that I can be the better person and not just deliberately make your dad angry.

Liz: I'm sure it wouldn't be that at all. My dad would just hate you on general principle because he's an asshole.

Rick: You really don't like your dad that much do you; why is that?

Liz: I love my dad, but at the same time I hate him and it's because he doesn't see me for who I am. He doesn't understand me and I think he never has. He only sees me for what he wants me to be; and yes if you are wondering there are a lot of things I do just to make him mad. My college education is partly based on that as well.

Rick: As well as some of your choices in your love life?

Liz: Sure, but I'm no different than a lot of people in this life.

Rick: Isn't it funny how finding that true love of our life is sometimes paralleled to making someone else mad, whether it's through jealousy or parental revenge or even just in spite? Can you imagine a person shouting to the moon (***in a funny impressionable voice)***, "well I'll show so and so and spend the rest of my life with someone that doesn't make me happy just to get back at them"? And you know that the other person doesn't even care what you do to try and get back at them for something that they didn't quite realize made you mad to begin with.

Liz: I think you have a good point, but I think you have also engaged in too many stupid philosophical conversations at the bar with Chad and Charlie to be making those types of impressions. There comes a time when your little conversations get the best of you and you start going off on some authoritative tangent that doesn't make sense.

Rick: I thought you said I had a good point?

Liz: I did, but sometimes you take it a little too far and then start sounding like a Baptist preacher on Sunday.

Rick: I never realized I did that with my little philosophical speeches; you're really beginning to sound like my **(Liz cuts him off).**

Liz: Your wife or perhaps someone that is beginning to know you very well?

Rick: (sarcastically) Yeah, I'm getting a little scared now. This thing between us is not going to work if I don't have some kind of mystery left.

Liz: You still have some mystery left, although not as much as you think, but I still want you to tell me more about yourself. When it comes to people I want to know well, I have to figure out if it's worth it. What can I say, like you I try to be a good judge of people and that comes from paying attention.

Rick: Then you're learning very well and as long as I still have a little bit of mystery left, then all of my charm is not wasted on you.

Liz: I don't think you'll ever have to worry about that; after all, I'm still here.

Rick: Yes you are ***(he leans in to kiss her).***

As they are kissing, loud footsteps are heard from stage left. Chad and Charlie come running onto the stage. Rick and Liz are startled and abruptly stop kissing.

Charlie: (sounding out of breath) Rick, you got to say we've been with you all night; we're being chased by the police.

Rick: What did you do this time?

Chad: (sounding out of breath) They caught us scalping tickets, but we were able to get away before they saw who we were. Two cops have been chasing us half way through campus.

Rick: Didn't I tell you not to scalp your tickets? I told you that you would get caught here on campus. I'm so tired of covering for you guys.

Chad: Come on dude, just say that we've been here with you all night, the police are going to be here any second and you know we would do it for you.

Rick: I wouldn't be stupid enough to do something like this so I could get caught for wrong doing.

Liz: Rick, leave them alone; we'll just say that they've been here with us all evening.

Chad: Yeah Rick, just cover for us or we'll have to call you again for bail money.

Rick: Your bail fund is empty, and I'm tired of covering for you. You should... ***(Before he can finish his sentence two police officers show up)***

Officer 1: (looking at Chad and Charlie) You two are under arrest.

Rick: Officer, what did these two men do?

Officer 2: They were scalping tickets at the concert and when we tried to arrest them they resisted by running away.

Rick: These two? These can't be the same men you're looking for because they've been here all night with me and her.

Officer 1: We saw them so don't try to lie for them (he walks over to Chad and Charlie to put handcuffs on them).

Rick: I'm not lying for them. Are you sure you saw these two men, or two men or women that look like these two people.

Officer 1: We saw these two scalping tickets outside the concert hall and we're not going to keep defending our actions to you.

Rick: Okay, but can you describe what they look like...(***there is a pause where the police officers just look at him and don't give an answer)...*** you can't describe what they look like can you? I guess that's okay, but I know what judge they will appear before if you do arrest them, and he doesn't act too kindly when people are arrested under false pretenses. But hey, if you're willing to deal with that and put a black mark on what I'm sure are two fine careers in the police department, then don't let me stand in your way or tell you how to do your job.

Officer 2: And what judge do you know?

Rick: Judge MacLean, he's a regular at the bar that I run and I've known him since I was a kid. And if you really want to know, these two characters have had this happen before. The last time this happened the police officer that did it, who was a twenty year veteran of the department, got into so much trouble he was demoted to a crossing guard for the remainder of his career. But you don't have to take that into consideration if you don't want to.

Officer 1: So you know Judge MacLean?

Rick: Yes I do, he's a good friend of mine (***Chad says under his breath to Rick "he's your best friend")*** He's my best friend if you really want to know.

Officer 1: I don't know, you could be lying. How do I know that the only reason you know him is because you appeared before him once and now you're just using his name to make us go away?

Rick: Hey if you want to take that gamble then go right ahead. What if you're wrong?

Liz: Officer, there's no reason to keep going round and round like this. These two men have been with us all night. I know that because this one (***pointing at Chad)*** is my boyfriend and these two (***pointing at Rick and Charlie)*** are together. We were on a double date tonight. Now do I look like someone who's going to lie to you?

Chad gives a surprised look to Liz when she mentions that she is his girlfriend and Rick and Charlie both stare in disbelief at her when she says that they are a couple.

Officer 1: Well I still don't know if you're lying or not, prove to me that you're not lying.

Liz: Okay if he wasn't my boyfriend would I be willing to do this ***(she leans and gives Chad a passionate kiss to which he is very surprised, but kisses her back anyway)***

Rick and Charlie stare again in disbelief that Liz is willing to kiss Chad. Their looks are examples of a person whose mouth is dropped wide open and is looking at something with big eyes.

Officer 1: That doesn't mean anything. What about these two (***pointing at Charlie and Rick***)? If these two were going out then they would be willing to kiss each other in front of us. I want to see them do it.

Rick and Charlie give the police officers dirty looks, Chad begins to laugh quietly.

Liz: (smiling) I guess you boys better show your affection for each other.

Chad: Go ahead, you know you two don't mind public displays of affection.

Charlie is giving his brother a very dirty look right now.

Rick: Alright we'll kiss each other if that's what you want to see.

Rick grabs Charlie and leans in to kiss him when the second police officer starts to protest. This is supposed to be a very comical seen while Rick tries to call the police officer's bluff. They don't kiss each other because the second police officer stops them before they do it.

Officer 2: Alright, that's just disgusting. We don't need to see that.

Officer 1: Okay I guess you're right, you wouldn't be couples if weren't willing to kiss each other, but that doesn't mean that you two (***pointing at Chad and Charlie***) weren't scalping tickets and you're trying to cover for them.

Rick: Seriously officer, do these two look smart enough to scalp tickets and get away with it?

Chad and Charlie give Rick a dirty look because of the comment Rick has made about them.

Officer 1: Well, maybe you're right, but I better not catch any of you or anybody that looks like you scalping tickets.

Rick: (with a sarcastic tone) Okay that doesn't make much sense officer, but we'll do what you say. So you have a good night now, and we'll try our best not to get into trouble.

Officer 1: I don't need sarcasm out of you right now, or I'll haul you down town.

Rick: Sorry Officer, it's about all I can do right now, but I don't think it's against the law, so you have a good evening.

The two police officers leave the park area shaking their heads and mumbling to themselves about what just happened. ***(They walk off stage left)***

Charlie: We're not smart enough to get way with scalping tickets, huh? You're a real friend.

Rick: Hey, I'm the kind of friend that gets you out of trouble. Besides, I almost kissed you to get the police officers to leave.

Charlie: Yeah, it's enough to make me vomit and I can't believe you were actually going to kiss me.

Rick: I had to do something to get you out of trouble, but I wasn't going to actually kiss you. I just wanted to call the cop's bluff.

Charlie: Well I think you succeeded in that; anyway I think your girlfriend here said all that needed to be said to make those cops leave. ***(To Liz)*** I can't believe you said I was gay and Rick was my lover. Do I look gay or put off that kind of vibe?

Liz: Do you really want me to answer that? I wouldn't complain too much. Whatever I said was convincing enough to make the police leave and to stop you and Chad from ending up in jail

Charlie: I guess that's true, but Rick being my lover is a little far-fetched. He really isn't my type and he's not that good looking.

Rick: That's good to know; I guess I won't have to worry about you hitting on me anymore.

Charlie: You know you love it. Hey my lame-ass brother hasn't said anything for a while, which is unusual. What happened to you Chad? Being kissed by a real live woman put you into shock didn't it?

Rick: (with a big smile) I guess Liz had quite an effect on him, but then again I think any woman that actually kissed him would probably have the same effect on him.

Liz: Oh thanks, that's a nice thing to say about me. I've never had any complaints before, especially out of you.

Chad: Guys, leave me alone. I don't go into shock every time a woman kisses me. I just get a little nervous. I'm just a little shocked that Liz actually kissed me.

Rick: Chad, we're all a little surprised about that.

Charlie: Chad, I'm just surprised that she was willing to make physical contact you with at all.

Liz: You guys leave him alone, he's not that repulsive.

Chad: See Charlie you were wrong, some women don't find me repulsive and just maybe they find me a little bit better looking than you.

Charlie: Hey little brother, bullshit comes in many forms.

Liz: Can the three of you ever say anything nice to each other?

Rick, Chad, and Charlie all answer "no" at the same time.

Rick: We can say nice things to each other. It's just not as fun as being mean.

Charlie: Well, I don't know about you guys, but all that running earlier made me thirsty. I need a beer, so I'm heading to the club.

Liz: (to Chad and Charlie) I think the both of you owe me one for saving your ass.

Charlie: I guess it's the least we can do for you, but Chad's buying. After all, he was the one who got to kiss you. (***Both of them start to walk off the stage to exit the scene; towards stage right)***

Rick: So I guess we're heading back to the club before we call it night?

Liz: Yeah, and it will give you a reprieve on being more honest with me, so that should make you enjoy it more.

Rick: I told you already, you got my one piece of honesty for the night, so giving me a reprieve on being honest isn't going to entice me to go to a club with you.

Liz: How about a chance at getting lucky tonight?

Rick: That might do it, but it has to be a definite chance instead of a made-up answer that women like to give a man just to get the man to do what they want them to do.

Liz: I guess you will just have to find out, and you can finish your story some other time.

Rick: At this point I'll probably have to; I won't have a chance to get out of it.

Chad and Charlie are nearly off stage as to show them walking off from Rick and Liz to create some distance.

Charlie: (from a distance yells) Will you two hurry up? We're thirsty and I don't have a key anymore.

Rick: That's true, I did have to take it away from him after him and Chad decided to throw a party in the club after hours and half our liquor was missing.

Liz: There's never a dull moment with you guys, is there?

Rick: You have no idea, which makes me wonder why you are still hanging around.

Liz: I guess I just like a little excitement in my boring life and there is certainly enough surrounding you. (***They smile at each other as the lights go down.)***

Lights fade to end the scene

End of Act Two, Scene Four

Act 3

Scene one

It's been a little over than a month since the scene in the park. Rick and Liz are starting to get more serious and they are spending almost every night together. She has been spending the night at Rick's place a lot, but they have not been fully intimate with each other yet.

The scene opens up in another evening in the club before Rick starts his first set. Chad and Charlie are having a conversation with Liz while Rick is cutting limes and Susan is talking with some of the customers that are sitting around the bar.

Charlie: You know Liz, Rick here used to be quite the ladies' man back in high school and he went through women like they were going out of style, even when he was in college. If I were you I'd dump his ass and let an actual gentleman take you out.

Liz: And Charlie, who do you suggest that I replace Rick with?

Charlie: I hate to brag, but you would definitely do better with somebody like me.

Liz: Really? Well, speaking of finding a gentleman, do you know if there's a service I can call to find one? I think finding one here is still a matter of question.

Charlie: Hey, don't be fooled by my rugged good looks.

Liz: That's nice, but the way I've heard it is Rick had the same girlfriend for most of high school and college, so these rumors that you keep making up aren't going to convince me.

Charlie: I'm just trying to point out the fact that ***(pointing at Rick)*** ugly here might not be the best choice for any future happiness you might be looking for with someone.

Liz: Charlie, are you still jealous that I kissed Chad instead of you that night?

Chad: Yes he is, and rightfully so, because what woman wouldn't want to kiss me?

Rick: Chad, that would be a sane woman, but seriously, you need to get your own women. Preferably women that you don't have to spend $2.99 a minute to talk to.

Susan comes walking over to where the conversation is. She is still behind the bar.

Susan: Rick, you need to leave Chad alone. Not everybody can be like you and pick-up any woman in this bar and have a wild night of making love with her.

Rick: I think you have that department covered.

Susan: I don't hit on every female in this bar and then try to take them home with me.(***Looking at Chad***) Chad, don't say anything, and just take that fantasy right out of your head. I'm not a lesbian, I'm bisexual and it's only a state of mind depending on what phase I'm in at that moment.

Rick: Susan, you can say whatever you want, but when you try and get a woman from this club to go home with you after extensive flirting, which for you is every woman you meet here, that makes you a lesbian and it has nothing to do with a state of mind.

Susan: I date men as well; you all know that.

Rick: Yes you do, but you also think everything in here is on the menu, and most of the time it tends to be women, so I think that makes you a lesbian.

Susan: No it doesn't, it just makes me bi-sexual which we all know is a fantasy that all you guys around here have about any woman you meet, because you all hope that there may be a chance for a threesome.

Rick: Okay being one of the only honest guys around I'll tell you this...

Susan: (looking at Liz) Is there even such a thing as a truly honest guy?

Liz: I really don't think there is.

Rick: I heard that, and no matter what you gals say I'm going to finish my sentence. Yes, as men we're always interested in getting to have a threesome, but when it comes to being bi-sexual you're still gay, so really what's the difference in being bi-sexual or a lesbian?

Liz: Honey, the difference is when you're a lesbian you can't stand to be with a man at all because they can't satisfy you, but if you're bi-sexual then it means that you do like men at least a little bit, and then there's that chance that you'll get to have that little fantasy that all men want.

Liz smiles sarcastically at Rick as he smiles back at her just to let her know that she has made a good point.

Rick: Yeah, I still don't know why I put up with you though.

Liz: It's because you love me and just can't stand to live without me.

Rick: Love is just a byproduct and tends to be overrated anyway.

Liz: But you know you can't live without women, and the sad truth is even though we can't really live without men, we can live without you a little bit longer than you can live without us.

Rick, Chad, and Charlie look at each other while thinking for a moment and then respond in unison.

All (Rick, Chad, and Charlie): No, we don't buy that.

Rick: Whatever fantasy you want to tell yourself, but this doesn't mean that women have some magical power over men as you would like to think.

Liz and Susan: Sure there is, it's called sex.

Bud comes walking over to the conversation.

Bud: You know none of you damn kids know even two cent's worth of what love is all about. I've never seen so many amateurs in one room when it comes to love. And before anybody says anything, the reason I know a thing or two about love is not because I'm old, but because I found the secret to keeping the passion going within your relationship ...and.. keeping a good sex life.

Chad: Ah, Bud we don't want to hear anything about sex from you. It's not really your area anymore.

Bud: Chad shut up and listen to me. If you listen for a change and quit running your mouth all the time then you might actually get a woman. I've been married to the same women for over 40 years and there's still passion in our relationship. We've had to work hard at it, but we both have found a way to keep loving each other. You see, that's the real answer to lifelong love: finding a way to love that person despite all their faults or annoyances, and finding a way be happy with that person. Now if I had to write a book on love I'd probably title it "Idiots Galore: The Wrong way to love" I'd have five case studies for the subject matter with all of your pictures on the front cover.

Charlie: Damn Bud that's a harsh thing to say to us. How do you know we're really all that bad when it comes to finding love?

Bud: I listen to your stupid conversations every night, it's a judgment call. If you want to know a little truth about love, it's like a fish. It's boring and annoying trying to catch the fish. You have to put up one hell of fight that doesn't even seem worth it when trying to reel it in, and then it's just stinks, especially when you have to let it go, or it can just die on you. I guess in the end love is just like a fish, it just really stinks, but we wouldn't know what to do without it.

Bud walks off to help some customers at the other end of the bar. Susan, Liz, Chad, and Charlie all just look at each other with somewhat bewildered looks on their face after what Bud just said.

Rick: I don't know about any of you, but I feel better now after that little inspirational speech ***(Rick just shakes his head at what Bud said*****).**

Susan: He really doesn't know me at all.

Rick: Susan, you're never with someone long enough for them to get to know the real you.

Susan: What can I say, I like variety, and by the way the Malone's are here tonight and it's their anniversary.

Rick: Really, how long have they been married?

Susan: Fifty years today, and they requested their song from you tonight.

Susan walks back out from behind the bar to check on her customers.

Liz: Who are the Malone's, Rick?

Rick: They're this elderly couple who've lived in this neighborhood all their lives and have known everybody around her from the time they were born or since they were children. They have been coming to watch me since I first started playing in this joint.

Chad: Don't forget to tell her that Mrs. Malone is one crazy old broad.

Rick: You only think that because she doesn't like you and she hit you with a broom one time. Frankly, she had every right to; you stole her pie off the window sill as she was trying to cool it.

Chad: Hey, she left it there and you know the rule of "finder's keepers." I wasn't just going to leave a perfectly good pie sitting there.

Liz: Chad, you stole an old lady's pie? What kind of person does that?

Rick: I think stupid is a good description and I believe that Mrs. Malone has every right to keep hating you. After all, the pie was for Mr. Malone's birthday, and considering how hard he's worked all his life at a legitimate job, he really deserved to come home and enjoy the pie his wife made for him.

Chad: How was I supposed to know that it was for Mr. Malone's birthday? When I see pie I'm only thinking to myself how good it's going to taste, not if it's for somebody's birthday.

Liz: That's a sad thing when somebody has to steal a pie from an old lady in order to get something nice from someone or just to feel loved.

Chad: Have you ever had Mrs. Malone's pie? It's worth stealing!

Rick: Chad, everybody from the neighborhood at one time or another has had a piece of her pie, but the difference is they don't have to steal it and they still can get a second piece without getting hit by a broom.

Chad just shakes his head as his way of saying he doesn't care what anybody says he is going to do what he wants to do.

Liz: Well besides the subject of Chad being a "low-life" who likes to steal Mrs. Malone's pie, what's the special song they want to hear from you?

Rick: Oh, I can't tell you that. It will just have to be a surprise to you just like if will be for everybody else in here, but if you like classic big-band and Jazz then you will probably like this song.

Liz: You just have to be difficult don't you?

Rick: Yeah, I do because it's fun to be that way ***(he smiles sarcastically)***.

Some more musicians walk through the door and begin to set up around the stage. They are Gus Davis' jazz band from the neighborhood they've been playing together for over 40 years and the band that Rick learned how to play jazz and the blues with. There is a sax player, horn player, trumpet player, drummer and bass player. Rick joins them and begins his set. The Malone's are seated at a table near the stage area.

Rick: (looking at the Malone's and talking to the crowd) Tonight I am going to start with a special request by a couple in here who are celebrating their 50th wedding anniversary. They are a couple from this neighborhood that I am sure we all know, and this particular song is one of their favorites. It just happens to be the song that they "courted" each other with, and tonight I'm going play for them even though I may not do it justice as the original artist that wrote many years ago did. But I will do my best ***(Rick smiles at the Malone's)***

Rick begins to play *As Time Goes By* with the rest of the musicians. This is meant to be an emotional scene where Liz begins to see something that she has never seen in Rick before. She is inspired by his music and the way he inspires the audience with it, more so than she has been throughout the story so far. Liz has a look on her face that says many things such as inspiration, happiness, and being in love. The Malone's (they do not have a speaking role) have to convey the same things with the looks on their faces. The Actors in this particular scene have to convey all these emotions within the expressions on their faces so that the audience knows what's happening with them. This scene is supposed to be an emotional scene. The lights begin to fade when Rick is on the last part of the song, and completely go out when he is done to end the scene.

End of Act Three, Scene One

Scene Two

Rick and Liz walk into Rick's apartment and are in the middle of conversation while laughing. During the scene, Rick and Liz spend their time in the apartment talking to each other, but they move around the apartment as they finish their conversation. This is what's happening here, but the scene will start with them laughing in the apartment and Liz beginning to speak.

Liz: I don't think I've ever known so many people with such comical lives as your friends.

Rick: They do certainly keep everybody laughing. That's probably why I still hang out with them. It certainly isn't for stimulating conversation, although everybody there has their moments.

Liz: Yeah, I don't think I've ever heard love compared to a fish before, but I guess that only happens in a bar.

Rick: Hey, anything goes in a bar; especially if its conversation. And that usually means nothing's taboo.

Liz: Since anything goes when it comes to conversation in a bar, and that should mean honesty, there is something I've been meaning to ask you, and after watching you tonight I really have to know now. How do you do it? How do you inspire so many people through music and make them feel the happiest that they probably have ever been when they're listening to you play?

Rick: I wish I could take most of the credit, but it's usually the music speaking through me. You know, Gus told me something a long time ago about music and the inspiration it gives off. You see, music is something that has an emotional connection with us. It doesn't matter what kind of music it is as long as we like it, but it lives in us and lives through us and that's what inspires us. For a musician, that same inspiration that it gives them projects out to the audience they're playing for, and part of the musician's job is to make sure that happens. I do it because I want the audience to feel the same thing I'm feeling when I play, and when I can make that happen I absolutely love it. That's why I play piano for people in a club and don't want to do anything else. I guess it's the same thing for an artist.

Liz: You're right, and art does come in many forms. The thing is, I've never known anybody who does so much in inspiring other people and making them feel good. Perhaps that's why I'm falling in love with you.

Rick: That's what an art form is supposed to do, whatever form it comes in. It's supposed to inspire us and it's supposed to make us happy, and that's what we're alive for. It's also supposed to help us find what makes us truly happy, and for me it's the music of life. I also tend to think it's supposed to help us find someone to love. Maybe that's also why I want to be with you.

Liz: (smiling) You know, with talk like that you might just get lucky tonight.

Rick: Who would've thought that a little bit of truth could actually get you laid instead of some cheap lie? I guess you're just a sucker for the truth, uh?

Liz: Rick, shut-up and just kiss me.

They kiss and the lights quickly fade as they are kissing each other passionately. It's still the same scene in the apartment, but the next morning when the lights come back up. Their cloths are little wrinkled from last night. They are having breakfast and drinking coffee.

Liz: You don't have much here in the way of food do you?

Rick: I don't really keep that much food around here; you know I have to keep up with the whole single man's syndrome of only having beer and ketchup in the fridge. But I do have coffee, which is the most important thing in the food category next to beer.

Liz: Well, you have to maintain some aspects of a normal guy instead of having the complete "great guy package."

Rick: We all have to be something and maintain at least a little bit of what society says is normal.

Liz: Doesn't every great artist make themselves great by not fitting into what society says is normal?

Rick: Sure, but that's only what we choose to see in them and be inspired by, because we know that we can't do what they do. We're inspired by the strength to stand outside the lines, so we don't see the aspects of normal that they do have. Hell, even Louis Armstrong was a normal guy in that he was a skirt chaser and slept with any woman he could get his hands on.

Liz: Boys will be boys no matter how much of an artist they are.

Rick: Yeah, we're kind of built that way. You know, there is something I want to know about you. Are you going to live your dream and be a "true blue" artist?

Liz: You still have to make a living at it, and that term "Starving Artist" is very true. Unless you're famous it's kind of hard to make any money selling your work. I don't know if I could really do that. I would like to, though. I would love to go to Europe and be a painter or sculptor. Even doing restoration work I think would be fun. I really hope I could get a scholarship so I could go to Europe, but if I don't I guess I'll have to do something else.

Rick: You're going to let a little thing like money get in the way of doing what you truly love? You're going to let it ruin your chance of being happy? Why give up so easily, especially if it is your passion?

Liz: I won't give up, but without money I'll have to reevaluate what I should be doing to survive in this life and be happy.

Rick: You know, Hitler was a painter and because people said he wasn't very good and had no future at it he found something else to do, like trying to take over the world. The sad but funny irony of that is he probably had those people killed later when he was trying to take over the world. But don't you think that the world would've been better off if he hadn't given up so easily trying to be a painter? Perhaps he could have been the next Rembrandt instead of a mass murdering shithead.

Liz: So what are you saying? That if I give up on my dream I'll resort to mass genocide to get revenge for my failure?

Rick: It's a possibility.

Liz: Kind of an extreme possibility don't you think?

Rick: It is, but a possibility nonetheless.

Liz: Well I'd like to think that I'm much more of a sane person than that and not the kind of person that resorts to such things.

Rick: Hey, we're all capable of things that we think we can't be capable of. It's just a matter of the right thing pushing us to our breaking point.

Liz: If nobody likes my work and I'm a failure as an artist, then I'll try not to go and kill everybody. But if I do, you'll be the first because I had this stupid conversation with you.

Rick: Fair enough I guess, but just remember that a lot of bad things can happen when you do give up on your dreams, and regret is not something that we should live with. That's probably the main reason I do what I do.

Liz: I do happen to agree with you even though you like to throw out some extreme possibilities of what can happen if we don't live our dreams, but I wouldn't use this kind of argument with my dad.

Rick: Are you saying that your dad doesn't care about living a passion or fulfilling one's dream?

Liz: It's not that he doesn't believe in those things, he just doesn't see the profit in it. With most things in life there has to be a dollar figure attached to it for him to believe. I can't fault him completely for that kind of mentality, because it did help him to make lots of money and pay for my education.

Rick: Everybody has their own beliefs, and we don't have the right to judge just because they're not our own beliefs, but it's good that you see the bright side to the way your father thinks even though I can tell you don't agree.

Liz: I don't agree with his thinking, but I also want you to know how he thinks if you ever meet him, which by the way you are invited to dinner tomorrow night with my parents and I.

Rick: Why do I have the feeling that you've told them already that I'm coming to dinner tomorrow?

Liz: I told them that if you didn't have anything to do tomorrow you would probably stop by for dinner and you would like to meet them since we have been seeing each other for the past two months.

Rick: Well it's not a total lie, because it's probably time for me to meet them, especially after last night (***Liz starts smiling)***. And yes, I would like to meet them. Do you think they will like me?

Liz: My mother will, but it may take my dad a little bit of time to warm up to you. Your lifestyles and ways of thinking are very different, and there are certain philosophical conversations that you should avoid with him.

Rick: I'll try to behave myself with your dad, but just remember there are no guarantees in this life, except perhaps death. I don't really think we can escape that.

Liz: Just try and be good. I want them to like you and I want them to be able to see what I see in you.

Rick: Hey, your parents are only going to see what they want to see in me. All I can do is be who I am and hope they like me for that. You're the only one that has to be satisfied with me, but I'll try and be good so hopefully your parents will like me.

Liz: That's all I ask.

Rick: One thing's for sure, it's going to be interesting meeting your parents, which by the way I hope you at least told them a little bit about me so there won't be too many surprises with me.

Liz: I told them a little bit about you, and yes when you meet them it will be interesting to say the least.

Rick: At this point I guess that's all we can say and leave this to fate, or karma, or chance, I Ching, or whatever philosophy we choose to believe that makes us feel good.

Liz: Yeah, I guess that's all we can say on that.

Rick and Liz both just nod at each other and smile while the lights fade ending the scene.

End of Act Three, Scene Two

Scene Three

We're back at the bar where Rick is at the piano writing a song and Bud is cutting fruit behind the bar. Chad and Charlie are playing dominos with the judge. Rick is humming the song he is writing and is smiling, showing off his joyful state. The song he is writing is called *There's Somebody like You* which will be played at the end of the play.

Chad: So Rick, everything going good in your life these days? You seem awfully happy, even more than usual.

Rick: Yeah, everything is going great just like it has been for the last few years, but thanks for asking.

Charlie: What my brother in trying to be sly or cool about and is failing to do is ask you if you got some recently because you don't usually hum or whistle unless you're really happy. For you it's usually when you've had sex.

Rick: No, I think you're confusing me with you and Chad. I do whistle when I'm happy about other things.

Charlie: You're right, we like to hum and whistle a little bit when we've actually had sex with a real girl, but so do you, and after knowing you for about twenty years we know the signs to look for when you've gotten laid. Also it's been awhile for you, and you seem a little more happy than usual, so that means it must have been extra special.

Rick: Is sex all you think about?

Chad and Charlie: Well, yeah. We're guys and that's what we do.

Rick: Then why is my sex life so interesting to you?

Charlie: Because it's more exciting than our own and it's much better living vicariously through you. You're the piano player, which means you're the sexy one.

Rick: I know that's true, and I'm glad to know that you can admit it, but you really don't have to keep up with my sex life.

Chad: So are you going to answer the question?

Rick: And what question is that?

Chad: You know. Did you get some recently?

Rick: I'm not going tell you, because unlike you, my personal life is not going to be broadcasted in this club. Besides, I'm a gentleman, and we don't tell about what happens in the bedroom.

Charlie: Oh, he must be in love with her because that's never stopped him before.

Rick: Shut up guys. Just because I don't want to talk about it doesn't mean that I'm in love with her.

The Judge: Okay, despite what these two morons ***(pointing at Chad and Charlie)*** are telling you or asking you, how do you really feel about this girl? Is it love?

Rick: I don't know if its love, but I do know she's great. She makes me feel good; she makes me laugh, and having her in my life just fits.

The Judge: Well, I don't know if you know this, but that's called love Rick. For those of us that have known you all these years, you have only talked about one other person that way before.

Rick: I know, and to be honest that's what scares me. I do know that with her it doesn't feel wrong.

The Judge: Well, love is a strange thing and sometimes the only way you know it is if it doesn't feel wrong. Rick, I think you might actually care for this young woman more than you want to admit to. But I don't blame you for not wanting everybody to know your business, especially in this club. Fiction is always the main theme in any kind of bar garnished with a little exaggeration, and that's not at all unusual in this place, Chad and Charlie.

Charlie: What can we say? We like stories, and this is a good place for them.

Bud: What's your favorite kind of story, Charlie? Fiction?

Charlie: It's whatever the hour calls for. Speaking of stories, what's the story behind this song you're playing Rick? I've never heard it before.

Everybody looks at Rick waiting for an answer.

Rick: If everybody must know, it's a new one that I've been writing. And before any poor assumptions are made, yes I've been inspired by Liz, so that's the story behind this song.

Bud: We all know who your inspiration is these days, and it's a good thing that you actually have some because the last thing we need around here is an unhappy piano player depressing the crowd.

Rick: Don't worry about me, Bud. I think you have the market cornered on misery and depression around here. Because of that, anything I do will always seem joyful.

Bud: It's a dirty job, but somebody has to do it.

Everybody in the bar at the same time starts saying things like "that's true" or "you know he's right".

The Judge: If you want some advice, don't let your pride get the best of you. Tell her what she means to you.

Old Man Henderson: What you should do is "mount" her then marry her. Things should always be done in the proper order.

Chad: Hey that's good advice; things should be done in a proper order.

Rick: And Chad, that's why you don't have a girlfriend. Now Judge, that's good advice, but I'm not going to take advice from the rest of you in this club. I'm not going to take advice from the desperate and lonely that come in here day after day to drown their sorrows about long lost love.

Chad: How do you know it's not the woman's fault and we just get screwed over because they can't understand how it should be?

Rick: This from the man who thought that four women walking in together were lesbians. ***(Everybody starts laughing).*** This is the reason I don't take advice about love from you.

The Judge: Now that's really good advice, Rick.

Chad: I don't know why you guys are so mean.

The Judge: Because it's more fun that way, and I deserve a chance to be mean to you for all the times you've been in my court and I've let you slide.

Rick: Chad, you really are a good guy, but we have to have someone to pick on around here and it just happens to be you.

Charlie: Don't worry little brother. I'll buy you a beer and you can feel better about yourself while drinking away you're sorrows. Many great people in this world like supermodels and rock stars do it every night. Just look at Hugh Hefner. He drinks like fish and is still surrounded by beautiful women.

Rick: Well, although this conversation has been enlightening, I have to go. Tonight I'm finally meeting Liz's parents. We're having dinner at their house.

The Judge: That's a big step in your relationship when you have dinner with the parents. That usually means the woman is thinking about the rest of her life with you.

Rick: Let's not get ahead ourselves here and start adding to the rumors that are floating around. Besides, I still like the single life and I'm not interested in being tied down. Remember, the "mojo" that influences the great philosophy of the piano player is powered by being single. I'd like to still maintain that.

The Judge: Someday Rick we all fall hard. Remember that's not a bad thing.

Rick: Alright, I'll at least consider that point of view, but if you'll excuse me, I'm off to see if this piano player can be liked in every circle.

Bud: I don't care what anybody says, you're a hell of a guy, Rick.

Rick: Thanks Bud, at least I'll always be liked by someone.

The lights fade to end the scene.

End of Act Three, Scene Three

Scene Four

Rick and Liz are walking up to her parent's house (this can be from stage left or stage right, but for this scene I have chosen Stage Right).They are carrying on in conversation before entering the house. The lights are dimmed a little bit so as to represent the street being lit up by street lights.

Liz: Now remember, there aren't too many things you and my father can talk about without ending up in an argument. Religion and politics are definitely out. If he seems to be antagonistic, just let it go. It's just his way and he's just trying to get you mad.

Rick: You know, your father doesn't sound like a very fun guy. Is there anything we are going to be able to talk about tonight?

Liz: Probably not, so maybe you shouldn't say too much tonight.

Rick: (laughing) Liz, I'm sure it's going to be fine. They'll like me, and you don't have anything to worry about. Look at me. What's not to like?

Liz: My dad will find something. Then he'll just harp on it until you get mad so then he can really not like you. That's why I'm telling you it's just best to ignore him and beat him at his own game.

Rick: Well here we are. I guess it's game time. No turning back now.

Liz: If you did at this point I'd have to hurt you.

Rick and Liz enter into the house where Liz's mother, Mary, greets them.

Mary: Elizabeth, you did make it and I see you brought your friend. Well, are you going to introduce me to your handsome gentlemen?

Liz: Yes, I'll introduce you, but try not be too embarrassing.

Mary: Honey, I'm not here to embarrass you. I just want to meet this young man that you've been talking about lately. I'm you mother so that's makes me entitled to meet your friends and embarrass you a little bit if I want.

Liz: Alright mother, this is Rick. He's the one I've been seeing for the last couple of months.

Mary: It's very nice to finally meet you. I think you're even more handsome than Elizabeth described.

Rick: Well thank you, it's very nice to meet you Mrs.**...*(Mary cuts him off before he can finish his sentence)***

Mary: Oh, please call me Mary. From the way Elizabeth has talked about you, I feel like we already know you in this house.

Rick: Okay then, Mary it is.

Mary: Come on in to the living room. Elizabeth's father will be down in a minute. So we've been told that you're a piano player.

Rick: Yes, I play piano at the *The Blue's Note.* I've been playing there since I was a teenager.

Rick and Liz sit down on the couch in the living room. The room is filled with artistic pieces and Antiques. Mary takes a seat in one of the chairs.

Mary: What kind of music do you play?

Rick: Mainly jazz and blues with a little bit of classic rock mixed in. I guess I really just play the classics; anything from the 1920's to now that can be played on the piano.

Mary: That's great, I always wanted to learn the piano, but never did. I was a flute player in college and in the college orchestra.

Rick: Really, it sounds like that was a fun experience.

Mary: Not really, the flute is not a fun instrument. The cool instruments to play on in an orchestra are always the saxophone, and maybe the violin.

Liz: What my mother is not bragging about and has every right to is that she did get to play in the Chicago Symphony for a little while as a replacement. My mother is the only one in this family that has any musical talent, but she has a lot of it to make up for everyone else.

Mary: I don't think it's worth bragging about, but I guess I was at least good enough to play once or twice for the Chicago Symphony. I will say this: I've always had a reel passion for music even though playing the flute was my mother's idea, but no matter what, it was still a great experience and a lot of fun.

Rick: I think that's the main thing with playing music; really having fun doing it and making sure it's a great experience. That's why I still play and I don't see myself ever giving it up.

Edward, Liz's father, comes walking into the room as Rick is finishing his sentence.

Edward: (jokingly or sarcastically) So what's all this talk I hear about music and the Chicago Symphony? Is someone getting me some free tickets or is that just wishful thinking? I mean, my only daughter could actually get me a present.

Liz: Oh dad, you know I'd get those tickets, but you already have season tickets so it wouldn't do me any good. You'll just have to get something else from me, but only if you're good.

Edward: I'm always good and I really deserve a present.

Liz: I don't know about always being good, but you might actually deserve a present. Although the jury is still out on that decision.

Edward: I've never had a child that gave me so much grief, but I guess that's why I love her so much anyway. ***(looking at Rick)*** Children are supposed to keep you on your toes. and my daughter certainly does. By the way, I'm Edward, Elizabeth's father.

Rick: I'm Rick. It's very nice to meet you.

Edward: Well, it's very nice to finally meet you. So you're the piano player slash bartender I've been hearing about? So what's life like as a piano player?

Rick: It's great. You get to play music every night, and you get to make people feel good and forget about their problems for at least a little while. There's a lot to be said for that, especially if it makes you happy doing it.

Mary: Elizabeth, will you help me in the kitchen? I think we should let the men talk before dinner.

Liz: Okay. Besides, I haven't caught up with you lately and would like to do that.

The two women leave the room (exit off stage). Rick and Edward watch as they leave before the conversation continues.

Edward: There can't be a lot of money in playing piano in a bar, or is my assumption wrong on that?

Rick: No, there's not a whole lot of money in this business, at least compared to the owner of a fortune 500 company, but there's enough if you don't need a lot of money to live on.

Edward: Hey, I guess the real question is "what's enough money" or "can there ever be too much of it."

Rick: (laughing) You've got a good point, sir. It's a question that we all have to ask ourselves at some point in life.

Edward: Rick, would you like a glass of Bourbon before dinner?

Rick: Sure, a little bourbon is always good.

Edward gets up and pours bourbon into two glasses from the mini bar in the living room. He walks over and hands a glass to Rick who is still seated.

Edward: Elizabeth has told me you're that really good point guard that De Paul had years ago, the one that almost got De Paul into the final round of the tournament two years in row.

Rick: I don't know if I was the one that really got the team in the tournament during those seasons. I mean, there were a lot of good players on those teams. However, I did play basketball at De Paul in the early nineties, and I guess I was a pretty good.

Edward: Well, I remember when you made that game winning shot to advance to the final four in '92. My daughter and I were there; it's probably one of the greatest sports moments I've ever had the pleasure of seeing. Why didn't you ever go pro?

Rick: A serious knee injury the following year in the opening round of the tournament ruined my chances. After two years of reconstructive surgery I decided not to play the game anymore. Also, basketball wasn't something I was interested in anymore.

Edward: That's right. I remember you getting injured and then nothing was ever heard about you again. You were supposed to be one of the top picks in the NBA draft and then you dropped off the face of the earth. What happened to you?

Rick: I spent the next two years rehabbing my knee and trying to walk again. Mainly I just disappeared from all that I had ever known before, except playing the piano.

Edward: You must have been doing something all this time, like a career or traveling the world, something adventurous or glamorous?

Rick: I wish I could tell you yes, but the only thing I did was become a piano player and lose myself in music.

Edward: Did you ever get your degree from De Paul?

Rick: No, I never did. I left school before my research was complete for my thesis in Psychology.

Edward: So you never graduated or got a degree.

Rick: No I didn't; I left and I never looked back.

Edward: So you quit just like that and never got an education?

Rick: I did quit college, but I still got an education even though I never received a diploma.

Edward: You still need that diploma for your education because without it you're just a dropout. Without it you'll just be a quitter.

Rick: What does a college degree really say about you? Can it show how intelligent you are or if you were actually educated? Maybe all it says is that you completed the requirements to have degree, but that piece of paper doesn't determine who you are or how intelligent you might be.

Edward: That piece of paper is a requirement for getting a college education; without it you don't have a college education.

Rick: Bill Gates never got a college degree, but he still invented the Windows software and people consider him a pretty smart guy. In fact, he's considered one of the smartest guys in the world.

Edward: Are you trying to convince me that you're intelligent even though you didn't get a college degree? I don't see any major successes to prove that like inventing revolutionary computer software.

Rick: No, I'm not trying to convince you of anything. You can come to your own conclusion or opinion about me after tonight. It doesn't matter what I tell you, you'll believe what you want to believe. All I'm saying is that a college degree doesn't mean anything important, or what I personally believe is important in life.

Edward: I guess you can choose any point of view you like, but there is still just one point of view that's the truth.

Rick: Wasn't it John Keats who said "truth is beauty and beauty is truth"? Although my point of view may not be one you're comfortable with, it's still mine and no matter what I'm going to still just be me.

Edward: I guess you're one of those who just likes to disagree with everyone. Or perhaps you're one of those intellectuals that just has to show everybody that you're smarter than they are and that you know best.

Rick: I'm not trying to prove that I'm the one person on this earth who knows best for how humanity should think, nor am I trying to be argumentative with you, but I think I'm right in my own personal philosophy and I'm going to stand up for my own beliefs, especially when someone is trying to condemn them.

Edward: I'm not trying to condemn your beliefs or your point of view, but I think you're a little mixed up and could stand to be more objective.

Rick: I didn't realize that I had a problem with being objective, but when it comes to being more objective the same could be said for you.

Edward just sits back and laughs to himself after Rick's last remark as to say well done for Rick's good points in the argument.

Rick: So what exactly does your company do?

Edward: We dabble in a lot of things, but mainly we're a technology company. We try to keep up with the latest innovations in technology and capitalize on it.

Rick: Do you like what you do?

Edward: Do you mean is it fun running my own fortune 500 company? In answer to your question, yes I love it and I couldn't see myself doing anything else. I love big business and being able to find a product that's good for society and capitalize on its use for the world.

Rick: I think it's good for people to find a profession that makes them happy and also makes them want to go to work every day.

Edward: True, but you still have to be practical about a profession. You have to make enough money to live on. I think the goal for everyone should be to make as much money as possible.

Rick: So you think having money is going to make someone totally happy? There's more in this life than just money. Why should people be in a job that makes them miserable every day when they come home even if makes them lots of money?

Edward: Rick, you're going to realize that having money can do a lot more for you than not having it. It will provide more opportunities for you and will give you a greater chance to be happy. Do you honestly think that a street musician is completely happy being poor and barely scraping by?

Rick: I'm not saying that every musician doesn't dream of becoming famous and making millions of dollars so they might not have to worry about anything in life anymore. However, one can still not have worries in life even on limited means. How do you know that every street musician is completely unhappy? There are some out there that are just as content and happy playing on a street corner hardly making any money than in a big concert hall because they do it for the satisfaction of their art.

Edward: Do you actually know any of these people that are supposedly happy and poor, playing music on the street?

Rick: Yes I do. I've known a lot of musicians over the years that fit that description. Most of them are still alive and have been totally happy without making very much money. A lot of them still have other part time gigs besides music, but they're doing what they have a passion for and for over forty years. The reason I know this is because I grew up with these musicians and it's where I truly learned how to play. You see, they're the true musical muses because the passion and inspiration for the music pours out of them onto the audience that listens. When it comes to something like that, money has nothing to do with it.

Edward: Well, inspiration is not going to pay the bills and it certainly doesn't better your situation in life. There are a lot of worries in life that can be taken away with a little bit of money.

Rick: On the last part you're right, if you're talking about your bookie and he's going to break your legs if you don't pay him. Although I tend to think that there are a lot of worries that people have in life that really aren't that big of a deal compared to finding a way to be happy and perhaps keeping our sanity, again money isn't always going to solve those kinds of problems. I know that what I'm talking about is more or less a utopia of sorts, but I think people get confused on what's really important in life, and that creates a lot of the problems that people have.

Edward: You know, we all have our delusions of grandeur, but as an intelligent human being we still have to be practical about things. This is one of the things that I have tried to teach my daughter. Its fine to pursue artistic endeavors, but the practical thing is to do a job that will make you enough money to live on in this life.

Rick: So you think there's nothing practical in trying to be the happiest person you can in life?

Edward is getting angry now in his tone as he is arguing with Rick.

Edward: Not at the expense of providing for your family or taking care of loved ones. Your own selfish pursuits cannot outweigh the needs of your family. Sometimes we have to sacrifice the things that might make us happy to ensure something better for loved ones. Making enough money to live on or a lot of money for that fact is just one of those things one does to ensure less worries.

Rick: Well, I think if we keep doing the things that other people need us do at the expense of our own happiness then we drive ourselves to some of the worst things in life like our own emotional destruction or insanity. I'm not saying that we don't sacrifice for other people while sometimes giving up what makes us happy, but we have to be true to ourselves. We have to do what's right for us, and that doesn't make us selfish. All those material things like money or fame or titles aren't things we can take with us. The only thing we have in the end that's worth something is memories with no regret and pride in the life we led.

Edward: It's a nice thought, but most of the time it's just a delusion made up by those who never had money. That's why artists, writers, and musicians tend to believe in notions like that. When you're starving and out of work those same people use ideas like that as an excuse to keep being lazy and not have to actually work in a practical profession. When you do something like that, all you're doing is taking away from society.

Rick: You don't think that any kind of an artist can actually give something good to society?

Edward: Not as much as somebody in commerce, especially when it is the commerce of essential items such as food.

Rick is starting to get a little defensive now.

Rick: If it comes down to the choice of living in a world of deluded ideas and notions or selling my soul to the devil spawn of capitalism where I would live each day as a bitter, angry sellout then I'll take the delusion.

Edward: I don't think I like your tone and I would appreciate it if you refrain from calling those who work in capitalistic society as sellouts. We are still exercising our most basic principles of freedom and democracy when it comes to business. If you work hard enough and earn it, then what you earn is yours and doesn't have to be split with anybody else in this country. Don't try and influence me with your Socialist bullshit.

Rick: I wasn't arguing for Socialism, I was merely pointing out that there are better things in life than the endeavors of capitalism. And you're right, the principles of capitalism are just as vital as artistic endeavors under the flag of democracy. All through this conversation you have been antagonizing me to get me to lash out or lose my temper with you. Why?

Edward: I 'm not going to lie, I am testing you a little bit because I want to see what kind of person you are, and so far I'm not impressed.

Rick: Why? Is it because I don't have the same beliefs as you and because I'm a lot different than you are?

Edward: No, it's because you have no logical sense of what man should do in life. Those little fantasies you have about just doing something that makes you happy at the expense of taking care of the ones you love doesn't have any real logic to it. Those fantasies are just foolish pursuits.

Rick: Who are you to decide what is logical? Just because I believe a little differently than you doesn't mean my thinking is illogical. Besides, the only person I have to take care of in this life is me. I don't have a family and I'm not arguing that when it comes to taking care of your family sometimes we have to sacrifice a little bit of our own happiness. Wait a minute. This isn't about me, is it?

Edward: What are you talking about?

Rick: All your ideologies and preaching about what we have to do in life is not really directed towards me is it? This is about what your daughter wants to do with her life and you think I'm some bad influence because I live my life different from how you think a good and wise person should live.

They both get up from their seats and are standing now facing each other as they argue.

Edward: I want my daughter to be realistic about what she needs to do for a career so she can take care of herself.

Rick: So this is about her isn't it?

Edward: No, it's about the both of you, and if you want to live your life in some "being happy all the time fantasy world" without making any money then do so, but I'm not going to have some saloon keeper filling my daughter's head with ideas that's it's okay to pursue entertainment as a way of life and that it's okay to be poor. If I hadn't given up foolish pursuits when I was young and worked hard to build my company, then my family wouldn't have the things that they do and I wouldn't be able to do things that I can.

Rick: What part of your soul did you have to sell to get there? Better yet, how much time did you miss spending with your daughter while she was growing up so you could have all this? Sometimes it's not worth it. Sometimes we give up the things that are more important for the things that we foolishly thought were the important things.

Edward: You have no idea how much I was here for my family all through the years, nor do you have a goddamn clue what I did to get here, so don't throw your judgment at me.

Rick: And you don't have a fucking clue what I've done with my life, so what right do you have to judge me?

Edward: I have the right when it concerns my daughter's happiness. I still have to protect her from those that might take advantage of her or be a bad influence on her. I still have to show her the right choice when it comes to a horrible man that can ruin her life, and so far, you fit the bill.

Rick: You can think whatever you want of me, but when it concerns Liz and me, the choice is hers and hers alone. She's an adult, and therefore you don't get to make those decisions anymore for her.

Edward: How dare you, you son of a bitch. How dare you try to tell me what right I have with my own daughter! If you called yourself a man then you would show me a little bit more respect when it concerns my own daughter. I don't want you to see my daughter anymore, do you understand me?

Rick: No, I'm not going to let you dictate that part of my life. The thing is, I'm not trying to disrespect you, but I think you seriously misunderstand what your role is as Liz's father at this point in her life.

Mary and Liz walk into the room to see what all the shouting is about. Both men are still standing and yelling now, but not too loud.

Mary: What is all the shouting in here about? Edward, did you start an argument with this young man?

Liz: Rick, what are doing arguing with my dad?

Rick: Edward and I were not arguing, but we were having a little disagreement.

Edward: A disagreement. You're practically telling me that I have no place in my daughter's life and I don't love her. I have never had anybody she's dated show me so much disrespect. I want you out of my house right now.

Liz: Dad, what are you doing? Just because he disagrees with you doesn't mean you have to throw him out of the house.

Mary: Edward, she's right. This is uncalled for.

Edward: Shut up Mary. This doesn't concern you. And as for you, daughter of mine, you are forbidden to see this guy anymore. Now get out of my house, Rick.

Mary shuts up quickly and looks surprised at Edward's remark.

Liz: Dad, you can't forbid me to stop seeing him just because you may not like him.

Edward: I can when I pay for your tuition and rent. I'm not going to have a goddamn bastard like this come into my house and tell me what I need to do with my own daughter and then proceed to insult my way of life.

Liz just stares in disbelief at her father's remark while Rick starts to put on his coat. He is shaking his head in disbelief at what has happened.

Rick: I'm just going to say one more thing before I go. That is not what I've been telling you all night and you know it. I'm not trying to disrespect you. All I have been pointing out is that there are different points of view and yours and mine are very different. When it comes to your daughter and I, you don't have any right to tell us how this relationship is going to be or forbid her from seeing me. For God's sake, she's a grown woman. I wanted tonight to go well because I'm falling in love with Liz, but the sad thing is, sir, I think you are bound and determined to hate anybody that might show her a different life than the one you want for her. If you're going to prevent something like that then you don't love her enough.

Edward: Get out of my house right now you son of bitch!

Rick: Ma'am, ***(looking at Mary)*** thank you for inviting me to dinner.

Rick looks and smiles at Liz as he walks out the door.

Edward: Liz I don't want to hear about him ever again if you still want me to pay for school and your apartment.

Liz: Shut up, Dad. This isn't your decision and you don't get to forbid me from seeing whom I want to see ***(Edward begins to say something and Liz points her finger at him)***. Don't even think about it Dad. I don't care what you threaten me with at this point. You have no right to interfere with this. I'll walk out right now and you'll never ever see me again. Then I'll tell your partners what you really have planned for the company. You remember, don't you? It's that little tidbit of information that they don't have a clue about.

She walks out the door to go after Rick. Edward has a surprised and angry look on his face. At the other end of the stage we see Rick and Liz on the sidewalk in front of the house. The other side where the house is, is darkened while the stage lights are only on Rick and Liz right now.

Liz: Rick, where are you going?

Rick: I'm leaving, because at this point dinner would be a little awkward if I stayed.

Liz: If you were going to leave without me, were you at least going say goodbye to me?

Rick: No, not really. I figured I'd call you tomorrow after everyone had a chance to cool down.

Liz: Look, I'm sorry about my dad, but I told you not to argue with him because that's what he likes to do with people.

Rick: Arguing? Liz, what happened in there was fighting, and the only reason it hadn't come to a fist fight yet was because you and your mother walked in. I'm pretty certain if you hadn't, your father in all of his anger would have tried to hit me because he hated me that much. I think he was determined to hate me before he ever got know me because I don't believe in the same ideals he does.

Liz: Now that's unfair. My dad just doesn't start out hating somebody before he has had a chance to talk with them.

Rick: No, the truth is never unfair, it just stings a bit when we're finally hit with it after spending so much time trying to ignore it. I've been in arguments before. They're just debates over facts and opinions, but your father was literally fighting with me over what I believed. How much did you tell him about me before tonight?

Liz: I just told him that you were a piano player and a bartender that loved what he did and wasn't trying to make millions of dollars doing it or trying to be famous.

Rick: You see, from just telling him that your father already had a preconceived idea of what kind of person I was because what I am is nothing like him. There is no understanding or objectivity with him.

Liz: It doesn't matter what I told him, and part of what you're saying is true, but you stood toe to toe with him and fought, which is exactly what he wanted you to do. I told you just to let him be that way and ignore it because tonight I wanted them to accept you.

Rick: It doesn't matter if they accept me or not, because your happiness with me is based on you liking "me" and you accepting "me." I did screw up with one thing. I fought with your father when I should have just swallowed my pride and walked away, but I had to prove that my ideals are just as right despite what people like him may think.

Liz: Is that what this is all about, you being right and your own philosophy of life being the right one? If that's it, then you're just as bad as my dad, and I don't want to be with another person like him. I thought you were different. That's why I have been with you all this time.

Rick: I don't have this lifelong mission to make people like your father see that I'm right about how life should be lived. And before you conjure up any notion that I'm like your father then you better stop right there, because I am nothing like him. I'm not saying I'm perfect, and sometimes I get into a pissing contest just for the sake of doing it, even though there's no victory in it.

Liz: I guess with men nothing ever changes. You'll always be those rams that have to butt heads just to prove who is king. But damn it, Rick, it's not your job to liberate my dad and his screwed up thinking. With somebody like him it's just better to walk away and let him be.

Rick: Or better yet, maybe somebody close to him should stand up and tell him that his attitudes about life and people are wrong. Maybe it's time for you to stand up to him and be who you truly are, despite what he wants you to be. Godammit, make him see you for who you truly are.

Liz: Look, I can't just can't get into his face like you and make him see who I am and what I want to be in this life. I have to be more subtle about it because I can't change a blinded man.

Rick: You mean you can't give up his taking care of you or maybe you can't live without someone taking care of you. When we want to be happy... truly happy... then we have to decide what we're willing to sacrifice to truly be happy. We have to decide what's worth more.

Liz: Screw you, you still don't get it.

Rick: Believe me, I do, and I do know people like your dad because I see them all the time in the club, and the irony is that they're always looking for some kind escape. It's usually found arguing with other patrons over trivial things. You know, your father is right about me in one way. I do live in some sort of fantasy world where having money isn't important and just being the happiest person you can be in every aspect of your life is what's important. Maybe one day you'll get that and do what it takes for you to achieve that.

Rick turns around and walks away towards the exit off stage.

Liz: That's it? You're just going to leave now?

Rick: Yeah, I am because I don't think we need to see each other until things get straight and until I don't feel like hurting you or your father.

Rick begins to say something else, but shakes his head and walks away off stage while the lights go down to end the scene.

End of Act Three, Scene Four

Act 4

Scene One

It's been over a week since Rick and Liz have spoken to each other or seen each other since having dinner with her parents. The scene is at the club with Rick cleaning up around the bar at the end of the night. Chad and Charlie are both there sitting in their usual places having a conversation with Old Man Henderson. Bud is at the other end of the bar stocking beer. Susan is cleaning tables in the club. There is not much talking going on except for Chad, Charlie, and Old Man Henderson so as to reflect the solemn tone of the scene.

Chad: So Rick, we haven't seen Liz around here lately and you haven't said anything about her since you had dinner with her parents. What's going on with you two? Did you screw up with her and get dumped?

Rick: Why do you automatically assume that I did something wrong and she broke up with me? Maybe she did something and I dumped her, or perhaps I just got tired of her so I broke up with her.

Chad: Because you're a guy, and we're always to blame for whatever problems happen in the relationship. Whether we did anything at all, we're at fault somehow, even if it's just for being a man. So what is it that caused this problem with her?

Rick: You have a good point, but I really didn't do anything except get into a fight with her father. Now I know this is going to cause some problems, but I don't think I'm totally to blame for anything. She didn't exactly stand up for me even though she knew I had every right to defend myself against her father.

Charlie: You don't think she might still be mad at you for fighting with her dad to begin with?

Rick: I'm sure she's mad, but I'm not going to try and find her just to apologize for something I didn't do wrong. Eventually she'll quit being mad, or she'll just stop seeing me. I can only do so much when it comes to mending whatever bridge is between us, and I'm only going to call her once. If she isn't there or won't return my phone call, then so be it. We just won't be together.

Charlie: Yeah that makes sense. Keep being stubborn and wait for the women to come around because you were the one who was right and she was wrong.

Rick: You don't think I'm doing the right thing?

Charlie: Look, I'm not saying that you didn't have any right to fight with her dad, but if you would have been the bigger person and walked away without escalating the argument, it might not have been so bad and she might not have been so mad at you. Your stubbornness tends to get in the way of you being happy, and be honest, is it really going to fix the problem?

Rick: I'll admit my being stubborn sometimes gets in the way of my happiness, and perhaps I should just swallow my pride sometimes. However, I can't just forget what happened. I feel like her father ambushed me, and I did what anybody would do in my place. I defended myself the best way I could. What makes me really mad is the fact that Liz won't stand up to her own father, knowing that he's wrong about her.

Charlie: Maybe she isn't ready to do it yet and you can't do it for her no matter how much you want her to break free. Look, you're the one that everybody looks to when they need help because we all know that you can take care of everybody, but we rely on you because we want your help. Liz may not want that from you yet.

Rick: How come you're the one that has all the answers tonight? I don't think I've ever heard you be this profound before. Usually it's me that has all the answers.

Charlie: Even piano players get lost from time to time, and I do have my moments. I'll tell you something else, too. Remember that girl I was seeing a few years ago?

Rick: (sarcastically) Out of the massive number of women you date, no I don't remember her. Actually I don't recall you ever dating anybody in the last few years.

Charlie: Yeah, you're funny, but regardless of what you might think in that I'm making her up or she dumped me, it didn't happen that way. I got mad at her for something that at the time seemed like a big deal, but really wasn't and I walked away from her for good. I never tried to call her or go see her hoping that she would come around and see that I was right, but she didn't. For once Chad is actually right about something when it comes to women. They don't just come crawling back. I think they don't do that just to spite men. My pride is what ended her and me, and I wish that I could change that. Buddy I just don't want that to happen to you and see you go through what you did last time when the love of your life walked out.

Rick: You're right, and I don't want that to happen again either, but I can't stop telling the truth and be somebody else just to please her father and her, too. All the philosophy I know is what I know to be true in life. Part of being me and being true to myself is that I have to be honest with everybody else. If I don't do that then I'm just a hypocrite.

Bud walks over after hearing where the conversation is going.

Bud: Nobody is telling you that you have to be untruthful, but there is a right way and a wrong way to be honest with somebody. I've never known getting into a fight to be the right way, have you?

Rick: Its true fighting never really solves anything, but sometimes the right thing to do is not to back down. We should always fight for the truth.

Bud: And did not backing down really solve anything with her dad? As Charlie pointed out, maybe the outcome would have been a lot better if you would've just walked away from her dad's argument. Rick, you may be a pretty smart guy who knows a lot about life, but you still don't know how to walk away from a fight even when you know you should. Your stubbornness does cause problems for you, and there are a lot of happy times you've given away because you didn't want to swallow that pride.

Chad: You know he's right, so what are you going to do about Liz?

Rick: What is this, group therapy? Everybody gets to gang up on Rick and solve his problems?

Charlie: I guess you can call it that. But hey, we're your friends and that's what we are supposed to do.

Chad: We're only doing what you do for us all the time and that's be our friend, which means you help us solve any problem we might have. It also means that you rely on us just as much as we rely on you. That, my friend, is a two-way street. So are you going to answer my question?

Liz walks into the door and is greeted by Susan. While Rick is thinking about how to respond to Chad's question Liz and Susan speak to each other. Rick has his back to the door so he does not see Liz walk in. Rick does not answer till Susan and Liz are done talking so the scene is not over-lapped with conversation. The lights fade on Rick while Susan and Liz are talking, but the lights are on the two women as they talk. When they are done and Liz walks over to the bar the lights will shine on the whole stage.

Susan: Hey, we haven't seen you in a while. Is everything okay with you?

Liz: Yeah I'm doing fine. So I guess everybody around here has all already heard about what happened.

Susan: Honey, everybody's personal life around here is an open book. This is a bar, there's no such thing as privacy.

Liz: Is it okay for me to be here after hours?

Susan: Sure it is, go on over. I think he'll need to see you.

Rick: I don't know Chad. I don't know if we can see each other anymore. I hope that's not the case though, because I love being around her and I haven't felt that way about anybody in a long time. I probably shouldn't have done what I did and I am sorry for it even though I still don't think I was totally in the wrong. I don't have the answer to me and her and maybe there aren't any answers.

Liz: (standing at the edge behind Rick) I don't know about you, but I would like to try and provide an answer to you and me.

Rick (turning around in surprise): So would I. What are you doing here?

Liz: I wanted to talk you and I also had good news that I wanted you to be the first to hear.

Everybody in the bar is staring at Liz waiting for the news.

Susan: Alright, everybody out of here. Leave these two alone. They have a lot to talk about.

Rick: Bud, I'll lock up. Thanks, Susan.

Chad: Why do we have to go, we're just going to hear about it later anyway.

Susan: Chad shut up and get you're but out of here.

Old Man Henderson: That's okay. Gossip when you're drunk is more entertaining, so I don't need to hear anything right now. Besides, somebody still has a happy hour somewhere.

Susan: That's good, because you weren't going to get to hear anything anyway, and that includes any gossip later.

Charlie: Rick, just be honest with her and yourself. Don't let that stubbornness get in the way.

Everybody is walking out the door (stage right) except Rick and Liz. Chad and Charlie are still talking and annoying Bud as they walk out.

Chad: I feel like pancakes. We should go get some breakfast before the "drunk crowd" shows up at the diner.

Charlie: Is eating all you think about besides getting laid?

Chad: What other fun things are there? There are only so many fun things to do in life and food and sex are probably at the top of the list.

Charlie: How is it that I'm related to you? I always wonder why God cursed me with being related to you.

Chad: Just for that you can buy everybody breakfast tonight.

Susan: In that case I'm definitely joining you for breakfast.

Bud: I think breakfast on you is a good reward for having to listen to your stupid conversations every night. I guess I'll be joining you guys.

Old Man Henderson: Hey, if you guys are buying breakfast then happy hour can wait, but can we stop buy the liquor store first? I need a little Irish coffee with my eggs.

Charlie: Hey, I'm not buying breakfast for everybody. Since when we do actually listen to my little brother?

Chad: Come on Charlie. You have the money because you sold all your Phantom of the Opera tickets tonight and we're going to the diner where Dallas that cute waitress you like to flirt with works.

Charlie: You're such an idiot. I don't know why Mom didn't leave you at the zoo that time. You would have fit right in with the monkeys.

The group is finally completely off stage and we don't hear any more of their conversation. Liz and Rick are left alone.

Rick: I don't know why I still hang around these people anymore. Sometimes I feel like just taking off and never returning, but then I might miss them.

Liz: You would miss them because they're family and believe or not they do take care of you. From what I heard, they know exactly what to say to you when you need to hear it. When it comes to people you love that's what they're supposed to do for you.

Rick: I guess you're right. So what brings you into my door this time?

Liz: I wanted to see you and tell you what I think is some good news. I also thought we both have had enough time to cool off. By the way, I did get your message.

Rick: We probably both have a few things to say to each to other. Before we go on, I should apologize for my behavior with your father. I still don't necessarily think I was wrong in what I said, but the way I handled everything was wrong and I think you should know that.

Liz: You were right in what you said and you were right about me.

Rick: I wasn't trying to insult you, I was just angry because you didn't defend me.

Liz: I know you weren't. You're right, I've never been any better than a servant when it came to my dad. Making him understand what I want for my life has been a long time coming. That's why I had a very long talk with him this week about my future and what my plans are.

Rick: How did he take it?

Liz: Well, he wasn't pleased, and I don't think he's going to waste his money on me anymore as he put it. However, I did make him understand that what he wants for me and what I want are two different things. The funny thing is he already had an office for me at his company, and apparently I was supposed to start in the next couple of weeks. Anyway, you were certainly the catalyst for that discussion with my dad and for me resigning before I even started.

Rick: I've been that for certain things over the years and although I'm sorry about how it happened, I'm glad that it did. It sounds like to me it might end up being a good thing.

Liz: I think it's going to be a good thing, and I also should have defended you or at least pulled you back before you really got carried away.

Rick :(laughing) Yeah, I definitely got carried away. You got to see me when I howl at the moon a little bit. Those are not exactly my finer moments, but then again I think we all have moments like that.

Liz: You're right about that, and it felt pretty good having one of those moments with my dad, as I'm sure it felt good for you when you had that moment with him.

Rick: Your dad, my new best friend; Oh yeah it felt pretty good. I can't lie about that.

Liz: Rick, I have lived for the most part a sheltered life and did what my parents wanted me to do. De Paul was more or less a compromise as long as I got a business degree. I was supposed to go to University of Chicago because my dad and mom went there. College was supposed to be my breaking free period and I have done that to an extent, but there are still some things that my dad has still had some say about in my life. The point is, it's not as easy for me to stand up and rebel. With my dad and the life he has provided for his family, it's very hard to go against what he wants for us. You don't have any ties, so you have nothing to lose by standing up to him.

Rick: You have a point, although the difference between you and me is that I've been standing on my own two feet without any help for a long time and you haven't. Don't get me wrong I'm not criticizing you for how it's been in your life, and believe me, I can understand why your life has been the way it has been, but there does come a time when we have to rise up and break free so we can find who we truly are.

Liz: And that's what I'm doing now because it's time. This whole thing sounds like something out of a movie. You know, the kind where some small town girl goes off to the big city to find her dream when her parents don't approve. Then she meets somebody who shows her what life is all about, and in the end she has to make that choice to live life under the submission of her family or break free to live her dream and her own life.

Rick: Isn't it funny how stories in movies truly mirror how life really is sometimes? Enough of that, I want to know what this good news of yours is.

Liz: I'll get to that in a minute because there's something else I want you to know. Now I don't want you to think that I'm some silly school girl who's easily infatuated with the first charming and funny guy that comes along. I may be easily inspired, but I'm still critical and objective when it comes to men. The thing is Rick, the past two months have been probably the best time in my life, at least that I can remember. I'm in love with you and I think I have been since the first time I ever heard you play. The night you played for the Malone's and I saw how you can touch people inside with music just confirmed for me how much I'm in love with you. I've never known anybody like you or known anybody that inspires me the way you do or makes me feel beautiful inside or who can make me feel like I can do anything.

Rick: I think I've known for a while, and to tell the truth I haven't done all those things to try and make you fall in love with me. I did it because I believe in you and I want you to be happy. I want you to find what I found and the reason I want all this for you is because I have fallen for you. These days I really can't see myself living without you. Perhaps that's why I've been so nutty lately.

Liz: Well then, here's my good news. I got the scholarship to the art school in Paris. I'm getting my chance to live my dream and to do something for me.

Rick: That's great! I had no doubt that you would get this chance. I bet the excitement is just overflowing inside of you right now.

Liz: Believe me, ever since I got the letter I've just wanted to scream for joy and tell everybody I saw, but I've actually waited because I wanted you to be the first one to hear about it.

Rick: So far I'm the only one who knows?

Liz: Yeah, not even my parents know, which will be interesting when I tell them because my dad thought I wouldn't get the scholarship and then I'd be forced to work for him. I wanted to tell you first because you're the one who's believed in me the most, and I want you to come with me. I don't want to do it alone. I want to do it with somebody that I love.

Rick: I can't go with you, Liz. This is something you have to do on your own.

Liz: That was so not the response I was expecting. I want you to be with me as I take this step. I'm not asking you to live my life for me, but just stand by me. After being with you I can't see being without you. Doesn't that count for something?

Rick: It counts for a lot and it makes me feel good to hear you say all this, but I can't go with you. No matter how much I can't live without you or how much I miss being around you, or hearing your laugh every day and seeing your smile light up the room I can't go with you.

Liz: Why not? If you can't live without me then why won't you go with me?

Rick: Because this is my home and this is where I belong.

Liz: Didn't you tell me once that for some people home is where they hang their hat; that for them home is never one place? Does is really matter where you are as long as we can be together?

Rick: You're right to an extent, but let me finish. Part of the philosophy I've acquired over the years is knowing that some people are meant to wander and find different places to make a difference. On the other hand, some are meant to stay in one place and that's where they find happiness and make a difference. I found out a long time ago that was me, and I would never leave this place. I wouldn't even want to because I am truly happy when I'm here. It's my "Hub in the Universe!"

Liz: How can you say that when you've never seen the rest of the world or experienced everything you can from it?

Rick: I'm not saying that we don't visit other places, but there is one place that we truly call home and always return to. The only way you can know that is if you do go and see what's outside your home. I've done that. I've been to places that I thought I would never go to, and even though I haven't seen all that I would like to, I do know where my home is. You haven't. You haven't been outside of this place to know if you will one day call this your true home.

Liz: Have you ever been to Paris?

Rick: No, I haven't yet, but maybe someday I will get there. And there's another reason why I can't go with you. You getting to go to Paris and have a chance at being a professional artist is your day in the sun, and I can't interfere with that. I had mine with basketball and although I'm a little disappointed that I never got to play pro basketball, I don't have any regrets about the chance I got and what happened to me. This is your chance to find out how bright you can shine in the spotlight and I can't be with you for that. Sure, it might be nice if we were together while you do this, but the journey of finding ourselves and what makes us happy has to be done alone.

Liz: Wasn't Linda with you and standing by your side while you were playing basketball?

Rick: Yeah, she was, but playing basketball at De Paul wasn't where I found myself. That other thing I was going to be honest about on the park bench was this; it was after I was done playing and after Linda had left that I found myself, but the journey that I took in doing that was done alone. Through all the depression and through all the agony that I went through in that part of my life I still had to do it all alone. Sure, there were my friends that were nearby and would get me a cup of coffee with some aspirin if I was hung-over, but in the end I was the only one that could find the answer to who I really was and what made me completely happy.

Liz: You're right about people having to figure out who they are and what they want on their own, but I still want you nearby to make me feel happy and safe, to tell me that everything is going to be okay and just because I want to be with you. I want to know something. What do you really have here that you couldn't walk away from, especially for love?

Rick: Now that's kind of a tricky answer because when it comes to love there really isn't anything that we shouldn't be able to do for it, and yes I'm one those that could walk away from a life where I'm happy if a loved one asked me to, but there's a flip side to this issue that were talking about. First of all, I could give you a thousand inspirational speeches about finding yourself and what makes you happy, but they're all going to have the same point: you're the only one who can do it and you usually have to do it alone. Now the hard thing about loving someone is setting them free or letting them go. That's the true test of loving someone. If you want to know how much I'm in love with you, I love you enough to do that.

Liz: I don't understand. Are you trying to tell me that for us to be together we have to give in to that old cliché where if you love somebody set them free and if they come back it was mean to be?

Rick: Something like that, but I also don't want to be responsible for you having to give up something that could be your dream come true, or your destiny if you will. I understand that loved ones sacrifice for each other all the time, but they can't sacrifice their own happiness or the things that make them complete because if we do something like that then we're destroying who we are and I don't think somebody who claims to love you can ask you to do that.

Liz: Now be honest with me are you just telling me all this because you don't want to live in Paris with me because if that's the truth then just tell me. I want you to be honest with me.

Rick: Okay, you're right, I don't really want to live in Paris, but that's not a reflection on you or me or not wanting to be with you. However, I'm not asking you to stay here for me, because if I love you like I've said before, then I can't. My little philosophical speech is not something I'm making up just to let you down easy. I mean every word I'm telling you, and as much as I love you and want you to stay, I have to let you go so you can find what makes you happy...what makes you complete. The only way to find those things is to go out there, take a journey into the world, and to take that journey into ourselves.

Liz: You know when you want something bad it's never easy and I guess I'm still one of those people who are still naive enough to believe that when two people love each other it's going to be easy, because love is all you need.

Rick: That's the thing *The Beatles* never explained in their song. Besides, when is it ever easy when it comes to the things we want or the things that might be good for us? It kind of reminds me of that old Buddhist philosophy, the harder the journey the greater the reward. But I'll tell you the real bitch of being in love. It's when you get a second chance and you still have to let them go. For me, I haven't felt this way in a long time and I never thought I would. I thought for longest time after Linda that there would never be anybody who could make me fall in love, but you did. And I don't want to let you go, but I know I have to.

Liz: I know you're right and that this journey is mine and mine alone, but I want to know something from you. With everything you know and have learned over the years; with all your philosophies of life, does it ever take you out of here, out of Chicago? Do you ever broaden your horizons a little bit anymore, or do you use all this philosophy as an excuse just to hide the fact that you're hiding from having to try something new?

Rick: Hiding? You think I'm hiding in this place?

Liz: If we're being honest with each other, then yes, I do. Think about it. Ever since Linda, have you ever gone anywhere outside Chicago? Have you ever left here to see the world?

Rick: Liz. I've been to a lot of places in this world. Let's remember this isn't about me. This is about you and the journey you need to take.

Liz: You might have visited a lot of places, but that was before she left you. Be honest. You haven't gone anywhere but here since then. If this is about the both of us finding ourselves and being complete so that one day we might be together, then be totally honest with yourself.

Rick: It's not hiding. I just don't have any reason to go anywhere else.

Liz: That's just a made up excuse to convince yourself that you're not really hiding from the rest of the world. If you're gonna talk about second chances, then second chances mean you have to get up after you've been knocked down and try again.

Rick: (in anger) Godamnit, I am not hiding! Quit making this about me!

Liz: If you're getting that mad over what I'm saying, then maybe I'm right, and this isn't only about me. This is about both of us and whether we have a future together.

There is a long pause after this.

Liz: Are you not going to say anything now? If you're just going to stand there and be mad then this is never going to work. Like you said, the truth stings sometimes.

Rick: Okay, maybe you're right. Let's say I've been using my life here as an excuse not to try again, but I'm still right about what I've said to you. It's funny, we can be so right about other people, and I've learned to have good judgment about people after being here so many years, but maybe I can't see myself as clearly as I always thought.

Liz: Rick, I'm not trying to know everything about you and put you in your place, but I want us to be to be totally honest with each other. You're right about me, and you were right about my dad. As much as I want you to go with me to Paris, you're right to say I have to do this alone, but if I'm going take a chance and evolve into something better than myself, then you have practice what you preach.

Rick: (smiling) I guess I can't get off the hook with this one, especially with all the preaching I've done up to this point.

Liz: No you can't, because if we're going to be together someday, then we have to both be at that point where we're ready for it, and I for one am looking forward to that day.

Rick: I guess when two people love each other then they keep each other in check, don't they?

Liz: You got it, piano man.

Rick: Then I'll make this promise to you. Although this is my "Hub in the Universe," my universe will get a little bit bigger and maybe one day it will be our time. You know I can't go with you though, right?

Liz: I know, and all I want from you is not to hide away from the world, but I don't want you to change from the person I fell for. You're picking yourself up again after being kicked down by taking a chance on me. I could be really, really psycho and boil your pet alive just to get you to love me.

Rick: Well I'll be sure to keep the family pet away from you if you ever get really mad at me. Even though I can't go with you, you're going to do just fine.

Liz: I hope so, but I'm still going to need you to believe in me if I'm going to succeed at this.

Rick: I'll always believe in you, and that will never change, but you don't need me and you never have. Liz, I don't want to let you go, but I know I have to. You've made that kind of difference in my life. You should know that after you leave here tonight there won't be a day that I won't look to that door waiting for you to walk back through it into my life again.

Liz hugs Rick and as she is hugging him she says to Rick,

Liz: Someday when its time, but I won't say goodbye, just I'll see you later. You are going to see me off at the airport aren't you?

Rick: I'll pick you up and I'll see you off, you can count on that. I won't say goodbye to you either, only I'll see you later. Hey, I might even say I love you

Liz: That's what I need to hear from you.

Rick: Yeah, you're not any different from any other women I've ever known. All you need to hear is "I love you."

Liz: You still don't know me completely yet, but maybe someday you will.

Rick: You know, there is one thing that we haven't done yet that I would like to do and that's dance with you. It just so happens that I have a jukebox in here so how about it?

Liz: (sarcastically) You got it, so why don't you play it for me Sam?

Rick hits the Jukebox trying to be funny and then it actually starts playing a song. The song that begins to play is *If you don't know me by now* by Harold Melvin and the Blue Notes.

Rick: Ah, the ironies of love, I guess we can't ever escape them.

Liz: Not in this place.

They continue to smile at each other as they dance and the lights slowly fade as they dance ending the scene.

End of Act Four, Scene One

Scene Two

It's a few days later back at the Club and the regular crowd is there for another night of music and drinks. Rick is looking through a packet of papers as Bud and Susan are helping the few customers they have.

Charlie: So is Liz gone now?

Rick: Yeah, I dropped her off at the airport this morning so she won't be around anymore.

Chad: Are you sad? I know I'd be sad if my girlfriend left me.

Charlie: You're sad when any women wants to get away from you, even if she's as big as the Titanic and got severely beat by the ugly tree. And just for clarification, she didn't leave him, she just went to Europe for art school. Can't you show a little sympathy?

Rick: It's alright guys. Yes, I'm a little sad because I told her what I needed to tell her and I still had to let her go, but that's the game of love sometimes.

Charlie: What are you going to do now?

Rick: Well, I am going to have a stiff drink tonight, and I'm actually going to start writing again and I am going to keep living. I'm also going to thank God for second chances and just for an added bonus I'm going to confession tomorrow. I'm sure I'll have to say a few extra hail Marys for having friends like you.

Chad: What are all the papers for?

Rick: If you must know, they're what I need to get back into De Paul so I can finish my degree. It's time to stop hiding and broaden my horizons a little bit. Boys, there's a bigger world out there and I'd like to see it.

Charlie: You're not on some weird spiritual kick are you? If you start chanting and becoming a vegetarian then I'm not going to hang out with you anymore.

Rick: So that's what it'll take to make you leave? Well, I should have done this years ago. I'm just kidding, Charlie. This is about becoming a better person and not hiding here anymore. I can still be the happiest I can be when I'm here, but I can't hide here anymore. I'm going to make some changes for the better in my life.

Charlie: That's a good plan, Rick. Chad and I are making some changes as well. We're getting out of the "back of a van flea market business" and we're going to open up a legitimate ticket shop. Besides, the Judge is retiring, so we won't have our inside connection in the courts anymore. Yeah, it's time to get a legitimate job now.

Rick: I think that's been a long time coming Charlie, but I'm glad to hear that you two have decided that it's time. Wouldn't do you much good to end up in jail again since you really don't have a "bail fund" anymore.

Charlie: Like you, it's time for us to make some big changes in our lives. But the fact that we really can't afford to go to jail anymore has had a lot of influence on us.

Susan and Bud make their way over to the conversation at the corner of the bar. Susan puts her hands on Rick's shoulders to comfort him and then leans in to say something to him.

Susan: Are you going to be alright now that she's gone?

Rick: Yeah, I'm going to be okay, and I'm going to go on being me. She made a difference, but she made a better person out of me and I'm going to let that show in my music and my life.

Susan: I know we're all going to miss her around here, but don't let the man she brought out in you go away. I for one have enjoyed him being around.

Rick: I won't Susan, and that also means you can't let the person you've become go away either.

Susan: Just to let you know, I've been inspired by both of you so I am going to make some changes in my life, but only for the better. For one, I'm only going to be with one person at a time in a relationship, but no matter what, I don't think I could ever stop being me. I have to in this place so I can keep some balance between sane people and morons.

Rick: You should know by now that there's no such thing as sane people in this place.

Bud: That was never truer until all of you started coming here, and since everybody is making changes in their life I better not see my sales go down or I'm just going to have to make you change back so this place can be like it always has been.

Rick: Don't worry Bud, we won't let the worst thing in the world for you happen. And remember, you're not that lucky to get rid of all of us while seeing your place change for the worst.

Bud: I know that's true, and believe it or not, I probably wouldn't have it any other way. Now I'm not going to admit that ever again so if you'll excuse me I have customers to tend to.

Bud walks off, but only a few feet away to help some customers.

Rick: You know, it's a long and strange journey we take in life, but I think that's the best part of it.

Chad: It's the Music of Life.

Rick: What did you say?

Chad: The journey in life, it's the Music of Life. Life, like a song, has its many verses to the same story. Sometimes we have different themes to the same story and we go through our ups and downs just like the notes reflect. We have our climatic times that help us see the true meaning of the story, but at the end we come to a realization that we've never had before. The story is life and in it is the Music of Life.

Everybody is looking at Chad with surprised looks at the profound thing he has just said.

Rick: That has got to be the most profound thing you've ever said. How did you even come up with that?

Chad: It just came to me. I guess we all have our moments.

Charlie: Have you been reading encyclopedias again little brother?

Chad: No, I'm just not as dumb as you look.

Charlie: If that's true, then someone please wake me up from my dream.

Rick: You know that's the absolute truth. The journey in life is just the Music of Life.

Everybody is smiling to end the scene; lights fade.

End of Act Four, Scene Two

Scene Three

It's the same scene from the beginning of the play and as the lights come back up Rick is still staring at the picture and the letter. Bud is still stocking beer in the bar. Susan, Charlie, Chad and Old Man Henderson some in the bar from Stage Left and take their usual places. Susan is behind the bar helping Bud; Charlie, Chad and Old Man Henderson take their seats at the corner of the bar.

Bud: Everybody don't bother Rick for a while, he got another letter from Liz.

Rick: (still staring at the picture) You know Liz, he was right. The journey we take in life is definitely The Music of Life.

Rick then begins to play his song inspired by Liz, There's Somebody Like You. As he is playing, everybody in the club is starting to sing out loud.

This last scene is one that can be done two ways. One is everybody can sing to themselves or everybody can sing together like in a piano bar. The whole song should be played and the lights slowly fade as the song comes to an end and this will end the play.

End of Act Four, Scene Three

- The End -

There's Somebody like You

Words and Music By Marcus Blake

Jazz: with upbeat and jazzy feeling

1st verse

G7 Cmaj7 Am7\C

There's somebody like you

A7 Em7__A7

Who haunts my dreams

A7 Em7__A7

Who makes me feel real

Fmaj7 A7 Fmaj7 A7

I couldn't laugh and I couldn't sing

A7 D7 G7__C

Without somebody like you

G7 Cmaj7 Am7\C

There's somebody like you

A7 Em7__A7

That I want to wake up to

A7 Em7__A7

That I want to take my fears away

Fmaj7 A7 Fmaj7 A7

Maybe I couldn't be sad, but only glad

A7 D7 G7__C

Perhaps with somebody like you

1st chorus

E7 Am7 D7

I've waited for so long to meet the right one

E7 Am7 D7

To have an honest chance at true love

Cmaj7 Am7 Cmaj7 Am7

Gm7\C

And I can't tell you why some were made to love and some were not

Cmaj7 Dm7 Fm6

But perhaps I can learn to love

A7 D7 G7__C

Because of Somebody like you

2nd verse

G7 C maj7 Am7\C

I couldn't find anybody like you

A7 Em7__A7

With a smile that melts my heart away

A7 Em7__A7

Or can level me with those eyes

Fmaj7 A7 Fmaj7 A7

I've kept searching all this time, but it's been hard to find

A7 D7 G7_C

Anybody that's like you

G7 C maj7 Am7\C

With somebody like you

A7 Em7_A7

It's been safe to say

A7 Em7_A7

My search is over

Fmaj7 A7 Fmaj7 A7

I've never had any luck, until I bumped into you

A7 D7 G7_C

Because there's nobody like you

2nd chorus

E7 Am7 D7

I've waited for so long to meet the right one

E7 Am7 D7

To have an honest chance at true love

Cmaj7 Am7 Cmaj7 Am7

Gm7\C

And I can't tell you why some were made to love and some were not

Cmaj7 Dm7 Fm6

But now I've learned what love is all about

A7 D7 G7__C

Because there's nobody like you.

ESSAYS

The American Experience

Seen Through a Writer's Eyes

If we walk throughout this land seeing all the different shades of American life what becomes "The American Experience," can it even truly be defined? What is it that distinguishes America from anything else, a sense of opportunity or the freedom that we demonstrate? Maybe "The American Experience" is something that is not ever defined, but displayed through the lives of the American people in all our triumphs and all our tragedies.

Maybe America is not even a mere object that is to be possessed or something that is easy to understand but just a mixture of ideas. If this is true then it is our ideals, and desires, and wide range of different philosophies that make up America's perpetual state.

The idea of America with all of its greatness may seem fragile or just a dream, but we prove it to be true and we prove its existence by how we live as Americans each day. The idea of America that I talk about is the corner stone of ideals that were set in stone by many founding fathers and that make up what was and is America. Freedom, liberty, equality, religious tolerance and individualism are but a few, and they shout through time from voices of the past to voices that are soon to come.

Contrary to some mythical tail they were not invented by us, but were always here only to be discovered by some idealistic soul. People who were no doubt influenced by some other idealistic soul who posed as a great philosopher seeing all that we could be.

Yes, I am talking about John Lock and his most basic beliefs of human nature. That all men are born free and have certain natural rights when they live within a state of nature that no government could possess or take away because they existed long before any government did. [1] That same philosophy is the core of what we are as America and has been ingrained into us from birth.

For many American writers have tried to make sense of the experience that is America, but perhaps they knew what we all know deep inside that mere words cannot describe "The American Experience." Only living it every day with all that we are and all we can be will truly define "The American Experience."

It is true that America is a melting pot, not only of different cultures, but different ideals. From all places in the world we have Americans, people who echo the same voice of individualism and people who come here to this undaunted land seeking the same desire. People who have that natural right to be an individual in every sense and are never discriminated against by the government they pledge allegiance to in a land that embraces individualistic endeavor.

Also, to have the opportunity and natural freedom that rings out and beckons those who have had and will have the courage to start over and seek what is attainable for all. Every person here has their own story to tell and one that encompasses family and generations. Every American family has played their part in "The American Experience" that stretches from a time long ago to now and to where we are going on this journey that becomes the experience.

It is "The American Experience" that becomes our sorrows and our joys as we all take part and that is never seen more clearly than through the artists who record those ideals of America for safekeeping. There are those in this nation who have fully embraced America through her tragedies and her celebrations. They have gotten just as much from America as America has gotten from them, which is part of the experience. People like our founding fathers or military heroes whose words echo out through history.

---

[1] Laslett, Peter, ed.; *Lock's Two Treaties of Government* ; Cambridge University Press: Cambridge, 1960 p. 348

But just the same there are words from other misbegotten heroes like the great poets or writers of America who make us see a picture that we may have not seen before. Even though they come close sometimes it may not be close enough, but we still see something that we have not seen before because of them. Walt Whitman who gathered all that he could from the experience that is America may have said it best.

No great Literature nor any like style of behavior or orator or social intercourse or household arrangements or public institutions or the treatment by bosses of employed people, nor executive detail or detail of the army or navy, nor spirit of legislation or courts or police or tuition or architecture or songs or amusements or the costumes of young men, can long elude the jealous and passionate instinct of American standards. Whether or not the sign appears from the mouths of the people, it throbs a live interrogation in freeman's and freewoman's heart after that which passes by or this built to remain.[2]

America is more than any institution or object that bares a name and even much, much more than we as her people. For even after we have long passed away America and the experience that's her will still be here living on for those delicate souls that choose to take part and live within America. For that idea of America like Camelot is greater than we as her people.

Although as Americans, as one historian put it, we search for symbols to describe America she is more than a flag, or a majestic bird, or weathered

---

[2] Whitman, Walt *; Leaves of Grass: Selected Poetry and Prose of Walt Whitman* ; Doubleday : New York, 1997 p. 27

monument to a long forgotten hero.[3] The quest for national identity does not lie within old relics or mythical tales or even a history book.

Who we are as a nation lies within the words we echo and the actions we live. A symbol is an easy way to identify something and if that is the only way to show America and "The American Experience" then that symbol should be the people of this great nation. People exercising so virtuously those ideals that we grab onto and that have become the cornerstones of our existence.

Demonstrating freedom at every turn like for instance standing next to a man who cries out boldly what you would spend every moment of your life denouncing, but letting him speak with the same right that is granted to you. Choosing freely and with conviction to engage in military service or not if it is decided by your own choice it's not for you.

To strive for any career opportunity you might dream about and not be made to do something else by a government. The actions and the words of the American people are the symbol for America and the essence of national identity.

However America is not people restricted to positions of authority or people with certain titles; it's also not people of a certain race or a certain level of means or even people who are descendants of American Aristocrats or American heroes that are the symbols of America.

For it is all that are fortunate enough to be called Americans, people of past and present. There

---

[3] Boorstin, Daniel J.; *The Americans: The National Experience*; Random House: New York, 1965 p. 325

is something that distinguishes America from anybody else and it is the people of this great nation. The American people exemplify that human spirit above all else, seeking to be individuals who live within their natural right to be free. They are people of all races, of all religions, or of any means like the poet who knows nothing of prejudice or is limited in his or her endeavors. One particular poet described the American people in this light

Other states indicate themselves in their deputies....but the genius of the United States is not best or most in its executives or legislatures, nor in the ambassadors or authors or colleges or churches or parlors, nor even in its newspapers or inventors.... but always most in the common people. Their manners speech dress friendships-the freshness and candor of their physiognomy the picturesque looseness of their carriage....their deathless attachment to freedom.[4]

There is truth in what was said of the American people by that poet and one might believe the American People are poets in their own way. When one lives and breathes by their emotions and inspirations while displaying them in the form of writing, or music, or art, or even by mere action they embody the spirit of the poet. Perhaps that is the greatest metaphor we can have of ourselves.

That same spirit carries on in all that we do and all that we have created in America. The place that we call home and it is that place where we find

---

[4] Whitman, Walt ; p.3

our peace and harmony, and find our own creative endeavor. For we as Americans are part of a nation that constantly reinvents itself.

The type of government we choose to rule ourselves with is a great example of that poetic spirit. A nation that is for the people, of the people, and by the people is truly unique in its own right. We were the first nation in the world to have such a unique thing as a constitution, even though other nations had documents limiting the powers of kings, to have a document that gave the power of the nation solely in the hands of the people was unheard of At the time.

We were a first among nations, a pattern to follow and something that gives definition "The American Experience." At one time that kind of concept was the most liberal of ideas and now it's the answer to oppressed nations and the most sought after by people. Our laws and Constitution are by no means perfect, but what truly is in this life?

The Constitution is the starting point of "The American Experience." It is the parameters to living our lives as Americans where freedom is absolute and governing is in the hands of the free. Our history and identity have derived from it and the challenges met have found answers within it. Our Constitution has given us the tools to be individuals, the freedom to find that poetic spirit, and to live as Americans.

After it was written Thomas Jefferson commented on it purpose and said in questions of Power, then let no more be heard of confidence in man, but bind him down from mischief by chains of the Constitution.[5]

To Jefferson and many like-minded individuals man was not meant to be ruled by one person or two, but to have the power to choose their leaders.

The constitution was never considered perfect and was subject to different interpretation and even change. All it does is give the people of this nation the right to determine their own course of action. To experience that is something greater than any earthly pleasure.

After many years of change and additions to the Constitution and the laws of the United Sates Justice Oliver Wendell Holmes said this about our most basic principle in America after dissenting a supreme court case, "If there is any principle of the constitution that more imperatively calls for attachment than any other it is the principle of free thought, not free thought for those who agree with us, but freedom for the thought we hate."[6]

Even the Constitution is not enough when living as Americans and with it being the starting point the end is only reached by living our lives with the most natural of rights, to live absolutely free. Can the Constitution and our most basic principles sum up "The American Experience"? No, but it is the beginning to understanding and living "The American Experience."

"The American Experience" is so much more than our most precious symbols of freedom such as

---

[5] Cummings Jr., Milton C; *Democracy Under Pressure*, Harcourt Brace College pub.: New York, 1997p48

[6] Cummings, Milton C.; p.57

the Constitution or the Bill of Rights. It's our everyday lives and how we live within this nation. To begin to understand "The American Experience" we have to see it through eyes of Americans and that includes people from all walks of life. There are millions of people here in America and each one has their own story to tell.

They all have their voice and they all play their part in that Experience that is America. Any nation if it has an identity has to be larger than symbols of ideals or laws. The American Constitution is a great symbol of freedom, but symbols never tell the whole story. The first line of a Poem or the introduction of a story will never convey what the author is truly saying. Many years after the Constitution had been written and after he had been President Thomas Jefferson again would comment on the Constitution's existence. He stated in later to Samuel Kercheval,

Some men look at constitutions with sanctimonious reverence and deem them like the ark of the covenant, too sacred to be touched They ascribe to the men of the proceeding a wisdom more than human, and suppose what they did to beyond amendment .... Laws and institutions must go hand and hand with the progress of the human mind ..... As new Discoveries are made, new truths disclosed, and manners and opinions change ... institutions much advance also, and keep pace with the times.[7]

---

[7] Padover, Saul K ed. "Letter to Samuel Kercheval" *The Complete Jefferson*, Duell , Sloan, and Pearce: New York 1943 p. 291

Bodies of law that become symbols of freedom or other political institutions must stay with the current of human reason and emotion. Human thought and reason will take many different roads in the ongoing journey of time. Can we really expect that change will never come and the way America and the world are viewed will remain the same?

Even the poet and writer never stay within the same mode of feeling, but are always branching out and finding new inspiration. Remember even though symbols like the Constitution seem magical they're only made of paper, wood, stone, or marble, and the ideas expressed with those symbols are what give them their power, their essence of life.

The reverence should not be for the symbol, but for the idea it expresses. This is why it is the American people that exemplify "The American Experience" more than anything else. It is different people bringing new ideas and inspirations to the foreground of American life.

On national holidays we celebrate American life, our history, and the many heroes that have contributed while reveling in "The American Experience." There are our founding fathers that changed from professionals and statesman of English society to revolutionaries risking all they had for a free nation. There are the millions American servicemen who fought in countless wars for our nation, some who were fortunate enough to only sacrifice their time and some who gave their life for American ideals.

These are just a few faces that help make "The American Experience" and contribute to the American persona. There are people like the factory workers in

Chicago or Detroit, the steelworkers in Pennsylvania or the farmers in Iowa, the ranchers in Texas or the fishermen in Massachusetts and California, and the many firefighters and policeman who protect and serve within our communities.

There are also countless governmental employees who keep this nation running now and for our progression into the future. Also let us not forget the many different ethnicities that have brought and continue to bring culture and different philosophies to the rural and urban areas of America.

There are people from every turn in the world who add something to the melting pot of America, immigrants who seek a better tomorrow for themselves and added just as much to the building of this nation as founding fathers and military heroes. We can never forget that those of us today have descendants from somewhere in the past who came here searching for a better chance in life and added to our American history in some way.

It is the American people that make this great nation; all the voices of the past and the present with all their stories that make our history. There is no monument or symbol that can truly tell everything that is America. It is only the American people that can tell her story and the Experience that is America.

There are many people throughout our history who are great examples of the American spirit and add greatly to "The American Experience." Some of them we know their stories well and have been told of their actions many times over the course of our lives.

Some are military heroes like Robert E. Lee or Ulysses S. Grant. Some are Astronauts who journeyed into places outside our world where only a few had been before. Some are rebels who challenge the mainstream to make things better or right like a Martin Luther King Jr. or a Susan B. Anthony. Some are even Baseball heroes who we watch with joy and show us the courage to never give up in victory or defeat.

There are even the American authors who have so carefully detailed the story of America and the character she embodies in their works. Our literary heritage is filled with the expressions of those writers and their impressions of American life through the ages. However there are more than just these heroes that were mentioned who make up America and "The American Experience."

There are ordinary people or common people who just live as Americans, who rise early every morning to work so they can provide for their family and ensure a better life for their children. They are people who provide services to others such as teaching others especially in places where education is not priority. There are those who build homes or drive forms of public transportation.

They're everyday people who work while living free, and never cry out as victims of society to receive that which they did not earn. They are people who work hard to better themselves making their part in America through education or self-improvement while sometimes receiving a little help to get there. They are people who live what seems like ordinary lives, but do extraordinary things, and that is to live as Americans and to be individuals, which may not be an easy thing to do.

There are many unsung heroes throughout this nation, but then again people are defined by their times and situations. It's what we do in the face of a challenge, whether we shriek away from it or revel in it and it's something that symbolizes the American spirit and adds to the experience of her.

It is the times that people live in and their actions during those times that define them as heroes while making them worth remembering in American history. Even though we celebrate the triumphs in America throughout our history we must remember the tragedies that occur as well. America is by no means perfect and the actions of every American past or present always admirable. There have been plenty of things in American history that we wish could be forgotten, moments in our lives that were not our finest.

Even so, those tragedies add to the American character and should be remembered because they provide a teaching tool if we are willing to learn. However out of the madness sometimes will come unlikely heroes who do extraordinary things. Abraham Lincoln is probably the best example of how the times in our history and the actions by one individual can define that person.

We tend to judge Lincoln as the model president and the best we ever had throughout our history. He became president in a time of great madness, a time when our nation would face its most serious test in its perpetual existence.

Lincoln was the right man for the job in helping save the United States and moving past all the anguish that our Civil War caused; he is also the best example for finding peace within conflict for any era. America has gone through similar times of strife and discontent throughout its history, times when our nation was hurt and filled with sorrow. Lincoln's words are probably the best source of hope and answers when America is in such a tragic state. In his second inaugural address he said this,

With malice toward none; with charity for all; with firmness in the right as God gives us to see the right, let us strive on to finish the work we are in; to bind up the nation's wounds, to care for him who shall have borne the battle, and for his widow, and his orphan - to do which may achieve and cherish a just and lasting peace, among ourselves, and with all nations.[8]

Lincoln is probably one of the best examples of a true American and somebody who displayed so much American character. He is one of those time-honored treasures that we remember when we think of characters that define "The American Experience." His words ring out through American history and are cornerstones in our American Literary Heritage.

Lincoln is not the only one though, that helps display that American spirit; there are people from different times who did different things, but still added something to America. There are ordinary men and women who have done extraordinary things and

---

[8] Johnson, Michael ed.; *Abraham Lincoln, Slavery, and the Civil War: Selected Writing's and Speeches*; Bedford/ST. Martin's pub.: Boston 2001 p.196

who are just as much of a hero as Lincoln, but whose story may not have been told yet.

America is not an easy place and not at all close to heaven as some might think. America might be the best place in the world to seek opportunity and freedom, but we have to strive for it more than anything that we strive and sacrifice for.

There have been many throughout history that has sacrificed for that freedom and opportunity for nothing ever comes without a price. But there are people in this great nation who are as selfish as the vulture and only seek to gain at the expense of others.

As long as human nature thrives here in this world nothing will ever be perfect, but there are places and some things that come close to it. Even America has its own “skeletons in the closet” that we do not look to favorably upon, but through dark times will come the greatest of things. One American poet commented on the fact that even though America was not perfect and had its own sins there was no place he could love better.

Claude McKay wrote this poem called America giving his interpretation of the Experience that is America,

Although she feeds me bread of bitterness
And sinks into my throat her tiger’s tooth,
Stealing my breath of life, I will confess,
I love this cultured hell that tests my youth!
Her vigor flows like tides into my blood,
Giving me strength erect against her hate,
Her bigness sweeps my being like a flood,

Yet as a rebel fronts a king in state,
I stand within her walls with not a shred
Of terror, malice, not a word of jeer,
Darkly I gaze into the days ahead,
And see her might and granite wonders there,
Beneath the touch of Time's unerring hand,
Like priceless treasures sinking in the sand.[9]

Many poets like McKay saw the realities that were not always good in America, but still found what made her great. There have been many writes in America who reveled within "The American Experience." like McKay, but still showed the dark nature that lied within.

Things like true equality among all Americans did take a while to come about and the laws that would protected the rights of everyone under the law were passed over a hundred years after this nation's birth. Even America's less than perfect nature makes the American story better and adds to the experience. Walt Whitman once said the United States themselves were essentially the greatest poem.[10]

Although even the greatest of stories or poems have to show the dark and bright themes to add full scope to its meaning. The American story is filled with both dark and bright themes and we do not just revel in the triumphs, but also our tragedies. We have to if we are going experience America for all that she is and to fully take part in the freedom granted by her. Even though America is not an easy place and the things we hold dear have taken a lot of sacrifice she is still the greatest gift.

Anybody who wants that freedom or opportunity here can have it if they are willing to work and even sacrifice for it. It was never meant for those selfish souls who are willing to have it only at the expense of others.

---

[9] Cooper, Wayne F. ed. *The Passion of Claude McKay: Selected Poetry and Prose*; Schocken Books: New York 1973 p.84
[10] Whitman, Walt p.3

There are a few that are like that, but if it is all or most of America that can only be answered by us.

For the greatest part of America are the American people, and that is people of all walks of life and from every place within America. America has still maintained and remained strong through all her tragedies. Even in our most desperate hours America has braved the storm and that is only because of the American people.

America has always been characterized by her people, everybody from our founding fathers, to the common people in America that are not always heard about, and to the writers and poets who show America for all that she is within their works. "The American Experience" as we have talked about is shown through the American people, but the experience and the spirit of America is also shown through the events in our history that help define who we are.

It seems that from the beginning this land has been filled with hope and the promise for liberty for all mankind. Even through all the different influences and changing of powers since the first European stepped foot in this country hundreds of years ago what we deem the American spirit has always been here.

That "do or die" spirit or that we can accomplish anything that we set our hearts to do. Maybe it was the untamed land and sense of excitement to forge a new home that developed that spirit. Maybe it was the sense of adventure or some deep soulful hope brought to such an untamed place by the first explorers here. No, I am not talking about Christopher Columbus, but Leif Ericson and his Viking seaman four hundred years before.

There are a lot of things that might define the American spirit that so hugely influences the Experience of America, but it might best be concluded that it is her people. Even before there was the United States a place that is filled with opportunity and freedom it was always here and the American spirit embodied it. The America and the experience that is her was within the wild and untamed wilderness and perhaps it was that wild nature of the land which symbolized "The American Experience" so well.

All that we had to do was cut away the unnecessary clay so that the shape within would take form. This land is the truest of gifts and maybe we did not act accordingly in settling or possessing it. There have been many unconscionable deeds and horrific acts done throughout our history. There have been many times American people have acted less than perfect, but with all things that are good there are things that are bad. America is the greatest gift for anyone searching to be all that they can be and a place filled with more wonder and possibility.

Robert Frost wrote this poem on the gift that is America showing his own interpretation on this place that we as Americans call home. This is what he said,

This land was ours before we were the lands
She was our land more than a hundred years
Before we were her people. She was ours
In Massachusetts, in Virginia,
But we were England's, still colonials,
Possessing what we still were unpossessed by,
Possessed by what we now no more possessed.
Something we were withholding made us weak
Until we found out that it was ourselves,
We were withholding from our land of living.
And forthwith found salvation in surrender
Such as we were we gave ourselves outright
(The deed of the gift was many deeds of war)
To the land vaguely realizing westward,
But still unstoried, artless, Unenhanced,
Such as she was, such as she would become[11]

To Robert Frost one America's most celebrated poets America was essentially the greatest gift and a gift

---

[11] Frost, Robert; *Complete Poems of Robert Frost* ; Henry Holt: New York, 1949 p. 116

here waiting to be accepted long before we were here. Though America was something meant for all kinds of people from all walks of life, never for just certain individuals.

Sometimes it would take a long time to realize that fact and that all the different kinds of people could live here in harmony, enjoying all that is America. Those American ideals like freedom and equality are for anyone who chooses to partake of those ideals.

America is not something we should take for granite for those treasured ideals and qualities that make America will always have to be preserved and sacrificed for. They do not come without a price or ever did. This is the part of America that does not make her easy because there are times that we have to fulfill that part of the deal we make with our country in partaking of the freedom and sovereignty granted by America. There are times that we have to give back and sacrifice our time, our valuables, our sweat, our blood, and maybe our life for this great nation. Sometimes we might ask ourselves if the sacrifices made are worth the gift from God above that is America and the answer is most certainly yes.

There have been plenty of Americans in the past that have risen to the challenge and done the hard things in sacrificing for an American cause. There have been times that we as a nation have united and sacrificed together to ensure those American ideals we so richly treasured here and all over the world.

Even our own revolution was a great sacrifice as well as treason to the nation we were a part of, but one that was worth it so we could have a place with all the ideals we live by and call it home. Sometimes we as a nation have had to and will have to rebel and go against the norm to ensure our liberty. It is that revolutionary spirit we carried then and still have that adds to "The American Experience", a spirit that says when we do not like something about our nation we change it for the better at all costs and sacrifice what is necessary. Sometimes it might even mean starting over if we have to.

The American revolutionary spirit is a part of all of us and we still carry it with us today, it is that same "do or die" spirit as we have talked about. John Adams many years after the American Revolution and his presidency commented on the revolution that he was so much a part of and said this, The Revolution was effected before the war commenced, the Revolution was in the minds and hearts of the people.[12]

It is still true today and we as Americans carry that spirit with us as we live "The American Experience." If you want to know the truth John Adams was talking about more than just the revolution, but all the ideals that made our revolution and how we still carry those same ideals inside of even today.

Many Americans have sacrificed all they had like many of the members of the Continental Congress for the gift that is America. Many people still sacrifice for that gift even today for where there is a dream to live and be free there is the dream of America. If there is any foreshadowing in history then one might have known that when the Declaration of Independence was being signed we were on the verge of something great.

There is no more clearer evidence than this, Dr. Benjamin Rush another signer of the document later asked John Adams "do you recollect the pensive and awful silence which pervaded the house when we were called up one after another to the table of the president of congress to subscribe what was believed by many at that time to be our own death warrants?"[13]

That silence was a savoring moment of something great and being done. Moments like that are part of "The American Experience" and it shows the character that America displays in all that we do. There is no place like America and there are not any unique individuals like

---

[12] Adams, Charles Frances ed. *The Works of John Adams*; Little Brown: Boston 1856 vol. 10, p.282

[13] Hawk, David; *A Transaction of Free Men*; Schribner's: New York; 1965, p.325

Americans. United, but diverse cultures that live as truly free men and women.

Each moment we live defines our character, how we act in times of tragedy and times of celebration. There have been a lot of great moments in our history that have defined America, times that showed who we really were. There have been moments that have not been our finest, but still have shown how we as America can rise above and be better. Although through all the moments and times that have made up our history they are only part of the story.

"The American Experience" as we have talked about is more than our history, our tragedies, and triumphs; it is the people behind those things that give definition to the experience of America. It is the actions of the American people that truly define her character and spirit. Not all actions that we celebrate, but the ones that are shameful and we are able to learn from.

It is true that most of the time it's through tragedies that America as a whole seems to shine more or at least that is when we really take notice. Although through times of triumph shows the sacrifices and battles fought, our true character becomes visible in reaching the triumph. There will always be sacrifices having to be made to ensure those American ideals like freedom and equality. Thomas Paine wrote this in explanation of the impending crisis' that wrought America yesterday and today,

These are the times that try men's souls! The summer soldier and the sunshine patriot in this crisis will shrink from the service of their country; but he that stands it now, deserves the love and thanks of man and woman. Tyranny like hell is not easily conquered; yet we have this consolation with us, that the harder the conflict, the more glorious the triumph. What we obtain too cheap we esteem too lightly: it is dearness only that gives everything its value.[14]

There are many times that try men's souls and it is how we act in those times that define who we are. We can let those times define us in a negative way or they can define us in a positive light, our actions will always speak louder than words.

If it is the American people who so much display what "The American Experience" is then we should look around and revel in the examples that are here today and there in the past. Even Americans that have gone before us still speak to us beyond the grave. Their voices are carried on through time in written works and memories passed down through the years.

There are many people from the past who display that ultimate American character and they are not just founding fathers or military heroes, but ordinary Americans like us.

They are People who reveled in the dream that is America and gave back to her just as much as they took from her. "The American Experience" is so much more than the symbols or monuments we use to display that American ideal, it is all the varieties of people living as free individuals and living as Americans.

For those of us that do like symbols or examples of the American spirit and although there are many to choose from maybe there is only one that is truly a symbol of "The American Experience."

---

[14] Foner, Philip S. ed. *The Complete Writing's of Thomas Paine*; Citadel Press: New York, 1969 vol. 1 p.58

It is popular opinion that there is only one American hero who truly was an example of the American spirit, Teddy Roosevelt. He was one man who truly lived his life as an American, fully partaking of all that there was in America and what she had to offer while giving plenty back to her.

As a couple of Historians pointed out, "He was like all our few truly great presidents: he seemed to embody the American state, he was an American and thought of himself as the United States like Lincoln, FDR, and Ronald Reagan.[15] The historians also pointed out, "He is remembered not for what happened so much as for what he was; he represents for a lot of Americans the traits that we consider best in American character"[16].

Teddy Roosevelt fully embraced America and lived his life to the very fullest with that "do or die" spirit that is so much a part of America. There is a lesson in that, something we all could learn in being Americans.

America is not easy and to have those ideals we love so much means we have to sacrifice and tolerate but that is the price for a free society. It is how we live our everyday that brings definition to "The American Experience" as well as echo's it out to all that will listen.

It is how we live that makes America an example above all others. The American people from all walks of life are special and can make anyone proud to be called an American. Walt Whitman once

---

[15] Harris, Joyce S`aenz; "A Century Later, Roosevelt Still Fascinates" *The Dallas Morning News*: Dallas Texas; November 4, 2001 p. 1j, 6j

[16] Harris, Joyce S`aenz ; p. 1j, 6j

wrote, "An Individual is as superb as a nation when he has the qualities that make a superb nation".[17]

It is the American people that make America great and makes "The American Experience" worth experiencing. Through all our triumphs and tragedies we show that American spirit and the dream that is America. With each moment of our lives past and present as well as the lives of future generations they become one more part of "The American Experience."

America is many, many things to different souls who are here while perfect we are not nor will ever be the one thing we are is a land filled with more opportunity and truly free. The greatest symbol of America will always be the American people. Shortly before Teddy Roosevelt died he wrote "Only those are fit to live who do not fear to die and none are fit to die who have shrunk from the joy of life and duty of life: both life and death are parts of the same Great Adventure."[18]

It is believed that Roosevelt was talking about America and the people with an American heart so this ideal would be echoed out to all of mankind. He makes a charge to those who live and especially those who live as Americans. Roosevelt's words is the truest source of inspiration for how life should be lived as an American and if we are true then we will not shriek from all that life has to offer especially in this place that is America.

Our American literary heritage is filled with memorable quotes and literary works from people

---

[17] Whitman, Walt p. 23 [18] Harris, Joyce S`aenz; p. 1j, 6j

who show all that America was and is today. There are powerful meanings behind the words of the American poet and writer that encompass the Experience of America. Through our history and literary works the beginning of the story is told, but it is through us the American people that the complete story of America will be told.

Like serene and heavenly poets we convey all that is America and her perpetual state. We will be a place filled with sorrow and filled with joy. We will celebrate our triumphs and we will morn and in our tragedies, but we will unite as Americans in the most perfect of dreams called America. In the Experience of America we have to live it, seek it, embody it, love it, cherish it, revel in it, celebrate it, hate it, and always remember it. For by doing this we become "The American Experience

References

1. Adams, Charles Frances, ed. *The Works of John Adams*; Little Brown: Boston; 1856 vol. 10

2. Boorstin, Daniel J.; *The Americans: The National Experience*; Random House: New York 1965

3. Cooper, Wayne F., ed. *The Passion of Claude McKay: Selected Poetry and Prose*; Schocken Books: New York 1973

4. Cummings, Milton C.; *Democracy Under Pressure*; Harcourt Brace College pub.: New York, 1997

5. Foner, Philip S. ed.; *The Complete Writing's of Thomas Paine*; Citadel Press: New York, 1969

6. Frost, Robert; *The Complete Poems of Robert Frost*; Henry Holt: New York; 1949

7. Harris, Joyce S`aenz; "A Century Later, Roosevelt Still Fascinates" *The Dallas Morning News*: Dallas, Texas; November 4, 2001

8. Hawk, David; *A Transaction of Free Men*; Schribner's: New York, 1964

9. Johnson, Michael; *Abraham Lincoln, Slavery, and the Civil War: Selected Writing's and Speeches*; Bedford/St. Martin's pub.: Boston, 2001

10. Laslett, Peter, ed.; *Lock's Two Treaties of Government*; Cambridge University Press: Cambridge, 1960

11. Padover, Saul K. ed. "Letter to Samuel Kercheval" *The Complete Jefferson*; Duell, Sloan, and Pearce pub.: New York, 1943

12. Whitman, Walt; *Leaves of Grass: Selected Poetry and Prose of Walt Whitman*; Doubleday: New York, 1997

www.ingramcontent.com/pod-product-compliance
Lightning Source LLC
Chambersburg PA
CBHW032058180726
48284CB00002B/336

* 9 7 8 1 9 3 2 9 9 6 6 0 9 *